MUSIC CONTEXTS
A CONCISE DICTIONARY
OF
HINDUSTANI MUSIC

MUSIC CONTEXTS
A CONCISE DICTIONARY
OF
HINDUSTANI MUSIC

Ashok Da. Ranade

PROMILLA & CO., PUBLISHERS
in association with
BIBLIOPHILE SOUTH ASIA
NEW DELHI & CHICAGO

Published by
PROMILLA & CO., PUBLISHERS
in association with
BIBLIOPHILE SOUTH ASIA
URL : www.biblioasia.com

C-127, Sarvodaya Enclave
New Delhi 110 017, India

First published 2006

ISBN : 81-85002-66-5 (Pb)

Typeset in AGaramond
Layout and processing by Radius Arc, New Delhi

Printed and bound in India by Uthra Print Communications,
New Delhi

To my Guru-s

Gayanguru-s
Pt. Gajananrao Joshi, Pt. Laxmanrao Bodas,
Pt. Pralahad Ganu and Prof. B.R. Deodher

Academic Guru
Dr. R.B. Patankar

PREFACE

I learnt Hindustani vocal music in the well-known *guru-shishya* tradition. Hence I never asked questions but absorbed innumerable insights which gradually fell into a well-knit pattern during a period of about twenty years. In a performance-oriented tradition this was but natural.

The training convinced me that theory and practice of music cohere better when performers themselves theorise. It soon became clear that the so-called 'illiterate' performers have been theorising all through the centuries, both verbally and non-verbally! They theorised and performed almost simultaneously. In the final analysis, relationship of all performing art to other life areas ensured that a majority of theorisations became verbalised to form a scholastic tradition.

Thus was created a majestic edifice of concepts and terms that echoes the life of music to a great extent. To understand these is to map the musical behaviour.

To bring together themes, concepts and terms led inevitably to the *Amarkosha*-format. The original plan envisaged including sections on music education and scholarship, folk and primitive music, popular music and music and culture.

I hope to do so in the near future.

Ashok Da. Ranade

Bombay
Vijayadashmi, 10 October 2005

CONTENTS

3.   MUSICAL INSTRUMENTS   281

1

MUSIC MAKING

Music, along with dance and drama forms the celebrated trinity of performing arts. Hence, 'making' of music is the life force of all music-related activities. Whether to learn, teach, practice, demonstrate, study, appreciate or even criticize music — for all these activities a firm foundation of actual music making is essential.

Music is made in many ways, under various circumstances and by different people. It has many modes of coming into being. Artistes, accompanists, the common, general audience as well as knowledgeable listeners — all have roles to play whenever music is created. The entire endeavour is governed by unwritten but definite norms — even though we may not be aware of them. Thus music in India does make partners of us all!

Music begins, flourishes, ends or it may linger behind. How do we receive music? Some take naturally to the flow of music, some step into the stream gingerly, some need to be guided into it, while very few allow it to pass by.

Fortunately, not many suffer the ignominy of remaining absolutely untouched by the Ganga of music — especially in India where musical literacy ranks very high. The main reason for the high musical literacy is that in India, six categories of music have flourished side by side for many centuries. The categories are Primitive, Folk, Religious, Art, Popular and Confluence. Even though the present brief is confined to Hindustani art music — generally known as 'Classical' music — awareness of the larger perspectives offered by the categorial sextet cannot be ignored.

For those who wish to be blessed by the touch of music, it helps to *know* or *understand* music — in addition to experiencing or feeling its magic. This effort is for those who seek to know about music in order to be in it — more fully.

1.1 Occasion

Sometimes music, by itself, is a sufficient provocation to make music! It is like the Everest, which is to be scaled because it is there! However, music is often made in order to mark an occasion — fittingly and properly. Unless marked with propriety, occasions are mere junctures of circumstances. It has been noted that for various cultural reasons music is a good marker. The nature of the occasion determines features such as motivation, environment, repertoire and format of the music made. Presentations of music undergo changes — qualitative as well as quantitative — according to the specific occasion concerned. It is therefore helpful to understand the overall character of the occasion for which music is made. It is obvious that place, time, circumstance and the goal — all have a bearing on the character an occasion acquires.

Some Historical Antecedents:

Individual entries in this section specifically deal with situation as obtained in the contemporary world of

Hindustani art music. However, it is obvious that the long performing tradition India enjoys has left strong traces of earlier practices in respect of selecting occasions for making music. Some historical data are noted here to provide perspective to the current model.

It is interesting to note that Patanjali's *Mahabhashya* mentions *samajja, samavaya* and *samasa* as three celebratory occasions for making music. The great grammarian-philosopher, Patanjali's (150 BC) commentary on Panini (400 BC) is a major work to throw light on early India. Panini in his turn was an archetypal grammarian whose approach to language and its codification made his aphoristic works *Ashtadhyayi* ('eight chapters') and *Dhatupatha* ('book of roots') veritable keys to decipher early cultural patterns.

In *Buddhist Tripitaka* (a post-Buddha compilation of Buddha's teachings done by his trusted disciples in three sections) has noted *samajja* and *giri-samajja* (or *giragga samajja*) as occasions of music making. Apart from terminological similarities with the Panini-tradition, Buddhist reference to making music on mountains may be taken to refer to specifically recreational music — obviously an early example of secular employment of music.

Occasions which received sanction for music-making in Buddhist tradition are important because generally Buddhism is not considered music-friendly! One such occasion is known as Kathindaan (कठिणदान). *Kathin* is the name of the yellow '*vastra*' to be worn by a Buddhist monk. The ceremonial giving away of this *vastra* is *Kathindaan*. Celebrated sometime in the period between full moon days of Hindu months of *Ashwin* and *Kartik* a donor — duly receiving permission from the Sangh to donate — would distribute *Kathin* to monks. Singing of devotional songs, holding of religious discourses and lectures by learned authorities also formed part of these celebrations (regarded very prestigious) and donors spent considerable money on these!

Yet another important antecedent is of the *goshthi-sabha*. By 200 AD, a complete *goshthi*-culture was evolved. There were various kinds of *goshthi*-s .in which an assembly could enjoy *vina* (lute), *vadya* (instrumental music), *geet* (singing), etc. To convene a *goshthi* was a prerogative of a *nagaraka*, an accomplished urbanite (*nagar* meaning a city). A person who could decorously conduct *goshthi* was known as a *goshthi-pati* (leader of the assembly). Vatsyayana broadly classified *goshthi*-s as good and bad. While the bad variety meant an opportunity for gambling or violence, the good *goshthi*-s relied on recreation and intellectual play among sophisticated participants. Among the good *goshthi*-s were included: *pada*-(literature) *goshthi*, *jalpa*-(story-narration) *goshthi*, *kavya*-(poetry) *goshthi*, *geet*-(song) *goshthi*, *nrittya*-(dance) *goshthi*, *vadya*-(instrumental music) *goshthi* and *vina*-playing (*vina* — a highly regarded lute in ancient India). So accepted was the *goshthi* format, that if learned and knowledgeable people gathered in a sacred place to respect memory of a saint, or a great personality etc. the event was described as *goshthi-shraddha*. Vatsyayana's description-cum-prescription about the *goshthi* culture is worth noting for it highlights interactive roles of life, culture and arts. For these *goshthi*-s, seven major contributors are listed: (1) Learned persons, (2) Poets, (3) Bards, (4) Singers, (5) Jesters, (6) Experts in history, and (7) Experts in *Purana*-s. Another feature was *Samaj*. *Samaj* was a performing concomitant of the *goshthi*. It brought together audience, authorities rewarding artists, experts/theoreticians and actual performers in a performing situation.

The most important aspect of the *goshthi*-s was a successful combining of performance and related discourse as a matter of everyday routine. Obviously, both could and would reflect on each other. Theorisation leading to scholastic tradition could remain closer to performing tradition — a fact making room for significant aesthetic consequences. The *goshthi* culture provided a living example of how a comprehensive Oral tradition can function towards a better and near-mandatory circulation of cultural ideas to ensure vitality.

The description of the daily schedule in the *Saraswatimandir* and the *Samaj* that took place in its courtyard, leaves us in no doubt about one more feature: all arts were to have a common platform in the prevailing culture. This could be expected to be conducive to inter-art exchanges. The composite artistic perspective and aesthetic vision, which comes to the forefront in *Natyashastra*, had a direct connection with real-life situation. Compositeness was not a theoretical position — it was a way of life!

Alternatively, the *goshthi* could be convened at the initiative of a *ganika* (meaning a courtesan) well versed in the sixty-four arts identified by works on ancient Indian culture with Vatsyayana's *Kamasutra* (200 BC to 400 AD) leading the way.

Whether in *Kamasutra* that describes the daily sch˙ lule of a *nagaraka*, i.e. cultured citizen, or in *Kavyamimamsa* of Rajashekhara (10th century), carefully arranged occasions for study, presentation and appreciation of different arts strikingly prove the importance accorded to performance of music in an appropriate setting.

By medieval times, a number of festivals were stabilised around agricultural operations such as seeding, harvesting or with ancestor worship and hero-worship. Some others were state or king sponsored e.g. Hastimangal (हस्तिमंगल) or Jayapan (जयपान). Around 1000 AD, a Jain work *Bhagawatisutra* could list 19 kinds of festivities and the typology seems relevant even today. With *maha* meaning festival, the names and the immediate related deity etc. could be tabulated as follows:

Name	Associated deity etc.
Indramaha	Indra इन्द्र
Skandamaha	Kartikeya कार्तिकेय
Rudramaha	Shiva शिव
Mukundmaha	Krishna कृष्ण
Bhutamaha	Bhoot, Preta, Pishaacha, Bhairav भूत, प्रेत, पिशाच, भैरव
Yakshamaha	Yaksha, Kubera यक्ष, कुबेर
Nagamaha	Naga नाग
Stupamaha	Bauddha Stupa बौद्धस्तूप
Chaityamaha	Matha, Vihara मठ, विहार
Vrikshamaha	Vriksha वृक्ष
Girimaha	Parvatyatra पर्वतयात्रा
Darimaha	Picnics in Valleys
Agadamaha	Wells कूप
Tadagamaha	Lake सरोवर
Daimaha	Pond पुष्करिणी
Nadimaha	Bathing in River नदीस्नान
Saramaha	Large Lake सरोवर
Sagarmaha	Ocean समुद्र
Agaramaha	Worship of Subterranean mines

Broadly it seems that festivals have four major types: (1) In honour of major deities, (2) Propitiation of minor deities, (3) In remembrance of religious leaders and heroes, and (4) Propitiation of natural elements and useful features of nature.

It is instructive to note some examples of festivities used for making non-serious and secular or even profane music as in some Carnival traditions in other cultures.

Udsevika (उदसेविका) was for instance an ancient festival celebrated immediately after *Indradhvajotsav* on *Bhadrapad Shuddha trayodashi*. Significantly it was alternatively known as *Bhootmatautsav* (भूतमाताउत्सव). In this festival *Udsevika* smears earth on her body and is married to Bhairav. They are respectively born from the minds of Parvati and Shiva and were married on the day of the *Utsava*. On this day, obscene speech and songs were in order; men and women rode on donkeys, dogs and bulls; old people behaved as if they were young and masqueraded as *gavali*, *domb*, or barbers or paraded bare-bodied. *Purana* such as *Skandapurana* extolled the importance of participating in it by stating that ancestors and gods do not accept offerings of those who do not participate in it!

Yet another instance is provided by the ancient *Udyanyatra* (उद्यानयात्रा). During the spring season for example, on a defined day people will go to gardens. Often professional singing/dancing women would accompany their patrons. On the way various games and sports such as animal-fights, will be in progress. On reaching the garden, people will sit on swings and *Samasyapoorti* (puzzle/riddle solving), *Kathavachan* (story-reading), etc. will form a part of the proceedings. Unmarried girls would go unescorted — though this was not without risk!

Amir Khusro is said to have profited from *samiti,* i.e. assembly of meritorious persons of Hindus (i.e. hailing from India) and *'Tatar',* i.e. assembly of experts from Turkastan to evolve genres such as *Kaul* and *Tarana.*

It is interesting to note that in the modern period leaders and reformers such as Lokmanya B.G. Tilak and cultural reformers such as Tagore in Bengal exploited the festival format for inculcating and spreading nationalism in India.

1.1.1   *Baithak* (H *baithana* = to sit)

Presentations of music (except in tribal, folk, religious or popular music making) are described as a concert of music, i.e. *Baithak.* Etymological connections hint at the modalities adopted during performances both by artistes and listeners respectively to make and receive music. Usually, both artists and listeners are seated on mattresses, etc., laid on the floor. This is in obvious contrast to the modern use of chairs for listeners and raised platforms for performers.

It helps to note that depending on the nature of the occasion *Baithak* can also mean a drawing room. For example, a patron, at his own sweet will and initiative may invite select persons to listen to an established or an 'up and coming' artiste. However, at a more institutional level, *Baithak*-s were not ticketed — at least till the beginning of the twentieth century. In all probability, one major patron paid or rewarded the artiste. However, to receive contributions from friends as a support was not entirely ruled out. Even today this kind of 'contributory' *Baithak* has not gone out of vogue.

The idiom of the language currently used by musicians and music-lovers alike confirms the strong musical association of the verb *baithana* ('to sit'). Musicians frequently employ expressions such as *aaj baithenge* ('today we will sit') etc. to indicate arrangement of a proposed music performance.

More closely examined the term *Baithak* also refers to the sitting postures adopted by performers. Posture is a particular disposition of bodily limbs, which performers prefer as facilitating their act. Obviously, certain postures are favoured as more conducing to music making than certain other possible postures. However, discussion of the performing posture would take us another area, that of actual performing activity itself. It is sufficient to note that performers have strong opinions on correctness or otherwise of postures to be adopted. This becomes especially noticeable when disciples or budding artists learn music.

As an institution, *Baithak* is traceable to *goshthi* (S. assembly).

1.1.2   *Barasi* (anniversary H < S *varsha* = year)

Music, it is felt, has the capacity to enshrine memory of revered personalities. Death anniversary of a musician or a revered saint may often be observed by organising a music performance. The main intention is to honour the person, revive memory of his work and admire his accomplishments for possible emulation. Expectably, compositions rendered on such occasions reiterate these and similar themes.

Barasi-s of Muslim saints, or *Sufi*-s, *Pir* (*pir = guru*, preceptor) inspire longer festivals known as *Urs* in which music forms an important component. On account of its rich musical content *Urs* is treated separately.

If the term *barasi* sounds secular, a term circulating with equal frequency is *'punyatithi'* (S *punya*= merit, virtue, *tithi* = a lunar day) and this term suggests a religio-emotional charge attached to both term and the concept. In the early decades of the 20th century it was considered auspicious to perform at *barasi*-s — at least for upcoming artists. To perform at such gatherings was to bode well for them, ensuring a bright future in their performing career.

It is interesting to note that in ancient India, if learned and knowledgeable people gathered in a sacred place to respect the revered memory of a saint, or a great personality, etc., the event was described as *goshthi-shraddha*. The conceptual relationship between *barasi* and this ancient format is obvious.

1.1.3   *Davat* (A)

A resident musician may host a ceremonial dinner in honour of a visiting musician. Recognised musicians are invited to attend the performance given by the visiting artiste on the occasion.

Basically, *davat* (invitation) has proved to be a useful institution as it introduces the visiting musician to local celebrities who then can spread his name in the right quarters.

Biographical accounts of musicians of the last century indicate that once musicians were convinced of their preparedness to professionally face the world a modus operandi was followed. On their own, musicians would set out to visit well known/established centres of patronage, pay respects to local and elderly musicians, call on patrons and await the moment of being noticed! Obviously, the system was well-tried out and accepted to be both appropriate and effective. Even a cursory examination reveals well-drawn out itineraries of musicians setting out to launch their careers. For example, when Pt. Balkrishnabuwa Ichalkaranjikar, (1849-1926), the founder of Gwaliyar School of Hindustani Music in Maharashtra and preceptor of Pt. Vishnu Digambar Paluskar, (a pioneering propagator of music in the 20th century) set out from Satara around 1866, he stopped at the following places: Karhad, Kurundwad, Ichalkaranji, Miraj, Phaltan, Dhar, Indore, Ratlam, Gwaliyar, Calcutta, Gidhare, Bitiya and Nepal. When, thirty years later, i.e. in 1896, Pt. Vishnu Digambar Paluskar (1872-1931) made a similar sortie, the stops were: Satara, Baroda, Kathiawar, Rajkot, Gwaliyar, Aligadh, Mathura, Delhi, Jullander, Amritsar, Lahore, Jodhpur, Montgomery, Lahore, Jaisalmer, Udaypur and Bombay. Princely states, industrial centres, sacred and religious places and seats of patrons, places where relatives and well-wishers were employed in prestigious institutions, etc., drama-companies — all together formed a network a musician would use to earn name, fame and money.

A slight variation of the model is also recorded. In the early years of the century a musician would invite other musicians at his place to perform one after the other — thus staging among themselves a kind of friendly contest leading to recognition and acceptance of comparative excellence. The ruling norm was simple: the better the musician, the later in the sequence would he perform! (A musician regarded to be the best would perform last.) This procedure naturally resulted in establishing a kind of 'rating system', if not a pecking order! The system was apparently flexible because a self-confident performer himself could declare that he would perform later, or after so and so! This was interpreted, as an implicit challenge to the prevalent rating and things could become embarrassing for the challenged musician as also for the host!

What is notable is that these occasions had an inherent provision for interaction among musicians — a feature, which could easily be expected to lead to a free and frank exchange of ideas (including healthy disagreements!).

1.1.4   *Hazri* (A)

It means 'presence before the respected'. On occasions performers present themselves in a temple before a deity, or in a royal court to perform. This act is described as *hazri dena*, meaning 'to give a performance out of respect'. This surely is a rather modest way of characterising one's own effort. The equivalent term in Sanskrit for the same practice is *'seva'* (meaning to serve, wait or attend upon to honour, to worship, and obey). It is interesting to note that according to Hindu religious tradition, at least two from the nine major modalities of devotion are music-related. They are *shravan* (listening to God's name and his praises) and *keertan* (singing God's praises).

On visiting a temple or a *dargah* of a *Sufi* saint, musicians may offer performances. They may also be appointed to offer performances with ritualistic regularity at certain temples. Both these types of performances are known as *hazri*.

The procedure was not of course restricted to temples. When Ustad Alladiya Khan (1855-1946) set out to make a name he reached Baroda. He could not give concerts to make his musical presence felt as Moharram was being observed. However, he went to a local mosque one evening to offer evening prayers and 'sang' *'marsiya'*. Usually, *marsiya* (comparable to any sophisticated genre of funeral music) are merely recited. However, there are some *mersiya* and *soz* singers who can employ many *raga*-s even in their recitation. Being a well-versed musician, Ustad Alladiya was well aware of this tradition of 'singing' *marsiya*-compositions. He did it in such a masterly fashion that Ustad Faiz Ahamed, the court musician who had also gone to offer prayers, came back impressed. He lost no time in declaring to his disciples that a great musician had arrived in the city!

1.1.5 *Karyakrama* (S *karya* = work, affair, business + *krama* = sequence)

The format connotes a single and independent presentation of almost any kind. The term came into circulation sometime during the twentieth century to describe a musical event. It clearly indicates a more formalised or officially inspired music making as also a more systematised organisation of the concerned event. Provided the arranged performances form a complete unit the term is valid irrespective of modality, purpose, audience-type and the involved organising agency.

1.1.6 *Mehfil* (A)

In essence the term is synonymous with the term *Baithak*. The word *Mehfil* generally means a place where a music or dance-performance is in progress. It is significant that *Sufi*-s (the Muslim mystics) describe the World itself as a *Mehfil*. It is known that *Sufi*-s virtually served as a bridge between Hindu and Islamic mysticism and by the eleventh century, they had created a firm footing for Sufism in India. It needs to be stressed that Hindustani art music is notably rich in *Sufi* associations and many of its characteristic features become intelligible if *Sufi* philosophy, terminology and way of life is borne in mind. The term *Mehfil* assumes significance in this light.

It is significant that while Shakespeare compared the world to a stage, the *Sufi*-s preferred a musical model for comparison!

One more word — *'majlis '* (A) is also in vogue. But it refers to only secular coming together of people for a common purpose. It is thus significant to note that Hindustani musical behaviour has preferred in *Mehfil* a word with both recreational and mystical associations to describe music making!

1.1.7 *Mela* (H < S *melaka* = that which brings together)

Music making in a festival celebrated to honour a Hindu deity, saint, etc., is popularly known as *mela*.

Some of the *mela*-s have been known for their long tradition. They attract musicians, music-lovers and devotees alike from far and wide. Invitation to participate in a *mela* is usually considered to be an honour. Participants also believe that to give a good account of oneself in a *mela* is to ensure lasting fame along with prosperity.

Usually, over a period, *mela*-s become institutions and develop their own lore and customs. Some conventions followed in *mela*-s may appear musical oddities, but being a part of the overall tradition, they have enjoyed reverent conformity. For example, *Harvallabh Mela* of Shikarpur encouraged simultaneous rhythm accompaniment provided by more than four *tabla* players to a single vocalist!

1.1.8 *Parishad* (S assembly)

Today *parishad* is understood as an attempt to bring together variety of performers for successive presentation in a series of individual engagements of short duration. It could be viewed as a step towards secularising and 'de-courting' (taking music out of royal court) art music to make it available to the general public at a reasonable as well as fixed price. The phenomenon is symptomatic of the democratisation processes that struck roots in India in the nineteenth century.

Prominent features of a *parishad* are:

1. Admission is by sale of tickets or by issue of special invitations.
2. Performers from various parts of the country are invited to perform according to a predetermined schedule.
3. As a rule, performers' fees are paid in cash though they may also be awarded honorary titles, medals, etc.
4. Individual artistes are allotted time-slots of varied durations, usually shorter than full-length concerts.
5. *Parishad* may run over many days and nights. To hold all-night performances on the last day is also a frequently followed practice.
6. In *parishad*, different kinds of artistes are heard and music becomes generally accessible. To attend *parishad* is also considered prestigious. However, it cannot be denied that heterogeneity of audiences, unevenness of presentations and the inevitable distancing of audience from artistes often reduce *parishad* to occasions of festivity, fashion and levity — music merely becoming an excuse 'to see and being seen' socially!

It is significant that of late, *parishad*s are attracting smaller audiences and even if crowds gather in them many serious listeners prefer 'private' concerts to 'big' conferences. Even though it is uncharitable to characterise *parishad format* as a mere show, it may be said that *parishad* often fails to mirror the real/total wealth of Hindustani music.

Examined historically, it could be said that in modern times models set up by the two great *Vishnu*-s, Vishnu Narayan Bhatkhande (1860-1936) and Vishnu Digambar Paluskar (1872-1931), have inspired *parishad*. The two established the vogue of *parishad* during the years 1916-1930. Efforts of these two pioneers were notably shot with an idealistic fervour. During the first All India Music Conference, which Pt. Bhatkhande organised at Baroda (1916) under the patronage of the then Maharaja of Baroda, Bhatkhande listed fourteen aims of his programme of the conference:

1. To take steps to protect and uplift Indian music on national lines.
2. To reduce it to a regular system such as could be easily taught to and learnt by educated men and women.
3. To provide a fairly workable uniform system of *raga*-s and *tala*-s, with special reference to the northern (the reference was to the Hindustani system of art music) system of music.
4. To effect if possible such a happy fusion of the northern and southern systems of music as would enrich both.
5. To provide a uniform system of notation for the whole country.
6. To arrange new *raga* production on scientific and systematic lines.
7. To consider and take further steps towards the improvement of our musical instruments in the light of our knowledge of modern science, all the while taking care to preserve our cultural identity.
8. To take steps to correct and preserve the great masterpieces of the art of music in the possession of great artistes.

9. To collect in a central library all available literature (ancient and modern) on the subject of Indian music and if necessary to publish it and render it available to students of music.

10. To examine and fix the microtones or *sruti*-s of Indian music with the help of scientific instruments and high class recognised artistes to distribute them among the *raga*-s.

11. To start an Indian 'Men of Music' series.

12. To conduct a monthly journal of music on up-to-date lines.

13. To raise a permanent fund for carrying on the above mentioned objectives.

14. To establish a National Academy of Music in a central place where top-class instruction in music could be given on up-to-date lines by eminent scholars and artistes in music.

Presented at length, and in the language used by Pt. Bhatkhande, the nationalist sentiment and his intense desire to prove the high status of Indian music could hardly be missed.

The other distinguished pioneer, Pandit Paluskar, also organised *parishad*. Their important features were:

1. In most of the *parishad*-s an exhibition of musical instruments was arranged.

2. Discussions were held on non-Indian musical features such as harmony.

3. A piano-concert was also scheduled in the 1921 conference.

During the years 1916-1930, about twelve conferences were inspired by the direct efforts of the two *Vishnu*-s. Since then, music *parishad*-s have become a regular feature of urban life. However, the original formulae appear to have lost their drawing power and their innate idealism also seems to have disappeared. Many new variations have been tried out. For example, to hold a *parishad* artistes of the same *gharana*, or those who could be conveniently labelled amateur, promising, etc., are brought together. Sometimes *parishad*-s devoted entirely to women musicians, or child artists are organised. *Parishad*-s focusing on a theme (e.g. monsoon *raga*-s, morning *raga*-s) is also a recurring phenomenon.

Parishad may also be described as a *sammelan, samaj,* conference, etc.

1.1.9   *Sama*

Sama = the term is usually translated as 'spiritual music'. However, literally, it means 'hearing'. In Sufism it means listening from the heart to music understood in the most profound sense — including poetry, melodies, rhythms while deeply plunged in the state of Love. As Sheikh Ruzbihan said "*Sama* is God's hearing; it is hearing from Him, for Him, in Him, and with Him. If it is not all of these at the same time, the person practicing *Sama* is not being faithful to God."

There are three kinds of *Sama*: that of ordinary persons, that of the elite and that of the elite of the elite. The ordinary listen with their carnal nature and that leads them to their perdition. The elite listen with their heart but are still full of desire. The elite of the elite listen with their soul and that is Love.

The chief features of *Sama* are:

- It is an offering to God as a mark of adoration and music is chosen to make the offering because music is the language of angels.

- Music is immaterial; both extrovert and introvert, mysterious and pure dynamics like God.
- The *Sama* is all encompassing as a presentation — having melody, rhythm, poetry, incantation, rites and choreography. It is often replete with symbolism.
- In *Sama* there is no distinction between spectators and participants and each expresses himself in a way agreeable to him.
- Music becomes part of Truth since mathematical laws govern it. Now Truth is complementary to Divine beauty — the attainment of which is the final goal of *Sama*.
- The *Sama* constitutes a departure from himself through a musical sacrifice.
- *Sama*, through music takes us back to our origin.

1.1.10 *Samiti*

See introductory note to the section.

1.1.11 *Tatar*

See introductory note to the section.

1.1.12 *Urs* (A.)

Yet another important festival in Indian context is *Urs*. Observed in Muslim shrines, and especially in *Sufi dargah*-s, *Urs* means music made and received ceremoniously, to some extent collectively and always with great enthusiasm. Sometimes these observances lead some performers/receivers to ecstatic states.

It is interesting to note that *Urs* originally means marriage festivities as distinct from marriage ceremony/rituals (i.e. *Nikah*). It also means dedication to god, deity etc. Hence, *Urs* takes place on death anniversaries of great saints and spiritual leaders, which provide the chief occasions for holding festivities. Saints' departure from the worldly scene is obviously interpreted as leading to union with God and hence the semantic association of *Urs* with marriage is not surprising. It also explains the ecstatic, buoyant and yet solemn nature of festivities in the *Urs*. Festivities that begin on the preceding day are known as Sandal (संदल).

A brief description of one of the major Indian *Urs* —the Ajmer *Urs* — in honour of Khwaja Moinuddin Chishti will help in getting a better idea of the phenomenon.

The *Urs* commences with the ritual of unfurling the flag with red border and green colour at the Buland Darwaja to the auspicious accompaniment of *shehnai* and *nagara*. This ritual is known as *'Parcham phaharana'*. On entering through the imposing gate one encounters a well-decorated space permeated with fragrance of roses, other flowers, incense sticks and *attar*-s. Devotees offer flowers in the mosque and later take back some of them as a token of Saint's favour/grace. During the six days of *Urs* Qawwali-singing continues nearly throughout the night.

Every evening, the *mazaar* (grave of the saint) is lit, *nagara* is played to gather the devotees for evening prayers. At late night, the *mazaar* is washed with essence of rose and *kevrah* before devotees are allowed to enter and spread shawl over the grave as offering. Another ritual is *'deg pakana'* which allows a devotee to contribute a share to the food cooked and distributed free to all. On special, appointed days, when bigger prayer meetings are held, the entire premises is washed with essences of rose etc. One may see women devotees washing the floor with their hair to express intensity of emotion.

In 1233 AD, on the first day of the Muslim month of *Rajab*, the Saint entered a room — forbidding disciples to disturb him. Five days later, not able to hold back any longer the disciples entered the room to find that the *Saint* had departed from the world. The exact day of his death could not therefore be ascertained. Hence, the *Urs* festivities are observed for six days.

1.1.13 *Utsava* (S *ut* + *sav* = intense offering)

Today, *Utsava* means a festival. Traditional life-pattern in India makes room for three types of occurrences when religion and performing arts can easily come together. The three are, *vrata*, meaning ritualistic observance, *parva*, i.e. days regarded important as they mark conjunction of certain planets etc. and finally *Utsava*, meaning festival. It is aptly defined as "नियताल्हादजनक व्यापार" that which certainly creates delightful activity. Amarkosha notes synonyms, "मह उद्धव उत्सव". Collective enjoyment and enrichment of the emotional life of the people has been the main goal and hence Vatsayana has described festivals as "संभूय क्रीडा". Quite a few festivals in the Indian tradition have been secular and some of them were patronised by kings. These were called Samajotsava or *Mela*. Even in *Rigveda* one such festival has been specifically mentioned. It was called Saman (समन्). Both men and women took part in it freely and poets, archers, prostitutes as well as marriageable girls participated! Horse-racing was also a part of it. In the ancient times the launching of the festivities was announced by beating a specific drum called *Chanbheri*. Festivals can broadly be described as periodically held celebrations with an accent on offering entertainment. This last type of celebration, *Utsava*, is important because it exemplifies a remarkable design inspired by religious as well as secular motives and manifestations.

Some festivals seem to favour music and other performing arts. Two good examples are *Vasant Panchami* and *Holi*.

Celebrated on the fifth day of the *Magh shuddha* according to the Hindu calendar, *Vasant Panchami* is a ceremonial welcome to advent of spring. It is also known as the day appointed for carrying out worship of Saraswati (the Goddess of learning), or alternatively for propitiating Lord Vishnu and his consort Laxmi (the Goddess of wealth). Wearing yellow garments, performing music and dance form an integral part of this *Utsava*. According to some authorities, this *Utsava* is associated with Madan, the god of love, and Rati, his consort.

When compared to *Holi* festivities, *Vasant Panchami* may appear to be a rather staid affair! *Holi* falls on the full moon day of *Phalgun* and the celebrations include throwing of coloured powder or coloured water on each other in addition to performing music and dance. In all manifestations connected with *Holi*, the element of eroticism comes to the fore. In rural areas even obscenity is accorded a right to surface during *Holi* festivities!

Vasant Panchami, Holi and such other *utsava*-s were highly favoured by rulers of the erstwhile princely states and by members of aristocratic families. These patrons offered musicians/performers generous support during celebrations.

Some examples would bring out the spirit of *Utsava* as a phenomenon.

Rajah Tukoji Holkar (III) of Indore was a great lover of the performing arts. We are told that till 1920-22 he used to celebrate *Holi* by arranging simultaneous performances at three places. The one taking place in open spaces allowed entry to all, the second variety organised in an enclosed space was open only to a select few while the third, arranged in his personal drawing room, was only meant for intimate invitees. The Maharaja paid artists in silver coins heaped in a fair-sized *'thali'* (plate) to express his appreciation of their performing excellence!

The other example is described in a biography of Ustad Mushtaq Hussain Khan (1878-1964) of the Sahaswan *gharana*. We are told:

> It was traditional with the court of Rampur to celebrate the advent of *sawan* or the rainy season. The people of the town foregathered in mango groves. Some relaxed in hammocks hanging from the branches of trees, some quaffed thirst-quenching *sherbets* listening to lilting melodies of the season, such as *kajri*, *jhoola* and *sawan*... Famous musicians gathered in the gardens and parks of the Nawab's palace and there were veritable feasts of *malhar-s* and *kajri-s*.*

Another interesting *Utsava* was the one celebrated by the Benaras-based royal houses and *nawabs*. Held on Tuesday (*Mangalwar* of *Chaitra*), *budhwa mangal* as the *Utsava* was called, saw expansive waters of the river Ganga adorned by rows of houseboats with the king's boat at the centre flanked by those of his courtiers etc. An awning was erected on the decks and colourful chandeliers illuminated the scene. Accomplished courtesans such as Badi Maina, Chhoti Maina, Rajeshwari Shivakunwar and Badi Moti performed. Courtesans from Benaras sang to the accompaniment of *sitar*, *tanpura*, etc., and therefore claimed more sophistication in their music performance.

In Benaras another interesting celebration with music-making at the centre was known as *Gulab-badi* (गुलाब-बाड़ी).

---

*Kshitish Roy, Sangeet Natak Akademi, New Delhi, 1964, pp. 21-22.

During the late 18th and early 19th century the post-*Holi* period, when roses were in abundance, *Chaiti*-s were sung in the fragrance-laden atmosphere and this music-making occasion was known as *Gulab-badi*. In it the seating arrangement utilised rose-petals, drinks were rose-coloured, lighting was rosy, rose-water was sprinkled on guests, the entire décor accentuated the same colour and costumes were also full of rose-colour and roses! Yet another instance when music was not treated as an entirely aural phenomenon!

After the 1890s, new *utsava*-s with political motivation and more evident nationalist prompting flourished and music always had a place in programme-schedules. The *Ganesh Utsava* launched in 1898 by the well-known freedom fighter and political activist Lokmanya Bal Gangadhar Tilak in Maharashtra and the *Durgapooja Utsava* in Bengal are good examples.

In the post-Independence era, the country celebrates 26th January (Republic Day) and 15th August (Independence day) as additional festivals.

1.2   Format

In the present context format is to be understood as an arrangement or deployment of music-making agencies accepted for presentation .The arrangement is designed to satisfy a particular performing purpose. Format is also related to the manner in which different members or components of the performing-set are distributed.

Elite or art, i.e. 'classical' music in contemporary India has not favoured choral or orchestral format. Ancient and medieval music making, however, clearly presented a different picture. Nowadays, group-performance is a phenomenon confined largely to folk, primitive or popular music.

In the final analysis, any particular format and the musical content related to it determine their mutual roles: an internal logic seems to operate and performing aims condition their interrelationship.

In the ancient tradition the mode of performing as a group was described as *kutapa*.

Kutapa was a special use of *vrinda,* i.e. a collective mode of music-making current in ancient India. If collective music making is used as a primary criterion then India seems to have a long tradition. For example, the Mahavrata ceremony in Grihyasootra mentioned priest's wives singing together. All epics refer to collective-singing. Sitabenga caves (200 AD) have a platform for instrumentalists.

However, most important is Bharata's *Kutapa Vinyasa,* i.e. placement/arrangement of *kutapa*. It is clearly stated that the arrangement has to take place before the commencement of the *poorvaranga* whish was the ritualistic pre-performance ceremony. The group performing it used to sit facing the audience and between the two *nepathyaka*-s. Among the players of chordophones, those playing *vipanci* and *vina* were seated separately. The *vina*-players employed *chitravina*. The role of *kacchapi* and *ghoshaka* varieties of *vina* was regarded secondary.

Three kinds of *kutapa* are mentioned: (1) *Tatakutapa*: This was to accompany the singers/songstresses. It actually consisted of *vipanchik, vainik*-s and *vanshavadak*. (2) *Avanaddha kutapa*: Consisted of *mradangik, panavik, darduraka*. (3) *Natyakutapa*: Consisted of singers, instrumental groups and different actors and actresses.

The *Kutapa* had the following stages: (1) *Pratyahara* = arrangement of instruments, (2) *Avatarana* = appearance of singers, (3) *Arambha* = commencement of vocal exercises,

(4) *Ashravana* = proper/methodical taking up of instruments, (5) *Vaktrapani* = rehearsing different styles of playing, (6) *Parighattana* = tuning of strings, (7) *Sanghottana* = taking up hand-poses for rhythm, (8) *Margasarita* = playing together of strings and rhythm-instruments. Bharata also specified seating arrangement.

Even the later *Sangeet Ratnakara*, refers to *natyakutapa* of three types: *uttama* (the best) = having 4 main singers, 12 accompanying singers, 4 flautists and 4 drummers (4-12-4-4). For *madhyama* (the medium) and *kanishtha* (inferior) varieties, the number of participants in similar categories was respectively 2-4-2-2 and 1-3-2-2.

In order to determine what kind of format operates in a particular performance, a useful question could be asked: Who sits/stands where and does what?

In art-music, all performers are seated. In a conventional distribution of the performing-set the chief performer occupies the central position, drone accompanists are normally at the back and on both sides of the main performer, rhythm accompanist operates from the main performer's right and melodic support comes from his/her left. Examined visually, the arrangement appears to function as a guide to the audience to focus its attention. Thus the distribution of the performing set helps better reception of the intended musical stimuli.

1.2.1   *Ekala* (S alone, singly)

An arrangement of the performing set in which one artiste performs with or without accompaniment is called *Ekala*. The format is employed both in rhythm-oriented and melody-oriented music.

Hindustani music making finds the format conducive at least on two accounts:

1. As is known improvisatory procedures are inherent to and important in art music: the format proves to be the most natural way of making music in this way. An artiste performing *Ekala* is unfettered and remains in full command of the process of music making. In case of a performer who concentrates on the tonal dimension, the accompanist operating in the rhythmic channel follows the former closely and vice versa.

2. Hindustani music lays greater store by succession and sequence, rather than by simultaneity and syncopation of musical notes. In other words, one note or beat at a time and one musical unit after the other, constitutes the general controlling principle. Elaboration, patterning and other musical strategies are explored in the *Ekala* format.

1.2.2   *Jugalbandi* (S *Jugal* = pair + A *bandi* = to bind)

While *Ekala* (solo) is the reigning format in Hindustani music making, no dynamic music culture can be expected to obstinately adhere to a single format. Variations in formats have therefore been effected through the ages. One such change in format is known as *Jugalbandi*. (The core meaning of the term *'yugul'* meaning pair is also carried to terms connected with other genres of music making e.g. in *dhrupad*.)

A co-ordinated music-making by a pair of main artistes, either in vocal or instrumental mode, with or without accompaniment, is known as *Jugalbandi*. To perform in pairs has been customary. In fact musicological evidence suggests that some musical forms received their special identity because a pair of chief performers presented them.[7]

It is usual to find two disciples of the same *guru* perform in the *Jugalbandi* format, obviously because they find it easier to co-ordinate. Examining the contents of Hindustani music one realises that all *raga*-music is concretised through presentations of grammatically correct and aesthetically relevant sequences. It therefore becomes necessary that successive phrasings of the two chief participants in a *Jugalbandi* result into a coherent, total pattern. Two individual insights creating a single concentrated vision is, in itself, a joy! In addition, *Jugalbandi* gives the pleasure of producing notable variety in tonal colour — an aspect in which Hindustani music is comparatively deficient.

In a standardised *Jugalbandi* combination, a pair of vocalists/instrumentalists accompanied by one rhythm-player present music. A variation might include two rhythm-accompanists inviting a description 'double *Jugalbandi*'! Other pairings in the format may combine *sitar* and *sarod*, *shehnai* and *violin*, *violin* and *bansuri*, *tabla* and *pakhawaj*.

It is necessary to remember that in *Jugalbandi* the basic composition such as *bandish*, *gat* etc. is presented jointly and without a pronounced segmentation. On the other hand duet format may include division of the composition itself.

1.2.3   *Kaccheri* = कच्चेरी

Though this format is more in vogue in the Carnatic system of art music it is finding takers in Hndustani music and moreover it displays some continuity with formats described in texts such as *Manasollasa*.

The word itself is derived from the Urdu word *Kachheri* which is significant as it has been often claimed that South

Indian music is entirely exempt from Muslim influence! As a format it is distinguished by the fact that even if there is one major vocalist or instrumentalist, and he is the main artist as in any other solo item, he is accompanied on varied instruments such as *violin, mridangam, ghatam, jhanz, dholak* and *khanjiri*. The format is traditionally governed by five sets of rules that control and determine the proceedings. Their names and areas of duties, etc., are as follows:

(1) *Gayak-vadak dharma* (गायकवादकधर्म): Rules pertaining to *raga, tala,* forms and behaviour protocol of accompanists, etc., are included in this set. (2) *Sabhapatidharma* (सभापतिधर्म): Every gathering has two presiding personalities — one knowledgeable in music and the other person respected in the society. They may intervene in the proceedings to ensure proper understanding of music and the successful completion of the venture. (3) *Samajdharma* (समाज-धर्म): Members of audience are to observe rules such as keeping quiet, give response at proper time in a proper way, to go out or come in, in such a way as not to disturb the gathering. (4) *Yajamandharma* (यजमानधर्म): When a patron arranges a concert in his house he should look after artists in every way, and pay them, as is considered proper. (5) *Karyadarshidharma* (कार्यदर्शीधर्म): An overall organiser has to ensure the proper sequence of the performance and provide necessary information about artists, items, etc., from time to time.

1.3 Performers

Hindustani musical literature employs a number of terms to denote performers, i.e. makers of music. Some of the terms give us inkling of their specialisation, versatility, etc. Some terms may also refer to the artistic excellence or mediocrity of the performers. There are some that range beyond music and point discreetly to their social status.

These terms in reality form a meaningful cluster. When properly appreciated, they provide an insight into the complex and sophisticated distinctions that exist among musicians.

Strictly speaking, the audience can hardly be considered to be in the performing category. However, audiences' contribution/input in presentation of art-music in India is immeasurable as it is chiefly qualitative in nature. By nods, claps, evocative utterances, occasional comments and extempore remarks, etc., the audience holds a culturally conditioned and subtly controlled dialogue with the performer throughout the entire performance. Anybody who merely 'listens' to Hindustani art music can hardly be considered its accredited audience! The 'real' audience has to 'perform' to earn that honour!

1.3.1 *Atai* (A)

Atai is a person who learns skills, etc., quickly or without anybody's help. However, the term has also acquired more specific though contradictory musicological meanings. For example, Fakirullah, in his *Ragadarpana* stated that the term indicated a person who knew the practical aspect of the art well but was weak in theory. On the other hand, a performer-patron of the status and musical ability of Ibrahim Adil Shah (II) (1580-1626 AD), described *Atai* as a musician of the highest order.

1.3.2 *Bajvaiyya* (H *bajana* = to play + suffix *ya. baja* S *vadya* = an instrument)

The term denotes a maker of instrumental music in general — either as a soloist or an accompanist.

1.3.3   *Bandijana* (S) Refers to a professional caste/class of performers active in early historical times. Performers from the caste made a living by singing praise songs.

1.3.4   *Buzurg* (P old, advanced in age, ancestor, parent)

The term connotes a performer who has long passed his prime but whose past achievements are still recognised by the musician community in general. With less frequency the term is also used to denote a connoisseur respected for his deep knowledge. *Buzurg* performers as well as listeners enjoy certain privileges in traditional musical events. For example, they would be offered front seat in a performance. Performers would also offer respects to them and solicit their permission before commencing to perform. In case a *buzurg* member of the audience expresses appreciation during performance, he would be immediately thanked in a proper manner.

It is interesting to note that the parent scale in contemporary Hindustani art music is *Bilawal*. The same scale is known in Persian makam system as *Buzurg*!

1.3.5   *Choumukha* (H S *chatur* = four + *mukha* = mouth)

The term is an obvious tribute to versatility of certain art-musicians. A male singer who can proficiently render four major forms in vocal music namely, *khayal*, *dhrupad-dhamar*, *tarana* and *thumri* is described as *choumukha*.

It is interesting to note that a medieval musical form was known as *chaturmukha* and *chaturanga*; a contemporary form possibly derived from the former includes elements that are predominant in the four forms mentioned earlier. The four elements are: meaningful words (associated with *khayal*), *sol-fa* singing (as in *sargam*), meaningless auspicious syllables (used in *tarana*). The core meaning of the term 'Choumukha' is also carried to other areas of music making. For example, a special kind of elaboration of rhythmic ideas in *Mridang/Pakahwaj* is described as 'Choumukha'.

It is presumed that a female singer displaying similar capacity would need a similar term!

1.3.6 *Dhrupadiya* (H *dhrupad* + suffix *ya*)

Dhrupadiya is a male singer specialising in performance of a musical form known as *dhrupad*. It is to be marked that the *ya*-ending formation is restricted to only two forms, namely, *khayal* and *dhrupad*. The reasons do not appear to be linguistic and hence the fact may prove predominance of these two forms within the art-music repertoire of vocal modality.

1.3.7 *Gandharva* (S)

According to the Naradiya Shiksha the term is derived in a rather metaphorical way. The three letters in the term stand for important musical features, thus *ga* = music, *dha* = instrumental accompaniment and *va* = instruments.

The term has a long history.

It is interesting to note that in *Rigveda* the term is often applied to a collective, a group of people whose abode (in company with Apsara) is water and skies. The *Taittiriya Pratishakhya* divides *gandharva*-s in two broad classes: *deva-gandharva* and *manushya-gandharva*. The former are divine, live in skies and are distinguished by handsome looks. The latter, human in origin and form, and known for their devotion are the ancient *gandharva* variety of music.

Gandharva-s are created by the supreme Lord of Creation and belong to the divine category. According to the Brahmana texts they are described as fond of luxury, lovers of women and beauty of forms — but they are also regarded slightly troublesome deities! They constitute a class of celestial musicians, of demigods specifically mentioned as singers or musicians of gods and reported to have 'good voices agreeable to females'. Early literature refers to them along with Magadha, Charana and Apsara. Names of *Gandharva*-s specifically assigned to Gods are: Vishvavasu, Ha Ha, Hu Hu, Narada, Parvat and Tumbaru. Narada we are specifically told, played *Vallari* and *Mahati* types of *vina*. The first was used to establish *murchana*-s of the seven notes to render *gramaraga*. The second kind of *vina*, he used to hang/tie around his neck during his famous peregrinations around the three worlds!

Their number has varied considerably in different texts. For example, *Atharvaveda* gives a figure of 6333, *Shatapatha Brahmana* enumerates 27 while *Taittiriya Aranyaka* has listed 11.

The epic *Ramayana* also mentions them as singers of praise-songs and divine artists. Their inclination to recreation, entertainment and generally to 'joys of life' is unfailingly reported. A rather curious etymological explanation in *Vayupurana* notes that the root *'dha'* means to 'drink' and hence the term refers to a clan which sings while drinking! However a more 'sober' interpretation from the same source talks of *gandharva*-s as those who sing the ancient *gandharva* variety of music. Another major *purana*, the *Markandeya Purana* states that *gandharva* belong to a professional caste of expert musicians with the status of demigods.

Interestingly certain geographical areas of the nine divisions of Bharatvarsha — as ancient India was known —

are also mentioned in the tradition as *Gaandharva*. For example, in the Vindhyachala janapada, there is one named *tumbaru/tumbul* — ostensibly name of one of the *gandharva* clans.

Gandharva-s have been depicted (as *vina*-playing on the right side of Buddha) in paintings sculptures near Mathura. Amaravati (200 BC), Nagarjuna Konda (200 AD) and the famous Ajanta caves also have their depiction.

During various periods in ancient India the term *gandharva* was applied to:

1.   Deities who knew divine secrets,
2.   Demigods who specialised in preparing *soma* — the divine drink — and who were notably partial to women,
3.   Those who (in addition to being inclined towards wine and women) were court musicians to Indra, the king of gods.

In later history a particular region was associated with them, a fact that would probably suggest that they were caste-musicians.

From medieval times onwards, *gandharva*-s were described as those who knew ancient as well as the modern vocal and instrumental music.

Today the term has been equated with performers who impress by unexpected sweetness in singing (due to performer's young age, etc.) and thus it is used as an honorific.

1.3.8   *Gaunharin* (H.)

Refers to professional women-singers especially from Benaras, who competently and competitively render *Kajri* (>) compositions.

1.3.9   *Gayaka* (S *gai* = to sing)

The term may denote:

1. one who is singing,
2. one who earns livelihood by singing, and
3. one who sings praises (of a patron).

As a critical term, *gayaka* is a value-neutral description of a performer who uses voice as his medium to make music. Of the three meanings noted above, the first suggests a vocalist, that is, a maker of music through voice. The second shade suggests a professional status (as opposed to an amateur). The third refers to a class of performers appointed to sing compositions in praise of kings, patrons, etc.

A female vocalist is described as *gayika*. It is to be noted that if performers are referred to as *ganewala* and *ganewali*, i.e. if Hindi (and not Sanskrit) terms apparently synonymous with the Sanskrit terms are used, there is a slide-down in the social scale. The Hindi terms connote performers from a lower class of professional entertainers who may also be assumed to have a lax moral code!

The medieval musicological tradition had a five-fold classification of *gayaka*-s as shown below:

Shikshakar	= a conscientious and able teacher
Anukar	= an able imitator
Rasik	= one who sang with emotion
Ranjak	= an entertainer
Bhavak	= an innovator capable of revitalising music

In *Ain-e-Akbari* court musicians are classified in three categories: *Gayanda* = singers, *Khavanda* = reciters and *Sazinda* = instrumentalists.

1.3.10   *Gayanda* = see *Gayaka*

1.3.11   *Gavaiyya* (H *gana* = to sing)

The term is understood as a special word in continuation of the term *gayaka*. A male art-musician of recognised mastery over the science and practice of music is called *gavaiyya*.

1.3.12   *Guni/gunakar* (S possessor of qualities or merit)

Generally the term refers to a performer acquainted with the current, as opposed to ancient, music and one who is also able to perform it proficiently.

1.3.13   *Kalavant* (S *kalavan* = one who knows art)

The historian Abul Fazl (1551-1596 AD) described a professional singer of *dhrupad* as *kalavant* and added that such singers come from a caste, which makes its living from music. In Rajasthan, *kalavant* denotes a caste-musician and a folk performer who sings but does not play an instrument. He also eschews dancing.

It is in this perspective that art-musicians took umbrage on being described as *kalavant*-s. In 1937, they registered an organised protest on being described as *kalavant*!

Today the term has become almost harmless as it is taken to mean 'an artiste'.

1.3.14   *Kalakar/Kalavati* (S *kala* = art)

Refer to a male or female artiste respectively. Etymologically there is no justification to confine the terms to music. Both are general terms covering all modalities, forms, mediums, etc., in music.

1.3.15 *Khavanda* = see *Gayaka*

1.3.16 *Khayaliya/khyaliya* (H *khayal* + suffix *ya*)

A male singer, who specialises in rendering the Hindustani vocal form *khayal*, is called a *khayaliya*. The *'ya'* ending is restricted to only two forms, namely *khayal* and *dhrupad*, and to that extent the prominence of the two forms within the Hindustani repertoire is emphasized.

1.3.17 *Mirashi* or *Mirasi* (A)

Mirashi or *mirasi* is a caste term. A person, who accompanies courtesans or 'nautch' girls (known as *Baiji* or *Tawaif*) on string or membrane-covered instruments, is described as *mirashi* or *mirasi*. Muslim caste-musicians residing in Punjab were also described as *mirashi*. Females in the caste, known as *mirasin*-s, are professional performers.

Today the term has come to mean an inferior musician accompanying a vocalist. Music education imparted by a *mirashi* is looked down upon. It is expected to be less authentic and less scientific.

1.3.18 *Nayaka* (S one who rules over others)

The term has many meanings:

1. A male musician from a caste known for training others in music and dance.
2. A person well versed both in theory and practice of music.

The second meaning is regarded less derogatory and it is more prevalent.

Hakim Muhammad Karam Imam, in his famous *Madanul Mousiki* (1853 AD) mentioned 12 persons who were accepted as *Nayaka*-s in his times. His writing is important as it gives an idea of a perspective near our times. The 12 *Nayaka*-s he lists are:

1. Bhanu	7. Pande
2. Lohang	8. Chajju
3. Dalu	9. Baksu
4. Bhagwan	10. Dhondu
5. Gopal Das	11. Meeramadh
6. Baiju	12. Amir Khusro

Other classes of musicians are:

Gandharva	=	practitioners of *Marga* music in ancient times and experts in *Deshi* music in later times
Guni/Gunakar	=	experts only in modern *raga*-s
Kalavant	=	experts in *dhrupad* and *trivat*
Qawwal	=	expert in *kaul*, *tarana*, and *khayal*
Dhadi	=	singers of *chargha*, etc.
Pandit	=	learned in the science of music

1.3.19 *Pandit* (S a learned person)

A person well versed in the theory of music.

1.3.20 *Peshewar* (< P *peshvar*)

One who professionally renders in front of, in the presence of others. The term is understood to be a contrast to the term amateur in pursuit of art. .

1.3.21 *Qawwal* (A *kaul* = aphorism, saying)

Generally denotes performer who sings *qawwali* songs. In Arabic, a singer of songs is known as *qawwal*. In Arabic *kaul* means a saying. Singers of *kaul* are known as *qawwal*. There were such singers in the times of Altamash (1210-1235 AD), i.e. even before the times of Amir Khusro. A reported tradition is that in the early 19th century, two *qawwal*-s — Shakkar and Makkhan — composed *qawwali*-compositions consisting of *sthayi* and *antara* sections, in *talas* which were not used by *dhrupad*-musicians. *Kaul* and *Kalbana* — the two types of praise songs are always sung together, they constitute a genre-pair. Abul Fazl has noted that like members of the Dhadi community, *qawwal*-s also used to sing popular songs. Persian songs were also sung in the *qawwali* style. Chishti of Ajmer inspired the *qawwal*-s to sing songs in Indian languages. Yet another opinion put forward is that Amir Khusro's influence was responsible for combining Indian and Persian styles and this is how *Kaul* and *Tarana*-s came into vogue. Those who rendered these forms were called *qawwal-bacche*. In the 15th century, Hussain Shah Shirky inspired these to sing *khayal*-songs. To respond to such *khayal*-s, current in his time, Sadarang Nyamatkhan began composing new *khayal*-s in the 18th century and these are today rendered in Hindustani art music.

1.3.22 *Shoukin* (A)

The term describes a person who studies or does something repeatedly to get joy out of the activity.

In music, *shoukin* means one who loves, studies and practises some kind of music with recognisable competence but does not enter the fray, i.e. the profession as a full-fledged musician. In all probability, a *shoukin* musician does not earn his living from music though he performs seriously and may also offer generous patronage to music and musicians. Compared to *peshewar* musicians, a *shoukin* or an amateur is judged less rigorously. It is probable that he enjoys more affection than respect from hard-core performers! The English word dilettante may come close to the import of *shoukin*.

1.3.23   *Vadaka* (S *vad* = to sound)

A performer who plays instrument to make music is known as a *vadaka*. He may or may not do so as an accompanist. Unlike the term *gayaka*, the term *vadaka* does not suggest any specific musical instrument nor does it suggest any socio-musicological status.

1.3.24   *Vyavasayika* (H < S *vyavasaya* = business, employment, profession)

A professional performer as distinguished from an amateur is known as *Vyavasayika*. Not only is he supposed to earn his livelihood through performance but more importantly, he is also expected to maintain high standards in effectiveness, proficiency, width of repertoire, etc. Demands made on *vyavasayika* musician are in all respects more exacting. Sometimes, *peshewar* is used as synonym for *vyavasayika* and vice versa.

1.4 Accompaniment

In the Hindustani system, music making is predominantly a solo activity. It is the individual performer who enjoys freedom and scope to project and elaborate his musical ideas. However, inputs from accompanists in varying degrees and of different kinds have a role to play. In fact, for a majority of performances in Hindustani music there is a conventionally constituted performing set which consists of three components, namely, main artiste/s, accompanist/s and audience.

Further, accompaniment is of three kinds: melodic, rhythmic and of drone.

Melodic accompaniment is obviously on the tonal axis. In essence it concentrates on progression of pitches employed and patterned in music. Rhythmic accompaniment focuses on 'beats' or measures as time-divisions and their patterns. Finally, drone is prominently designed/intended to continuously provide 'fundamental' or the selected note on which musician constructs selected scale, upwards and downwards. Of the three, the drone is the more constant/invariable. The other two are obvious variables in the sense that if the main artiste so chooses, he would allow introduction of improvised interruptions as well as link-phrases. This would create scope for melodic and rhythmic accompaniments. However, the basic tenet remains that by intention and arrangement, accompanists are followers, not leaders.

In a way, distribution of the accompanying set reflects primacy of vocal music. For example, the following conventional performing sets may be noted:

Main artiste	*Accompaniment*
Vocalist	rhythmic, melodic and drone
Instrumentalist (rhythmic)	melodic and drone
Instrumentalist (melodic)	rhythmic and drone

While describing the desirability of musical instruments, Sharangdeva, the medieval musicologist, made an admission of rare candor. He stated that rhythm instruments enthuse, encourage and bring joy to those in pain. He then goes on to add 'all instruments help in concealing shortcomings of the artiste'. It is obvious that accompanists may find themselves engaged in this musical philanthropy oftener than could be imagined!

1.4.1   *Jawab sangat* = (H *jawab* = answer, *sangat* = accompaniment)

In vocal or instrumental music, a *mukhada* is inserted after a *tan* or *paran*, etc. If and when accompanying rhythm instrument follows in a similar manner it is known as *Jawab sangat*.

1.4.2   *Lehra* (H *leher* = ripple, small wave)

For solo performances on rhythm instruments, especially on membranophonic instruments such as *tabla* as also for solo dance items, a recurring tonal pattern encompassing a predetermined number of beats is cyclically supplied in the required tempo on *sarangi, harmonium, violin* or on some such other melodic instrument. This repeated melodic pattern is known as *Lehra*.

The essence of a *lehra* is its constancy and sequentiality intended to provide a firm reference. It is not musically/melodically elaborated, even though a *lehra* player occasionally may tend to add a few embellishments to the melodic frame. It is untiringly presented as a reference circle to the solo-player as per his directions. It truly constitutes a minor musical wave!

Vocal *lehra* is a theoretical possibility but rarely exploited in music.

1.4.3   *Rebha* = A performer who sang praise songs was known as *Rebha*.

1.4.4   *Sazinda* (P *saz* = instrument)

An accompanist who provides accompaniment on a tonal or rhythmic instrument is known as *Sazinda*. Reportedly, the term indicates low status of accompanists, as they play with courtesans, etc. In *Ain-e-Akbari* court musicians are classified in three categories: *Gayanda* = singers, *Khavanda* = reciters and *Sazinda* = instrumentalists.

1.4.5   *Sangatiya* (H S *sam* = together + *gam* = to go)

Sangat indicates a purposeful coming together of two entities, which can otherwise be independent of each other.

In sophisticated musicological parlance *sangat* means to accompany but not by repeating what the chief musician has done. Nor is it a mechanical imitation of the soloist. In essence, *sangat* indicates an act of providing tonal or rhythmic complement to the main artiste, suitably and attractively matching or responding to his expression. In case the accompanist chooses to mechanically follow the soloist, his contribution is best described as *sath*, which merely means 'to be with'.

The term under discussion is however not to be confused with *sangati*, though both terms are etymologically connected. In music, *sangati* is a special relationship of agreement between two or more tonal phrases or patterns positioned/placed at a fair distance from one another and preferably in different halves of the scale-space.

1.4.6   *Sath* (H < S *sahit* = with)

Sath connotes a type of imitative and less creative accompaniment to the main artiste (also see *Sangat*).

1.4.7   *Sur* (H < S *swara* = note)

The drone accompaniment that characterises Hindustani art music of both vocal and instrumental modalities is known as *sur*. Basically, drone supplies a continuous fundamental in the scale selected by a performer. Sometimes, the fifth of the fundamental and the lower octave are also included in the *sur*. Considered as a whole, the *sur* turns out to be more of an atmospheric agent than a mere supply of one basic note, etc.

Tanpura for vocal music, *tamburi* for string instruments, etc., *sur* for *shehnai*, *sruti*-box or harmonium are some other examples of instruments employed for providing *sur*.

Drone provides *adharswana*, that is, a resultant sound from a cluster of notes or from a single note intended to serve as a foundation to music making. The principle of tonality (fixing the fundamental) and regarding *shadja*, *pancham* as immovable notes played important roles in determining the character of *sur* as it is obtained and employed today.

Usages such as *sur dena* (to give a *sur*) or *sur bharna* (to fill a *sur*) suggest the elements of continuity and fullness that every *sur* is necessarily expected to possess.

1.4.8   *Talapani* (S *tal* = to fix, found, establish *tala* = clapping, slapping + *pani* = hands)

It is a useful term. Unfortunately it has gone out of circulation. A person who provides accompaniment by marking *tala* by handclaps is called *talapani*. He may or may not recite the *tala* syllables aloud. Even today, a *talapani* is seen in action in presentation of *pakhawaj* solo. It is of interest to note that a *talapani* is not in action with *tabla*, etc., these being modern compared to the *pakhawaj*, the drum of ancient origin.

There is room to believe that *talapani* operated even during the Epic period of ancient India.

1.4.9   *Talapachara* (S *tala* = rhythm + *apachara* = departure)

A person, who provides rhythm accompaniment to a group of singers in a procession, by marking *tala* with handclaps and / or by reciting *tala*-syllables aloud, was called a *talapachara*, literally meaning 'to walk with *tala*'.

1.5 Forms of Music (Vocal)

The term 'form' is used in two closely and conceptually related but distinct senses. Thus when we pass a judgement on a particular performance of music as 'formless', the usage points to a wider, more conceptual connotation. The term 'formless' indicates that the performance in question lacks a sense of direction; or that it is marred by irregularity in construction; its components may suffer from a loss of balance finally leading to the remark 'there is no form in this entire activity'. This exemplifies 'form *in* music'.

On the other hand, a performance may reveal a definite sequence; its expression may display a purposeful selection of performing modes; arrangement of components may exhibit application of unambiguous criteria. As a result, it will deserve a conclusive comment such as: 'the performance is/ was, of vocal, classical, *khayal* music'. This latter judgement is an instance of clearly noting recognition and appreciation of 'form *of* music'.

How does the early Indian tradition look at the issue?

The 'doubtless' Sharangadeva in his *Sangeet Ratnakara* perceives the musical content to be divisible in six aspects (*ang*), which differ in their degree of essentiality. The *ang*-s are identified as:

Name	Meaning
Swara	Note/s in music
Biruda	Words of praise
Tenaka	Meaningless syllables regarded auspicious
Pada	Meaningful linguistic unit/s
Pata	Letters selected on account of their onomatopoetic properties to represent basic sounds of *avanaddha* (membrano-phonic) instruments
Tala	Basic and highly structured rhythm cycles formulated and accepted as basic and generative in Indian music— in practice as well as in theory

It is obvious that these aspects are expected to give a 'form' to the concerned music manifestation — this being the first and wider sense of the term 'form' explained earlier. However, actual inclusion/exclusion of some of these aspects results in emergence of a 'form' of music — in the second, narrower sense of the term 'form' as explained earlier. This narrower sense is suggested by the term *prabandha* in the ancient tradition.

Ratnakara notes the possibility that all six aspects may not be present in all forms of music and therefore a fivefold classification is presented, depending on the number of aspects included as shown:

Class name	Number of aspects
Medini	Six
Anandini	Five
Deepani	Four
Bhavani	Three
Taravali	Two

A strong commonsense is revealed in the unstated norm that there cannot be a form of music with less than two aspects. Music with a single aspect would at the most be a promise of music, not realised music!

This section is concerned with the second and narrower meaning of the term 'form' and it therefore focuses on forms of music. The concept of form is immediately related to the important aesthetic issues such as form and content, experience and conception, as well as the perennially debated theme of tradition and innovation. However, the discussion is pitched at a less ambitious level, that of explaining contemporary practice of music. In other words, only those forms of music rendered in customary musical situations such as concert, practice and learning are discussed.

The number of music-forms in art music does not exceed fifty-odd even if vocal and instrumental musical repertoires are considered together!

This may appear surprising, obviously in need of some explanation!

A brief look at early history may therefore prove helpful.

The medieval musicological scene could boast of at least seventy-five major forms of music (even if subtypes are set aside). The late eighteenth century chroniclers of musical practice refer to about thirty-five forms of music.

If one goes by references in modern, music-related literature pertaining to Hindustani music one can compile a whole list of musical genres which may appear to be a mixed bag as it contains song-types from at least four categories of music, namely art, religious, folk and popular. These genres are listed below to give an idea of the varied performing fare available when categories, arts and genres were not rigorously differentiated:

Forms discussed:

1. Arya
2. Ashtapadi
3. Badhawa
4. Bana
5. Bandish
6. Bandish ki thumri
7. Baradasta
8. Barvi
9. Beha/er
10. Bhajan
11. Chaiti
12. Char bait
13. Chaturang
14. Chaupai
15. Cheej/z
16. Chhanda
17. Chutukla
18. Chutkula (Choutukla)
19. Dadra (paired with Nukta)
20. Dhamar

21. Dharu
22. Dhrupad
23. Dhun ke Bhajan
24. Doha/Duha
25. Dutekiya Bhajan
26. Fati/eha
27. Geet
28. Ghazal (paired with Reekhta)
29. Gurcha
30. Holi/ri
31. Holi/ri geet
32. Huddikhwani
33. Jaccha
34. Jikri
35. Jod
36. Jut
37. Kajli/ri
38. Ka/ilbana
39. Kilbana-naqsh
40. Kaul/kool (paired with Kalbana)
41. Kavitta
42. Keherawa
43. Khayal
44. Khayalnuma
45. Kool
46. Lachau/v thumri
47. Lakshangeet
48. Langda Dhrupad
49. Led
50. Lehra
51. Manqabat
52. Marsiya
53. Maulood

54. Palna
55. Phag
56. Phagua
57. Phataha
58. Phoolband/h
59. Phoolpad
60. Prabandha
61. Qawwali
62. Raas
63. Ragasagar
64. Reekhta/Rekhta
65. Sadra
66. Samaji Bhajan
67. Samvadi Bhajan
68. Sargamgeet
69. Sawan
70. Sohar (Jaccha)
71. Sohla/Sohe/ila
72. Soz
73. Sozkhwani
74. Stobha
75. Stotra
76. Stuti
77. Sumirani (Kajri)
78. Swaravarta
79. Tapkhayal
80. Tappa
81. Tarana
82. Thumri
83. Trivat
84. Tuk
85. Vishnupada
86. Yugul /(bandh)

However, this multiplicity as well as the attrition of array of genres in art music is in a way deceptive. Firstly, the contemporary categorisation of music into primitive, folk, art and popular, etc., was not applied in the early years. Secondly, classification of arts into literary, performing and the fine arts is also a comparatively later attempt. These two factors have a direct bearing on enumeration of forms of art music listed as genres in vogue. For example, a genre of ritualistic dance-music might be considered nowadays as of the 'folk' category unlike in the medieval perspectives on music. Similarly, today a poem with each line composed in a different language may be considered a form of literature, and not of music. This is no place to lay down theoretical principles that govern crystallisation of music into forms of art-music. However, it would be helpful though somewhat simplistic to state that accent on tonal or rhythmic material, emphasis on meaningful or intellectual patterning and importance of simplicity of statement or complexity in rendering appear to provide significant criteria relevant to performance as well as appreciation of contemporary art music.

1.5.1   *Arya* (S *root ru* = to move, go)

It must be admitted that *Arya* does not enjoy status of a musical form suited to concert stage. It is one of the 'singable' and ancient metres regulated by the number of syllabic instants it consists of. Its connection with art music is mainly because of its employment as a pedagogical tool. In the tradition of Hindustani art music Arya was pressed into service to coherently string together grammatical features of *raga*. It is to be noted that through collections of Arya-s, the so-called uneducated musicians of the last century often had access to musicological scholastic tradition otherwise available in Sanskrit texts alone. The flexible structure of the Arya has obvious musical possibilities. It is no accident that it was used in *Gatha Saptashati* (seven hundred *Gatha*-s), the famous collection of songs by king Hala in *Maharashtra Prakrit*. Arya is abundantly sung by *keertankar*-s in the *Naradiya* tradition of the religio-musical discourses even today.

1.5.2   *Ashtapadi* (S. *ashta* (eight)+ *pada* (stanza)

Broadly speaking the term indicates a composition of eight stanzas, each consisting of eight lines. Jayadeva, the well-known poet-composer (12th century) brought prestige to the form and established it because of his unique dance-drama *Geet Govinda*. Jayadeva probably lived and composed between 1150-1200 AD. He belonged to the Vaishnavite cult that emphasized the worship of Vishnu (i.e. one of the three Hindu gods of the divine triad Brahma, Vishnu and Shiva). However, Jayadeva and his much-celebrated *Geet Govinda* register important deviations. *Geet Govinda is* recognised as a composite expression (i.e. consisting of dance, drama and music) in a form identified as *prekshanaka* (which was within a subtype called *uparupaka* in the theatric discussions). It is the first, major, poetic work in which *raga*-s for individual compositions are indicated, suggesting repeated performances. The complex structure of 12 cantos, 24 songs and narrative *sloka*-s employed 11 *raga*-s, had three characters in all: namely Radha, Krishna and Sakhi, i.e. a friend of Radha. It is also important because of the important place accorded to Radha, Lord Krishna's beloved. The work celebrates ecstatic, unconventional and highly, aesthetically manifested love-relationship of Radha and Lord Krishna (the only major musician-god in the Hindu pantheon!). The eight-stanza verse-form (hence known as *ashtapadi*) is employed and epi-sodes are thematically linked to lead to the climax of the *raas* dance (a circular dance form). Krishna, a popular Hindu god and an incarnation of Vishnu, dominated all Indian art forms throughout this period. Jayadeva's achievement was musical as well as cultural.

The main components of the genre are *dhruva*, *abhog*, *pada* and *biruda*. Another tradition holds that the king of Gwaliyar, Mansinha Tomar (1486-1516 AD) brought into vogue a genre called *Vishnupada* & hence *ashtapadi* as well as the *ashtachhap geya pada* in the Pushtimarga tradition were compelled to draw a furrow of their own. Yet another opinion is that all these forms constituted a musico-cultural answer to the *ghazal*, which Islamic *Sufi* saints popularised. In the 19th cen-tury Vasudevbuwa Joshi, a disciple of Ustad Hassukhan of Gwaliyar School of Hindustani Music revived the *ashtapadi* by composing them in *raga* and *tala*. Since then, Gwaliyar singers of *khayal* include *ashtapadi*-s in their repertoire.

1.5.3   Badhawa (H)

Originally, it is a genre of folk songs from Rajasthan in celebration of marriage, especially congratulating the bride-groom/bride for the happy union and prospective happi-ness. However, many *khayal* compositions are in circulation today, which deal with the same theme. Till the recent past art musicians used to sing such compositions with the avowed purpose of aptly and musically celebrating the oc-casion when patronage to art music was mainly princely courts and houses of feudal chiefs, etc. Today, though such compositions are sung, even musicians may not be aware of their original thrust! To that extent such compositions have become less functional and more art-oriented.

1.5.4   *Beha/er* = (H)

It is a folk song type in Braj with many subtypes such as Purana, Kanhaiya Khayal ki, Hathrasi, Rohatak and Kasganji. The genre is presented in competitive musical meets known as *dangal* or *akhada*. Even though songs from the genre are not from a musical genre presented from concert stage the songs display many musical features of art music. For example, purposeful use of *raga* and *tala*, elaboration of musical ideas, exhibition of musical skills to win over audiences, employment of well-designed stylistic/idiomatic formation are easily marked. In Hathrasi *beher*, for instance, very slow tempo is employed unlike many folk songs. Its refrain rises from the lower *pancham* to *madhya sa* with notable majesty before continuing melodic progressions. They are also passed on as per norms governing the famous *guru-shishya* tradition along with related customs and conventions.

1.5.5   *Bana* (H = Bridegroom)

Originally, it is a genre of folk songs from Rajasthan, which describe the merits, and good looks of the bridegroom who is about to get married. However, many *khayal* compositions are in circulation today, which deal with the same theme. Till the recent past art musicians used to sing such compositions with the avowed purpose of aptly and musically praising the bridegroom when patronage to art music was mainly princely courts and houses of feudal chiefs, etc. Today, though such compositions are sung, even musicians may not be aware of their original thrust! To that extent such compositions have become less functional and more art-oriented.

1.5.6   *Bandish* (H binding together)

The literal meaning of the term does not reflect the qualitative musical distinction it enjoys. Every single musical composition, or a *cheez* as it is called in vocal music, is not accorded status of a *bandish*. A *bandish* is a composition, which, due to its inherent completeness, can claim to be a map of a full musical growth, comparable to a seed carrying within it the complete potential of a full form. Hence knowledgeable persons in the world of music immediately accept a performer who is able to establish and prove mastery on *bandish*. Indian musicians rightly lay emphasis on knowing as many of *bandish*-s as possible. In fact a musician who scores high in this respect is described with a special adjective — *kothiwale* (a veritable storehouse).

The word composition would only be a loose translation of the term *Bandish*. In a way the Hindi meaning of the term, i.e. 'binding together', is a good description of the function *bandish* carries out. Musical content must have a ground plan on which an artist would be expected to build with the help of musical material at his disposal. *Bandish* performs this task. As indicated earlier, the term is usually used to refer to basic compositions a vocalist employs to launch musical improvisations/elaborations. However, there is little justification to restrict the term *bandish* to vocal music alone. Such compositions do exist in instrumental melodic and rhythm music. A number of composition-types and therefore compositions allow elaboration of musical ideas contained therein according to established methods, to lesser or greater length depending on their potential. Hence, phenomenon of *bandish* must be discussed with the qualification that it might also be relevant in instrumental music.

What are the components of a *bandish*? One cannot perhaps do better than enumerating and briefly describing major formal features of compositions in Hindustani vocal music taken in its entirety. It is to be noted that all features identified as components may not figure in each composition but no composition would be possible without at least some of them present. To begin with the structural blocks would help.

    i) Obviously, all music must have a marked beginning to indicate the commencement of the musical activity, irrespective of whether music is melodic or rhythmic. The early tradition rightly regarded this portion as essential and named it *udgraha*.

   ii) Optionally, a portion of music which functions as a joining passage follows the commencement of music. This is described in medieval musicology as *melapaka*.

  iii) This connecting portion of music links the beginning with the core of the musical expression concerned, regarded essential and aptly named *dhruva*, meaning permanent.

  iv) The core musical passage is followed by music, which is understandably at some distance from the beginning, as otherwise no progression towards the climax, would be possible. This phase has been appropriately named *antara*. There being occasions when musical movement ceases before climax is reached, *antara* is regarded optional.

   v) Finally, compositions have portions designed to round off the entire musical effort and the com-

ponent is called *abhoga*. This too is regarded optional.

After identifying structural features of a more
fundamental nature, one may turn to mention
those more directly connected with the material
of music. It is noteworthy and natural that the basic idea of *bandish* has a long ancestry. This is well
reflected in the fact of commonality or similarity
of structural blocks as perceived in India, at least
since medieval times. In order to bring home the
essential continuity of performing tradition as also
the continued attempts of grammatical tradition
to catch up with the former, structural features or
blocks of *bandish* are described here by referring
to terms current in the earlier period. Even if these
terms are not used today, what they connote tal-
lies with what we actually do while making music — an interesting juxtaposition.

vi) In a composition, element of *swara* refers to the
body of musical notes that represent the melodic
aspect of music. A composition may or may not
be in a *raga* or a combination of *raga*-s. However,
it can hardly do without a recognisable melodic
dimension. At the same time, it must be remembered that rhythm music uses melody to the mini-
mum and to that extent *swara* is less effective as
well as prominent.

vii) *Tala* is a highly processed rhythm. Music making
is possible without using *tala* or its combinations
but it cannot do without some kind of rhythm,
however weak, slight or irregular it may be. In
such cases, rhythm is manifest merely as an ele-

ment that marks divisions in an otherwise continuous activity.

viii) *Bandish*, may or may not use meaningful language-
units, that is, words, etc. This particular component is identified as *pada*. In this context it is to be
noted that use of meaningless sound-syllables has
a long tradition in India. In fact, they are called
tenaka and regarded auspicious as well as benefi-
cial. Besides, instrumental sounds, that is,
onomatopoiac representations of instrumental
sounds have also been employed in musical composition to add colour to the proceedings. Such
'words' are described as *patakshara*-s.

Very often, the name of the composer, of his patron, deity, or guru, features in compositions. This component is
called *biruda*.

Bandish or composition is not to be confused with a form
or genre of music. To draw a parallel with literature, a *bandish*
is comparable to a piece of writing acceptable as a piece of
creative literature as distinct from critical, informative, etc.
However, the accepted piece is further to be understood as
a novel, short story, or a play, etc. This second level of existence of the *bandish* is the genre-level. At this level, a composition would be identified as a *khayal*, or a *thumri* and so on.
A genre adds to, subtracts from, or modifies structural features described so far.

1.5.7   *Bandish ki Thumri* = > *thumri*

1.5.8   *Barwi* = (H) *Khayal* >

1.5.9   *Baradasta* = (H) *Kajri* >

1.5.10   *Bhajan* (H *bhaj* = to serve)

It may be recalled that the all-encompassing devotional movement sweeping over the country from the eighth century gave music a place of importance in devotion as a mode. It also ensured that rituals, ceremonies, festivals associated with devotional sects, cults, employ music of different kinds and in different capacities to allow maximum participation and reach. The result was a pan-Indian flowering of song, dance and drama. Numerous song-types crystallised into musical structures of immense variety, according to regional genius and prevailing linguistic-literary traditions. When such song-types are employed (with or without ritualistic context) as items in musico-devotional acts, they can usually be brought under the generic term *bhajan*. The content is usually praise of God and his attributes.

A unique category of composers was responsible for the type of music *bhajan*-s propagated. These composers are aptly described in India as saint-poets. Almost every region in India produced a galaxy of them; and, as a rule, they were prolific composers. Some of their compositions are still in circulation as *bhajan*-s and presented under the same name from concert stage. The saint poets employed definite *raga*-s and *tala*-s; however, in all probability tunes, which they might have used, are not necessarily current today. However, structural formulae could be expected to have remained mostly unchanged. It would therefore be relevant to note major constructional features of *bhajan* as a genre.

The two main structural features related to the medieval musical tradition are: *Pada* and *Biruda*.

Pada: the term refers to the meaningful, literary stanzas in the *bhajan*-s, which are generally short in length.

Biruda: It is a salutation to the deity, etc.

However the current regional traditions have additional structural features.

Tek: It is a unit formed by the first two lines. This is generally repeated after every stanza in case of a multi-stanza composition. It may be described as refrain of the song. In it the last syllable is prolonged to introduce musical elaboration/vocalisation. Normally, a sign called *avagraha* (like the English letter 's') is employed.

Jhad: It is a section in which two or more lines in a metre different than in the *tek* are employed. This section is also known as *antara*.

Chouk: A section of the song with four lines. It also occurs in song-types such as *choubola*, *Jikdi/ri*.

Tod: This section consists of a melodic component which makes a change over from the metres used for sections coming after the *tek*-metres back to those of the *tek*.

Mudra: It is the name of the composer. It is usually included in the last line of a *bhajan*.

Examined musically the traditional *bhajan*-tunes are found to employ repeatedly, certain *raga*-scales, such as, *des/h, sarang, bhairav, kalingda, mand, kalyan* and *mallar*. Preponderance of regional melodies (e.g. *mand*), seasonal melodies (e.g. *mallar*) and those from the ancient six *raga*-s (e.g. *bhairav*) is significant. A similar usage is detected in various folk musical traditions in India. The similarities go a long way in explaining the hold of the devotional and the folk categories on people in general. *Bhajan*-s employ rhythm with eight or sixteen beats. The tempo is neither slow nor fast. A gradual increase in the tempo towards musical climax is a general characteristic.

The instrumentation displays preference for one/two stringed instruments, which function as drone-cum-rhythm providers. Struck, rather than scraped percussive instruments are favourites. For example *jhanjh, manjiri, chipli, daph, dimdi,* would come to mind.

It is obvious that *bhajan*-s were originally meant to be solo/choral renderings in homes and temples. Their concert appearance is a comparatively recent phenomenon traceable to the early years of the twentieth century.

Due to a strong and pervasive influence of *Bhakti* movement and cults, *bhajan* assumed varied formats in the Braj-speaking area. These types resulted in differences in musical rendering and hence an illustrative discussion is necessary. Different Indian regions have today evolved their own *bhajan*-traditions and they would need separate treatment in an exhaustive analysis of the genre.

In the Braj tradition many subtypes of *bhajan* are in circulation. A brief discussion of some of them will make the complex situation clearer.

Samvadi bhajan-s: Samvad means dialogue. As the term suggests these *bhajan*-s are in a dialogic format. Expectably they narrate stories from history or mythology.

Samaji bhajan-s: This type came into vogue due to the Arya Samaj movement. This was a reformist movement and hence the content of the *bhajan*-s is social. Instead of Braj, these *bhajan*-s also rely on a variety of Hindi described as *Khadi boli.*

Dhun ke bhajan: It consists of four stanzas called *antara*-s. In this type of *bhajan* the tune is composed first and then the text is fitted into it.

Jikdi/ri bhajan: This *bhajan* type is identified after *bhajan* groups rendering them in *Chaitra* (the first month) and *Phalgun* (the last month) according to the Hindu calendar. They are also rendered for recreation and for *shok uthana*. In the folk tradition of poetry it is also pressed into service to

discuss philosophic, scientific matters. Unlike the other types
of *bhajan*-s, *Jikdi bhajan*-s do not begin with the *tek*. Sakhi
and Gatha are rendered first, to be followed by *tek* and then
follows the singing. Usually it consists of four *Jhad*–s

Rangatiya bhajan: In these *bhajans*, parts of other folk songs
such as *Alha* and *Hori* are also incorporated as components.

Dutekiya bhajan: It is simpler in construction than the
rangatiya discussed earlier.

1.5.11   *Chaiti* (H < S *Chaitra* = the first month of the Hindu
         calendar)

Folk songs in Uttar Pradesh and adjacent areas sung
during the month of *Chaitra* are called *chaiti*. Traditionally
they are women's songs with separation from lover/hus-
band as their main theme. According to a reported tradition
the song originated in Chapra and Ara areas.

Special constructional features of these songs include
beginning a line with the word Rama and ending it with
'ho Rama'. When sung to the accompaniment of instruments,
chaiti is known as *jhalkutiya*.

In musical repertoire described as semi-art *chaiti* has today acquired a place. Musically it follows all formulae used
in *thumri* (>) singing. In other words, efforts are made to
employ evocative tunes, tones and temperaments. Thematically *chaiti* centres on describing pangs of separation.

1.5.12   *Char Bait* = A song type in Urdu which has four
         stanza-s of four couplets each.

1.5.13   *Chaturanga* (H < S *chatur* = four + *ang* = aspects, or in
         popular etymology: *chatur* = four + *rang* = colour)

Chaturang is an inclusive form consisting of four aspects.
It consists of meaningful words, meaningless sound-clus-

ters, letters indicative of note-names and finally, sound clusters selected from those used in elaboration of ideas in rhythm-music in playing *pakhawaj* — the prototype of rhythm instruments in ancient India. In the medieval traditions a similar form was known as *chaturmukha*, that is, 'one having four mouths'. Incidentally, *chaturmukha* is one of the names of Lord Brahma, who has four mouths facing in four different directions.

Now such forms are rarely heard. *Chaturang* has a definite value as a musical curiosity though its musical potential is limited. It is usually sung in medium to fast tempo and uses *raga*-s employed in the *khayal* (>) corpus.

1.5.14 *Chaupai*

A four lined composition in praise of king. It has only two elements identified as *pada* and *biruda*.

1.5.15 *Cheez* (H thing, item)

Cheez means a composition in vocal classical music. Its main components are meaningful words set in a definite *raga*-structure along with a particular *tala*. Unlike *bandish* (>), *cheez*, as a concept, is less value-oriented. It refers to the ground plan of the musical idea, which a musician intends to explore further. It is interesting to note that when composite sensibility was the ruling impulse in formation of theoretical aspect of Indian performing arts, *vastu* was a term used to refer to the plot of a dramatic venture. *Vastu* and *cheez* are near synonym in the contemporary Hindi!

1.5.16 *Choutukla*

Sheikh Bahauddin Barnavi (1511-1628 AD) has specifically mentioned it as a genre difficult to render.

1.5.17   *Chutkula = > Khayal*

In the late half of the 15th century Hussain Shah Shirky of Jaunpur is credited to have brought the genre into vogue. It is described as difficult to sing.

1.5.18   *Dadra*

Primarily *dadra* denotes a *tala* (>) of six beats. However *dadra* also refers to a form of semi-art music set in *dadra tala* with the characteristic lilt of the *tala* neatly emphasized.

Set to tune in *dhun-raga*-s (>) normally employed in *thumri*-singing, *dadra* is invariably linked with the *thumri*, as *dhamar* (>) is with *dhrupad* (>). In fact it would not be farfetched to suggest that forms named after *tala*-s indicate their subsidiary position in the hierarchy of forms. In tone, tune and temperament *dadra*-s are fittingly paired with *thumri*-s.

It is also a type of folk song in Bundeli language in Bundelkhand.

1.5.19   *Dhamar*

Primarily the term denotes a *tala* (>) of fourteen beats. However, *dhamar* is also a variety of *dhrupad* (>) set in *dhamar tala*. The convention is to render a *dhamar*-composition after presenting a *dhrupad*. *Dhamar* is to be rendered in a tempo faster than that of the *dhrupad*. Contentwise, composition is usually secular and mildly erotic content is not ruled out. It is interesting to note that compared to the *choutala* as the *tala* mainly associated with *dhrupad*, *dhamar*, as a *tala* moves with less gravity. Before *khayal* came into vogue, these compositions appear to offer more freedom than the *dhrupad*.

1.5.20   *Doha* (n. H < S *dohad*, or *dwipad*, indicating two units)

Primarily a metre with a stanza of four lines, with alternate lines of thirteen and eleven letters respectively. It must be admitted that *doha* does not enjoy status of a musical form suited to concert stage. It is one of the 'singable' and ancient metres regulated by the number of syllabic instants it consists of. Its connection with art music is mainly because of its employment as a pedagogical tool.

Doha is of musical interest because it has been conventionally and aphoristically employed to codify grammatical rules and norms of music. They are usually couched in Braj and Prakrit languages of North India. Musicians memorise and quote them often. It is to be noted that through collections of *doha*-s and *arya*-s, the so-called uneducated musicians of the last century often had access to musicological scholastic tradition otherwise available in Sanskrit texts alone.

Traditionally a *doha* has text (*pada*) and *biruda* (the name of the composer) as its two main features. It is noteworthy that saint-poet composers from various devotional sects in northern India invariably employed *doha* to propagate didactic messages about ethical, religious, moral aspects of life to common man.

1.5.21   *Dhrupad* (H < S *dhruva* = firm, stable, unshakable. *pada* = stanza, place or position)

A plausible surmise is that in its origin *dhruvapada* was a recognised song-type used to sing praises of god and describe His attributes. The word *'dhruva'* means 'stable, constant, unshakable' and hence it is an apt description of god. A song in God's praise would naturally be called *dhruvapada*. *Dhrupad* is a later distortion of *dhruvapada*.

Yet another strand of the meaning is to be noted. *Pada* refers to the textual aspect of music. Thus *pada*, i.e. text used in a composition type called *dhruva* is *dhruvapada*. In medieval composition-types such as *Ela*, text set in its song-section called *dhruva* would thus be entitled to be identified as *dhruvapada*.

In the celebrated *Geet Govinda* the term *dhruva* is clearly mentioned. It appears that on account of the popularity of the *Geet Govinda*, the sequence of *dhruva* and *pada* became pervasive in dramatic music from the 11th to the 15th century. This feature influenced attitudes even in later times. Therefore, when *khayal* emerged during the Mogul period, the older, earlier music of *raga* and text (as a whole) was classified as *dhrupad*. It is as if the term *dhruvapada* became 'generic' in its thrust instead of suggesting a 'specific' form. It is interesting to note that even today dramatic songs from early works are called *daru* in the Telugu tradition.

However, in later song-types the term *dhruva* was confined to the first two lines of a composition and the rest portion was called *pada*. In this sense *dhrupad* refers to the burden of a poem or refrain of a song. It thus constitutes a prosodic feature. It remains unchanged and occurs repeatedly. *Dhruvaka* in the ancient texts is an equivalent. *Dhuya* in the Prakrit tradition is an obvious derivation with a similar meaning.

It could be said that the two semantic thrusts, of constancy and completion of a section/composition, came together and consequently *dhrupad* has come to mean composition in praise of God. Against this background, it is natural that *dhrupad* is understood today as a form of Hindustani art-music venerated for its long history and association with the divine.

In *Sangeet Ratnakara, prabandha,* i.e. a composition-type called *dhruva* is stated to have three components: *sthayi, antara* and *abhog.*

In the *sthayi* is *udgraha,* which contains two sections of identical melodic structure. *Antara* has one section and it is in a pitch higher than the *sthayi. Abhog* has two sections both having an identical melodic structure but the second section is sung in a pitch higher than the first. In addition, the *abhog* is to be rendered after the *udgraha* and *antara* have been sung twice. *Abhog* includes the name of the praised hero, king, etc. This is followed by singing of the *udgraha* once again and then comes the end of the rendering.

Ratnakara has given 16 varieties of the *dhruva prabandha:*

No.	Name	Syllables	Tala	Rasa	Result
1.	Jayant	11	Adi	Shringara	Longevity for all
2.	Shekhar	12	Nihsaraka	Veera	Supernatural powers
3.	Utsaha	13	Pratimanth	Hasya	Progeny
4.	Madhur	14	Hayaleela	Karuna	Enjoyment
5.	Nirmal	15	Krida	Shringara	Growth in lustre, Intellect
6.	Kuntal	16	Laghushekhar	Adbhuta	Getting the desired
7.	Komal	17	Jhanpa	Vipralambha	Supernatural powers
8.	Chara	18	Nihsara	Veer Rasa	Utmost delight/joy
9.	Nandan	19	Ektala	Veer+Shringara	Getting the desired
10.	Chandra-shekhar	20	Pratimantha	Shringara	Getting the desired
11.	Kamod	21	Pratimantha	Hasya	Long life for the hero
12.	Vijay	22	Dwitiya	Hasya	Enjoyment
13.	Kandarpa	23	Adi	Hasya + Karuna Shringara	Victory, enthusiasm
14.	Jaymangal	24	Kreeda	Shringara+Veera	Victory, enthusiasm
15.	Tilak	25	Ektali	Shringara+veera	Victory, enthusiasm
16.	Lalit	26	Pratimantha	Shringara	All supernatural powers

Kallinatha, the perceptive and authoritative commentator of *Sangeet Ratnakara,* foresaw the possibility of having a musically 'good' or significant composition, which however did not strictly adhere to rules and thus did not fit the typology of the 16 varieties Sharangadeva has identified in his *Ratnakara*. He therefore referred to two kinds of 'meaningfulness' – *aksharartha* and *padartha*. He said that a composition irregular (*aniyama*) in respect of number of syllables (*aksharasankhya*) could still be a *dhruva prabandha* if the *pada* aspect is according to rules. If on the other hand, it is irregular in respect of *padasankhya* (number of words/text), it can still be considered a *dhruva prabandha* if it consists of other components such as *rasa, tala,* etc. In other words, musical evaluation/assessment is not entirely based on presence/ absence of structural components.

Dhrupad as is current today — mostly in vocal music — is to be understood on this background.

Despite tantalising traces noted from the earlier period, an unambiguous evidence of the prosperity of this genre places it securely in the fifteenth century. Legendary figures such as Baiju Bawra, Gopal, and Tansen are the known and prominent performers of *dhrupad*. It is reported that the line from Tansen's sons was influenced by *rabab* a plucked chordophone and consequently musicians from this lineage became protagonists of a style (*bani*) called *Gaudhar*. On the other hand, those hailing from his daughter's lineage were influenced by *vina*, a chordophone with a more sustained note production. As a consequence the *vina*-influenced performers became protagonists of *bani*-s known as *Dagur, Nauhar* and *Khandahar*.

One more position advocated is that with Raja Mansinha's (king of Gwaliyar) efforts Braj language and music were fruitfully brought together and this made *dhruvapada* possible. *Dhrupad* gave an 'answer' to the *ghazal* which was brought into vogue by the *Sufi* saints and Vishnupada provided an 'answer' to *qawwali* popularised by the *Sufi* saints.

Going back a little, *Geet Govinda* had employed the term *dhruva* with reference to the first two lines of a stanza, the rest being described as *pada*. In the medieval *Sangit Ratnakara*, a compositional genre called *dhruva prabandha* is specified in great detail. The structural features as laid down in this monumental work establish a clear link between the contemporary *dhrupad* and its proto-type in the *Ratnakara*.

Capt. Willard listed four *tuk*-s (parts) of a *dhrupad* as: (1) *sthul/sthayi/bheda,* (2) *antara,* (3) *abhog,* (4) *bhog.*

However, the four structural features or parts of *dhrupad* as stabilised today are:

Name	Function
Sthayi	To begin a composition and establish its *raga*.
Antara	To follow immediately after the *sthayi* and explore the *raga*, and during the process to accentuate the upper half of the scale in the process.
Abhog	To give a sense of completion and to round off.
Sanchari	To trace a free movement.

The form follows a performing sequence with a marked strictness.

Singing of a *dhrupad* commences with *nom-tom*. Meaningless syllables such as *ri, da, na, nom, tom, yala, li,* etc. are employed in the *nom-tom* to unfold the selected *raga* successively in slow, medium and fast tempo without employing song-text and *tala*. It has been occasionally argued that the phase identified as *nom-tom* employs in reality (though with some distortion and sometimes in a truncated form) the auspicious *mantra*-phrase *anant hari om* with tonal patterns superimposed on it. Hence, the words in the phase can hardly be described as 'meaningless'. However, admittedly a majority of musicians do not seem to use these or such other words. Secondly and more importantly, historical perspective suggests that the use of non-sense syllables such as *nom-tom* is an extension of the medieval concept of employing meaningless syllables as auspicious words. The usage was then known as *tena-shabda*.

After the *non-tom*, comes the second phase in the singing of *dhrupad*. In this phase, the four parts described earlier are sung in a selected *tala* to the accompaniment of *pakhawaj* (>), a horizontal two-faced drum. In the third phase the song-text is sung in double, treble and quadruple *tempi*. Finally, improvised rhythmic as well as melodic patterns created by 'playing ' with the song text are introduced in varied as well as changing *tempi*. Conventionally, the *dhrupad* eschews singing with bare vowels such as 'aa', 'ee' and it also denies singers the luxury of executing *tans* (>) — those fast paced vocalisations, which attract listeners by their dazzling effects!

Traditional *dhrupad*-s, when examined for their thematic content, appear to devote considerable space to praise of gods, paean to kings, descriptions of alluring or somewhat 'frightening' beauty of nature (as of the dark monsoon clouds), descriptions of musicological rules/truths about *raga*, *tala*, *swara*, etc. In other words, the thematic content focuses attention on non-personal and semi-religious elements. The overall tone of the versification is serious. Normally, in initial stages the tempo, aptly described by the term *vilambit,* is kept slow. In a gradual movement towards musical climax it is purposefully increased to medium-fast. Conventional singing is virile and manly: it is rare to come across a female *dhrupad* performer.

Dhrupad mostly employs *choutala* (12 beats), *soorfakta* (10 beats), and *aditala* (16 beats). Almost every traditional *raga* has a *dhrupad* composition in it. In fact, one test of the authenticity of a *raga* is supposed to be availability of a *dhrupad* in it! A composition in *dhamar tala* is called *dhamar* (>) and one, which is set in *tala Jhaptala*, is known as *sadra* (>). A composition, which describes Lord Krishna's frolic in spring festival and which is also set in *tala dhamar*, is known as *Hori dhamar* (>).

From an aesthetic point of view *dhrupad* clearly lacks in musical flexibility because of its prescriptive syntax, which governs all phases of musical elaboration. In addition, the genre also suffers from a rather artificial bifurcation between tonal and rhythmic aspects.

Significantly other sub-types appear to move in direction of partially removing some of the shortcomings of the major genre. For example, *dhrupad* is traditionally followed by *dhamar* (>), which, at least to some extent does away with some of the restrictions shaping rendering of *dhrupad* (>also *dhamar, sadra, Vishnupada, langda dhrupad*).

Dhrupad-terminology:

Abhog = The final compositional section intended to round off the structure and give it a completeness.

Antara = A section which succeeds immediately after the *sthayi* — the first section in a composition.

Bani = Four major styles of rendering *dhrupad* compositions initially identified after dialects in which the songs were composed. Hence, the *bani*-s known as Gubarhar,

Khandar, Dagur and Nauhar were reasonably identifiable according to the following derivations: Gubarhar-Gaurari-Gwaliyari, Khandari — the region around Khandar fort, Dagari — Region around "Dagar" near Delhi, and Nauhari — from Nauha region.

Biruda = One aspect of the traditional six-aspected *dhrupad*. It consists of a section in praise of the king or the described hero.

Deshi = Regional langauges as opposed to Sanskrit.

Kalawant = Traditionally, as Abul Fazl mentioned, singers of *dhrupad*-s were known as Kalawant while those who sang *Vishnupad*-s were known as *Kirtaniya*.

Kirtaniya = see *Kalawant*.

Pada = One aspect of the traditional six-aspected *dhrupad*. It consists of meaningful linguistic expression which acts as a link between music and *rasa*, i.e., the sentiment-spectrum of the composition.

Pata = One aspect of the traditional six-aspected *dhrupad*. It consists of sound-syllables produced from various instruments, onomatopoetically identified and rendered in a composition.

Sanchari = A compositonal section in which free ranging *raga*-phrases are employed to explore the *raga* fully.

Sthayi = The section in which the constant/stable and characteristic phrases of a *raga* are introduced.

Swara = One aspect of the six-aspected *dhrupad*. It consists of intoned notes melody.

Tala = One aspect of the traditional six-aspected *dhrupad*. It consists of the time measures employed to give form and rhythmic structure to melodic composition.

Tenaka = One aspect of the traditional six-aspected *dhrupad*. It consists of meaningless auspicious syllables used musically in a composition enhancig the melodic colour.

Tuk = Individual sections of the *dhrupad* composition. They are four in number: *Sthayi, Antara, Abhog* and *Sanchari*.

Vishnupad = This was a genre of songs in praise of Vishnu, sung in temples in Mathura and brought into vogue by Raja Mansinha along with *dhrupad*-s.

1.5.22 *Fatiha* = Islam and Music >

1.5.23 *Geet* (S. = 'that which is sung' H.= song)

The first meaning is too wide in the present context of discussion of genres. A composition characterised by tune, metre, rhythm and language is *geet*.

The traditional terminology describes one who drafts the linguistic composition as *matukara*. One who takes care of the aspects of tune and rhythm is known as *dhatukara*. Finally, the rare person who is able to take care of both tune and text is called *vaggeyakara*. On the other hand, a person versifying later to match an already composed tune is known as *kuttikara*. The last variety is granted a lower status.

An important classification of the form introduced by the musicological tradition obviously stresses an overall rhythmic-melodic orientation of the genre *geet*. Those with a rhythmic weightage were called *padashrita* (dependent on language-units), while those emphasizing the melodic aspect were named *swarashrita* (dependent on notes).

It is to be regretted that the traditional theoretical positions about *geet* are not in easy circulation. Today any lyric/ poem sung to a certain tune, with or without the applications of *raga/tala* or such other concepts in art-music is described as a *geet*. The term has obviously become more accommodative, literature-oriented and less precise than suggested by the traditional musicology.

1.5.24   *Ghazal* (P = a love-song)

The original meaning of the term was 'a love song in Persian'. Later, the Urdu literary tradition, while deriving inspiration from the Persian continuity, extended its thematic range and admitted *ghazal*-s developing other subjects.

More specifically *kasida* in Persian literature was the precursor of *ghazal*. In fact poems in praise/adoration of a person had their origin in Arabic literature. From it, the stream of poems dealing with youthful love evolved separately and it acquired the name *ghazal*. An early poet in this tradition was Rudki (10th century).

Literally, *ghazal* means to talk of love with women. However, from the beginning, love of God was also an inevitable strand of the thematic fabric of the form. The *Sufi*-s were responsible for the early prosperity *ghazal*-s enjoyed. After the rise of Sufism the theme of this double-edged love prospered. Two concepts *Ishq-e-majazi* and *Ishq-e-haqeeqi* assumed significance. In order to propagate love of God among the sensitive and elite sections of the society the *Sufi* saints of the *Chishti* order often used suggestive poetry with great effect.

Sufism originated in *Koran* but according to many scholars it came to glory after Buddhism and Vedanta philosophy spread in Persia and Afghanistan. To understand one aspect of the appeal of *ghazal* it is necessary to remember that Sufism presents Mysticism in Islam. *Sufi*-s are Islamic saints who wear woolen garments (*Suf* = wool). Some important technical terms which are also helpful in appreciating many poetic resonances and images in *ghazal* are as follows:

Tasawwuf = *Sufi* doctrine.

Khanqah = Meeting place of the *Sufi*-s.
Shariat = Religious rules/norms.

Marqat = the restlessness, disquietude resulting from abandonment of intellection and logic to attain the supreme state.

Hakikat = Complete identification/communion with God
Pir/Murshad = Guru, preceptor.
Mureed = Disciple
Zikr = Repetition of God's name
Sama = Audition, a gathering of devotees employing singing and dancing for attaining God.
Hal = Ecstatic state

The *Sufi*-s registered a presence at Aurangabad in Maharashtra during the early 9th century. In India Urdu *ghazal* commenced its career in Aurangabad (Maharashtra) with Wali's poetry. Though he used Persian metre, he used many Hindi (i.e., a variety known as *Dakkhani*) words. These compositions were known as *Rekhti*.

On account of the metrical conventions as well as norms governing other structural features, *ghazal* certainly puts restrictions on the use of *tala*-s. The literary genesis of the form is proclaimed by its prosodic features, which in turn influence the rhythmic framework employed. It is no surprise that *ghazal*-s continued to be associated with *mushaira*-s (poet's conferences) in which poetry is recited.

There is evidence to suggest that till the 1920s, *ghazal* was sung almost as a *tappa* (>). From the earlier recitation-phase this was surely a step ahead but the non-correspondence between the romantically inclined content and the intellectual intricacy of *tappa*-singing, warranted a change. Gradually however the *ghazal* came to be sung to the accompaniment of instruments *a la thumri* (>). At this stage some musical embellishment was introduced, yet no musical elaboration was expected or attempted, even though certain *raga*-s seem to recur in the tunes employed. Today both *raga*-orientation and musical elaboration are on the increase.

Constructional features that have a bearing on singing of a *ghazal* are:

1.	*beher*	metre
2.	*radif*	end rhyme
3.	*kafiya*	word preceding the end-rhyme
4.	*misra*	line
5.	*sher*	couplet
6.	*ashar*	a number of *sher*-s
7.	*katah*	*ashar*, brought together thematically
8.	*matala*	first *sher*
9.	*makta*	last *sher*
10.	*takhallus*	*nom de plume*
11.	*husn-e-matala*	the most important *sher*

A non-rhythmic singing of *sher* in the *ghazal* presentation is often introduced on the spur of the moment. *Matala* is repeated often. End-rhymes are emphasized and *misra* is placed in varied tonal contexts.

1.5.25   *Gul* = A song-type from Persia sung in Pashto *tala*.

1.5.26   *Gurcha*

In most cases it was a song by caste musicians of the Dhadi caste to eulogise brave, heroic deeds. A subtype of it consisted of longer lines and then was known as *'bugud'*. If composed in Charani language, it was known as *bur*. Interestingly, similar songs in Braj and language current in

Gwaliyar region was known as *Sadra* – a term also used to indicate a kind of *dhrupad* composition.

1.5.27   *Pushtimarga* and *Haveli Sangeet*

Pushtimarga Ashtachhap:

Reportedly Vallabhacharya revived an older stream of music propagated by Vishnuswami around 1250 AD. It was however left to Vallabhcharya's son, Goswami Vitthalnathji (1516-1698 AD) to systematise the religio-musical procedures of the cult and to ceremoniously establish the eight musical *acharya*-s (preceptors) in 1607-1608 AD. All eight *acharya*-s, together with the main *guru*-s could be said to have established a line of musical growth, which continues to contribute for the last five hundred-years or so. It has been plausibly argued that the *Pushtimarga*-contribution to the Hindustani art music predates that of the Gwaliyar king Raja Mansinha and the famous *dhrupad*-s associated with him. Hence, a detailed discussion is intended at a later stage. The tabulated information about the *ashtachhap* composers would be adequate to justify claims made for their help in shaping Hindustani art music.

The tabulated information is given here with a view to allow a synoptic view of the *ashtachhap* universe of music, music-making and the socio-cultural wholeness of the vision as also for the specific musical contribution. Various leads provided by these tables can of course be pursued further. However, the intention is to lay down a total map for consideration, as the music seems to demand that kind of mapping.

The following table shows: number, name, birth-year, caste, name of the initiating *guru*, year of initiation and place where the composer was based.

Pushtimarga Ashtachhap

No.	Name of poet	Birth year	Caste	Name of the initiating guru	Year of initiation	Place where the poet composer was based
1	2	3	4	5	6	7
1.	Kumbhandas	1581	Gaurava Kshatriya	Vallabh-acharya	1612	Jamuna-vati
2.	Soordas	1591	Saraswat Brahmin	Vallabh-acharya	1623	Parasouli
3.	Krishnadasa	1589	Kunbi Patel	Vallabh-acharya	1624	Billichhu Kund
4.	Paramanandadasa	1606	Kanyakubja Brahmin	Vallabh-acharya	1633	Surabhi Kund
5.	Govindswami	1618	Sanadhya Brahmin	Vitthal-nath	1648	Kadam Khandi
6.	Cheetswami	1629	Mathuriya Chaubey	Vitthal-nath	1648	Puchhari
7.	Chaturbhujadas	1643	Gaurava Kshatriya	Vitthal-nath	1654	Jamuna-vati
8.	Nandadas	1646	Sanadhya Brahmin	Vitthal-nath	1663	Manasi-ganga

No.	Name of poet	Leela name	Image worship	Time allotted for *kirtan*
1.	Kumbhandas	Arjunsakha	Govardhannatha	Rajbhog-samaya
2.	Soordas	Krishnasakha	Mathuresh	Utthapana
3.	Krishnadasa	Vrishabhasakha	Madanmohan	Shayana
4.	Paramanandadasa	Toka sakha	Navneet Priya	Mangalasamaya
5.	Govindswami	Shridama sakha	Dwarakadhish	Gwala samaya
6.	Cheetswami	Subala sakha	Vitthalnath	Sandhya arti
7.	Chaturbhujadas	Vishala sakha	Gokulnatha	Bhoga
8.	Nandadas	Bhoja sakha	Gokulchandrama	Shringar

No.	Name	Expiry	Compo-sitions	*Raga*-s	*Tala*-s	Instru-ments
1.	Kumbhandas	1696	4000	33	6	18
2.	Soordas	1696	42	9		
3.	Krishnadasa	1692	1200	42		
4.	Paramanandadasa	1697	1400	42	20	
5.	Govindswami	1698		36	23	
6.	Cheetswami	1698	200	36	12	
7.	Chaturbhujadas	1698	36	29		
8.	Nandadas	1696	400	36	19	

Haveli Sangeet:

Vallabha sect used music extensively in the practice of *pushtimarg*. The eight poets who composed for the sampradaya were collectively called *ashtachhap*. They included: (1) Kumbhandas, (2) Soordas, (3) Krishnadas, (4) Parmanandadasa, (5) Govindswami, (6) Cheetswami, (7) Chaturbhujadas, and (8) Nandadas.

1.5.28 *Holi/hori* (H < S *Holika*, meaning a spring festival)

It is a song akin to *dhrupad* (>) though it has often only two sections instead of four sections, i.e., *tuk*-s of the *dhruvapada*. It is set in principal — almost all major *raga*-s (in which it is similar to *khayal*) with love-pranks of Radha and Krishna as the main theme. In most cases *dhamar tala* is employed. Alternatively, other *tala*-s such as *jhumra* and *deepchandi* are used. Significantly these *tala*-s also have fourteen *matra*-s (beats). On account of the importance given to the *dhamar tala*, *hori* is also known as *dhamar* (>).

If the theme of the composition is the well-known colour-festival known as *Holi* in India, *holi* is to be included in the *thumri* (>) group of semi-classical forms; otherwise the pronounced *dhrupad*-orientation is   recognised as a criterion for classification.

Holi, as a festival, is known for celebration, which includes kindling of the sacred fire to symbolise burning of the she-demon Holika. Alternatively, it alludes to the mythical burning of Madan, Lord of love, by Shiva whose penance Madan had disturbed. *Holi* is celebrated on the full moon day of *Phalgun* in the Hindu calendar.

1.5.29   *Holi geet* = > *Phag*

1.5.30 *Huddikhwani* = A folk song type sung while driving camels.

1.5.31 *Jaccha* = From Farsi *Jaccha* = a woman who has recently delivered a baby, see *Sohar*.

1.5.32 *Zikri* (H.)

One of the genres, which *Sufi*-s of the *Chishti* order reportedly brought into vogue by combining vernacular/regional languages and music in order to effectively propagate religious tenets among the populace. The other two genres mentioned in the same context have been *nukta* and *khayal*.

1.5.33 *Jod* (H. pair, equal)

It is a subtype of composition in genres like *khayal* as also in genres of rhythm music. A *'jod'* composition is identical with another existing composition in every respect except the text. (See *Yugalband/h*)

1.5.34 *Kajli / kajri* (H *kajal* = eye black)

It is a genre of female folk-songs sung in rainy season in Uttar Pradesh and adjacent regions. Women sing these songs while sitting on swings hung on trees. It has many, different tunes. Usually on the third day in the second half of *Bhadra*, women sing *kajli/kajri* songs all through the night to an accompanying circle-dance.

Varied etymology is reported. (1) The *kajli/kajri* songs are sung in the month of *Shravan* when the clouds are as black as *kohl* and hence the name. (2) Bharatendu opined that Daduray — a benevolent king in Madhya Bharat died and women in his kingdom evolved a new song-genre called *kajri* to mourn him and hence the name. (3) the third etymology is associated with the *Kajri vrata* observed on *Kajri Tritiya* by women. (The day is also described as *Satva teej* as preparations made from *Sattu* flour are eaten on that day.) There is a myth associated with this observance. Once in the court of Gods Mahadeva mentioned with ridicule that Mahakali is as black as *kohl*. She got annoyed, deposited her *shyam* colour in young green crops, burned her own body and then took re-birth as a daughter of Himalaya — thus again managed to be Shiva's wife! Hence on the appointed day women worship Harikali in corns, sing songs the whole night and then immerse the *Devi* in water bodies. Some maintain that the day on which these songs are sung – i.e. the third day (*tritiya*) in the month of *Shravana* is called — and hence the name. Though no definite chronology can be given — Bhojpuri saint-poets and especially Laxmi Sakhi (1840-1913 AD) has composed many *kajli* songs. *Kajli* songs from Mirzapur are well-known. As the saying goes: लीला रामनगर की भारी कजली मिर्जापुर सरनाम. Competitive presentations of *kajli* take place in that area and both male and female parties participate with enthusiasm.

As a form in semi-art music, *kajli* has found a place along with *chaiti* (>). Both are similar in many respects. The compositions are in Urdu or Farsi and mostly composed in *raga*-s *Pilu*, *Khamaj*, *Jhinzoti* or *Kafi*.

Many *akhada*-s, i.e. specific performing groups with their own respective *guru*-s or *shayar*-s (poets) perform *kajli* in competitive presentations on specific occasions. Performances begin on *Ganga Dashhara* (the bright tenth day of the month *Jyeshtha* in the Hindu calendar) after worshipping the *dholak*. Concluding performance usually takes place on the *Anantchaturdashi* day. (However, some *akhada*-s continue performances till the *Ashwin Krishnashtami*). According to the earlier practice, groups used to gather together at a predetermined place — and they arrived at the place as singing parties. Then one *akhada* will compete with the other.

Sometimes one *akhada* may invite the other to compete by sending over to them *elaichi* (cardamom)! In Benaras too the vogue of arranging the *dangal* (as the competitions are called) is an old custom. Two *akhada*-s position themselves at about 40 feet distance, facing each other. At the beginning, one of the *guru*-s stands up and sings *sumirati*. The second replies/answers by singing a composition in the same metre, in the same tune and on the same theme. Then the second *akhada* sings and the first answers. While a *guru* is searching/preparing for an answer the co-singers (called *devadiya*-s) continue to sing the *tek* (refrain). Instruments employed in the *sumirati* rendering are: *dholak, chang,* and *lakadi.* When the competition reaches its climax *bardasta* and *phataha* songs are sung. The latter often consists of obscene verses critical of the opponent. *Bardasta* compositions are extempore compositions composed to answer the opponent. Similar *dangal*-s take place between *shayar*-s and professional singers called *gounharin*-s.

However, as a form of popular music, *kajli* has developed another variety more deliberately processed and formalised. This type of *kajli*-s are composed and taught by expert *ustads* to professional singing women called *gounharin*-s. Each *ustad*'s school is known as *akhada* (i.e. a meeting place of professional entertainers). Organised and trained parties are pitted against one another on occasions described as *dangal*-s to make competitive presentations of the *kajli* compositions.

1.5.35 *Kaul*

A song in Arabic which was sung by *qawwal*-s was known as *Kaul*. Later began the vogue of composing the song with Persian words combined with sayings of *Sufi* saints. Sometimes even the *tarana bol*-s were included in it. *Kalbana* and *naqsh-o-gul* were types of the *kaul*. A tradition holds that Amir Khusro composed *tarana* and *kaul* with the help of *samiti* and *tatar*. *Samiti* meant a group of Indian (Hindu) knowledgeable people and *tatar* meant similar persons from the Tatar region of Turkastan. *Kaul* means 'sayings' (*sookti*). Those who sang the *kaul* were later known as *qawwal*-s.

1.5.36   *Kavitta* = (H < S *Kavitva* = ability to compose poetry)

A poetic form in Braj is always composed in *ghanakshari* — a metre with specific prosodic properties and history. Artists known as *kalavant* in Emperor Akbar's court were acknowledged experts in singing of *dhrupad* as well as in reciting *kavitta*. It has been recorded in the tradition that *kavitta* recitation inevitably included certain rhythmic feats such as singing in tempo variations known as equal, one-and-one-fourth times and one-and-one-half times of the original. It is interesting to note that elaboration of *dhrupad* also consists of manifestation of such rhythmic skills. Among Hindus, occupational caste formed by such reciters was known as *Bhatta*.

1.5.37   *Keherawa* = A song usually sung in *tala Keherawa* and mostly to the accompaniment of dance.

1.5.38   *Khayal* (H song, A idea)

Sometimes the term 'khayal' is also written as 'khyal'. However, in order to distinguish it from the folk genre of similar name from Rajasthan and to establish its identity as a form of Hindustani art music, it is necessary to be more specific and focused in using and spelling the term properly.

Literally this term of Persian origin means 'an idea'. Today the term is employed to indicate a dominant song-type and a major genre of Hindustani vocal art music. Further, *khayal* from Rajasthan is of many kinds, the common feature being a presentation that, in the final analysis, is a package that brings together dance, drama and music. Yet another interesting detail is that, yet another region, Bihar has a long tradition of singing songs called *khyalgeet*-s set in *tala*-s such as *jhumra*.

Some scholars have also etymologically traced the term to *'khel'* meaning game (H. *'khelna'* = to play. < S *'Krida'* game).

What is noteworthy is that in both derivations, reference is made to the intentional presence of greater freedom of elaboration which *khayal* allows as a form of Hindustani music making of the art category. A contrast to the rigid sequences of *dhrupad* (>) is also brought into relief because *dhrupad* is reported to have made room for the *khayal* during the sixteenth century.

History:

As is to be expected in every long-living and comprehensively developed tradition, many musical features of the genre have numerous antecedents though they are scattered in time and differ in contexts. The fact becomes clear when characteristics of musical genres are discussed.

For instance, take the use of regional language for a song-text — a feature *khayal* displays.

Even before Matanga (8th century) compositions in genres such as *Ela* or *Dhenki* were in Prakrit tongues. After Matanga, *dhruva*-s in Bharata's music became *dhruvapada*. From ancient times composing verses in Prakrit as contrasted with the Sanskrit *dhruva*-s was in vogue. To an extent the practice gained currency because certain features of versification in Sanskrit tradition posed problems. For example, the Sanskrit versification abounded in use of words with hard and distinct aspiration, complex nasalisation, compounds words and euphonic combinations. Use of regional language in *khayal* had therefore a predecessor.

The medieval *Sangeet Ratnakara* mentions a genre called *Akshiptika*. This was rendered in *gramaraga* and related *tala* — bringing out yet another resemblance with the contemporary *khayal*. It is also contended that other song-types such as *dwipadi*, *chatushpadi*, mentioned in *Ratnakara*, also anticipate *khayal* in some measure.

Finally and more importantly, phases of music-elaboration such as *Sthayabhanjani*, *Pratigrahanika* and *Roopakamanjari* or *Roopakalapti* in *Ratnakara* describe rhythm-'free' elaboration of *raga* and this also is reflected in the present day *khayal*.

Now let us consider the matter of elaboration of a musical idea in a *raga*, which is mentioned as the distinguishing characteristic of the genre. It is fair to say that a preliminary version of '*raga*' phenomenon as an elaborated musical idea presented for further development is surely foreshadowed in strategies such as *murchana*, *nyasa*, and *upanyasa* because these strategies arrange or sequence notes to express an implied idea. It is also deducible that the *tala*-less '*shushkageet*' (called '*upohana*'), which was put into service to determine the fundamental note, was the origin of the later concept of *nom-tom*, used today for a specific mode of *raga*-elaboration in genres such as *dhrupad*. (In a still earlier phase of music-making, i.e. in the singing of *Sama, pranava* — the sacred joint syllable *omkar* was recited to determine the fundamental note.) The point is that syllables otherwise regarded meaningless always had a place in music-making processes in India. Even before the singing of *dhruva*, the *Jati*-s were determined with the help of *nyasa* and *ansha*.

The element of freedom associated with *khayal* also has numerous antecedents. In the medieval phase of Indian music itself, phenomena listed as *uparaga, bhasharaga* and *deshiraga* register a movement away from limits imposed by instrumental music and instruments in order to secure freedom in musical elaboration. It is instructive that the element of freedom is often and appreciatively emphasized in relation to *khayal*. Perhaps the tendency to seek freedom from restrictions of earlier and established forms of music is an ever-present cultural tendency!

The use of *tala* in *khayal* also seems to be a part of a tradition longer than usually imagined. *Dhruva*-s in Bharata perhaps provide a very early example. Adherence of the *dhruva*-s to *tala* could be deduced from rules enunciated about definiteness of the number of syllables they should have. The *dhrupad*, which came into vogue during the Mughal period, and which is regarded a major predecessor to *khayal*, confirms this same lineage. It is often argued that a very special feature of *khayal* is the tendency to deviate from *dhrupad* in every possible way! In this context it is often and rightly pointed out how, even within the *dhrupad* genre itself there is a provision for more loosely structured and less 'heavy ' presentations — as exampled in *dhamar* (a spring song) and *sadra* (praise song). These forms must have proved appealing because of their festive content as well as swifter movement.

At this stage it is advisable to turn back to *Ratnakara* once again. It describes five classes of new compositional types. From these five, the last two are mentioned as 'lowly' and more interestingly, one of them is identified as '*Khallottara*'! Is it not thought provoking that the two major characteristics of *khallottara* are noted as: firstly, it changes the chief, prevailing characteristics of *raga* and secondly, it modifies prosodic features of the established poetic type. (*'khalla'* means a trench and *'uttara'* means a ford. Obviously, this does not seem to have any connection with the musical matters we are considering here!) It is tempting to ask: Is the term *"khallottara"* a Sanskritisation of the term *khayal*? Ratnakara also refers to *dhavalgeet* — a song-type celebrating marriage. Even today many *khayal*-texts have the same theme. Though *khayal*-s are not sung at the time of marriage many of them certainly are in celebration of marriage. Some experts hold that Saint Namdeo, who came 50 years after Ratnakara, has mentioned this genre.

In sum, it is possible that many ancient musical features and procedures have found their way in some form or the other in the contemporary performance of *khayal*!

It is on this background that one has to examine claims of Amir Khusro (1254-1325 AD) and alternatively, Sultan Hussain Shirky of Jaunpur (1457-1476 AD) as inventors/originators of *khayal*.

It appears that Khusro cannot be credited with this momentous invention because: (1) He himself never makes that claim in his writings. (2) Even in *Ain-e-Akbari*, he is only credited with the invention of *kaul* and *tarana*.

Capt. Willard, that pioneering Indologist credits Sultan Hussain Shirky of Jaunpur with the invention of *khayal*. He also mentions that compositions in a dialect spoken near Khirabad (and which consisted of two sections) were known in his times as *khayal*. In fact he goes on to state that a similar song-type with only one section is called *'chutkula'*, while a song-type with two sections and composed in Purbi dialect is called *'barwi'*. In this context, the *Sufi* saint Sheikh Bahauddin Barnavi (b. 1412 AD) is also often mentioned as a contributor to the process of evolving *khayal*. The saint's proficiency in singing *dhrupad* and *tarana* as also in playing

been, imarati and *rabab* are mentioned. The saint was a contemporary of Sultan Shirky.

It is therefore appropriate to say that *khayal* emerged as
a cumulative result of complex interactions between principles of *dhrupad* and *dhamar,* folksongs of Uttar Pradesh,
Punjab and Rajasthan as also musical exchanges between
singing modes/idioms of *ghazal, qawwali,* and *marsiya.*

The contribution of the *Sufi* saints needs a separate mention. In Arabic, *khayal* means 'contemplation'. Compositions
in *raga*-s in Indian languages often consisted of iconographic
descriptions of deities and of *raga*-icons. *Sufi*-s were fond of
music and they commenced singing of similar descriptions
of Allah, Mohammad, Peer, etc. in compositions in Indian
regional languages. They also employed *raga*-s for the purpose. Thus *khayal* became a synonym for *dhyana,* i.e. contemplation. In other words, the *Sufi* saints maintained a continuity of themes, sought to combine with it the prevailing,
Indian and structural components such as *sthayi* and *antara.*
New content and familiar form appears to be their motto.
Hence *khayal, jikri* and *nukta* were for common people and
ghazal was meant for the elite.

This *khayal* was evolving in Delhi by borrowing features
of *qawwal* style. The other, Lucknow-style, identified with
Sadarang and *Adarang,* came on the scene later. [For those
interested in micro-level research into *khayal*-corpus, it is
instructive to note that Pt. S.N. Ratanjankar had referred to
khayal-s in Yaman (*Salona re*), Bhimpalas (*Jai jai dhola dhar ki*)
and *Bageshri* (*Preet lagali mori re*) as *khayal*-s exemplifying
the Lucknow-style.] In times of Mohammad Shah Rangile
(1719-1748 AD), the *khayal* style was employed to subdue
qawwal-s. In Rangile's times *Sadarang* and *Adarang* brought
in the texts of *khayal*-s the typically Indian manifestations of
love and especially those systematised in the '*nayikabheda*'

theory of literature. Thus in place of *qawwal*, the *kalavant* came to the forefront. It is reported that in the 19th century, two composers, Shakkar and Makkhan used *tala*-s which were not used in *dhrupad* or *khayal*. Yet another step was taken when the legendary *ustad*-s, Haddu Khan and Hassu Khan, in Gwaliyar, marked the *khayal* with a distinctive style, which came to be known as Gwaliyar. It is worth noting that from Sadarang, composers of *khayal* instituted and followed the practice of using suffix *'rang'* in their names. The convention is followed almost universally even today! Even in the South terms such as *'parimalrang'* and *'suvrang'* came in to vogue.

When compared with *dhamar*-compositions, *khayal*-compositions impress by their capacity to entertain listeners and allow artists more room for freedom of expression. As in *dhamar*, *khayal* has two sections, but unlike the *dhamar* the *mukhada* of a *khayal* does not begin from the *sama* beat. Mostly the *sama* of the *khayal* is on its *vadi* note. The *khayal* text employs a language simpler than that in the *dhrupad*. And in progression, it is more convoluted and certainly displays more delicacy of approach. The aphoristic statement that *dhrupad* took inspiration from the *been*, *khayal* from the *sarangi* and *tarana* from the *sitar* interestingly brings out essential qualities of the idioms involved.

However that may be, the present-day *khayal* is an undoubted result of an overall process of musical liberalisation. The seeds were sown at least four centuries before *khayal* attained a new stability in the work of composer 'Sadarang' Nyamatkhan and those who followed.

Structure:

Today *khayal* consists of two *tuks* (parts or sections), namely, *sthayi* and *antara* as contrasted with the four parts of the *dhrupad*. The first part called *sthayi* usually ranges over and covers the first half of the gamut and the second half, *antara* mainly explores the upper ranges. Together the two sections are expected to explore the total *raga*-frame. A composition of one single part was, according to Capt. Willard, known as *chutkula*. In case a *khayal* has three parts, the part located between *sthayi* and *antara* is known as *manjha* (middle, intervening). Each separate line of a *khayal* is called *charan*. Normally a *khayal* does not have more than four or six lines, but there is no rigid rule about it. The oft-repeated, and important part of the first line of a *khayal* is called *mukhda* (S dim. of *mukh* = face). All the words used in a *khayal* are collectively known as *bol* (words).

Definition:

Khayal may be defined as a genre of Hindustani vocal art music in which song is composed in a definite *raga* to be sung in a particular *tala* and the composition is intended to provide basis for further elaboration of the *raga* concerned.

Following are its chief characteristics: (1) It is composed in a specific *raga* and *tala*. (2) Its two main varieties are *bada* (big/expansive) and *chhota* (small/less expansive). Usually, the former is set in slow tempo and the latter in fast tempo. Both are expected to be rendered in a manner befitting the original tempo etc. (3) The genre is considered ideal for elaboration of *raga* mainly through purposeful employment of a strategy described as improvisation — i.e. a method of presentation distinguished by rendering, that is not pre-composed. (4) Both *bada* and *chhota khayal*-s have two sections each. They are respectively known as *sthayi/asthayi* and *antara*. The overall aim of the *khayal* is ' depiction of the full musical image or development of the full musical idea of a *raga* through phases of rendering/elaboration identified as *alap, bol-alap, bol-laya, bol-tan* and *tan*. Normally, the sequence followed in rendering is as listed here but it is not obligatory to strictly adhere to it. The proportion of accentuation of these phases may also vary according to individual, stylistic and *gharana*-wise preferences. (5) Sometimes a *khayal* composition may have three sections. In that case the middle section is called *manjha*. (6) It is usually argued that *khayal* came into being after the *dhrupad* and practically compensated for the felt aesthetic and other deficiencies of *dhrupad* as a genre.

The singing of *khayal* however does not mean singing of a *khayal* composition. A *khayal* does not attain its full stature unless the composition is further elaborated. The usual plan of presenting an elaborate *khayal* may include the following phases:

a.   *Sthayi pesh karana* = Initial singing of *sthayi* and *antara*. This is designed to establish the range, mood and nature of the *raga*.

b.   *Alap*: Slow-tempo statement or spelling out of the various melodic ideas contained in a *raga*.
     Each *alap* terminates with the *mukhada* and a new *alap* is begun. There is no limit to the number of *tala* cycles each individual *alap* may require. Employing the *mukhda* and coming to the *sam* — the first beat of the *tala*-cycle — indicates completion of each *alap* as a statement of a particular musical idea. Usually the vowel-sound 'a' is used to sing *alap*.

c.   *Bol-alap*: The phase combines *alap* and enunciation of words of the composition concerned. This is expected to add one more dimension to the elaboration, because meaningfulness of words becomes a potential force in shaping musical ideas. The words and notes together afford a qualitatively different take-off even as sound-clusters.

d. *Bol-laya*: Instead of combining *bol*-s with *alap*-s they can also be brought into relief as units of rhythmic patterns without disturbing the *raga*-frame. Due to this exploration the *bol*-s themselves would offer a rhythmic quality when treated as sound-clusters. In this manner the *bol-lay* phase pays a purposeful attention to lay stress on selected *bol*-s to create rhythmic patterns. As a result, this phase successfully heightens a different aspect of words.

e. *Bol-tan*: This phase is marked by an alliance of words with melodic progressions in fast tempo. The latter are known as *tan* (>).

f. *Tan* is usually the climactic phase. Fast tempo tonal patterns (ideally) ranging over three octaves seem a natural climax to music-making. *Tan*-s function as instantaneous recapitulations of *raga*-s on account of their accent on speed and intensified creation of varied patterns within the relevant *raga*-scale. On account of their general climactic quality *tan*-s are not confined to *khayal*. They are musical highpoints and are therefore employed liberally in all musical categories and numerous other musical genres. They obviously fulfill a wider performing need.

The six phases outlined so far do not constitute rigid divisions and inevitably performing tradition in the overall musical behaviour clearly indicates overlapping *avatar*-s of these phases! Yet the phases, in various musical contexts, differ in proportion, placement and qualitative impact and hence one phase cannot be mistaken for the other. A *khayal* sung in a slow tempo has an intrinsic capacity to comfortably accommodate all or majority of the six phases. This variety of *khayal* is therefore aptly known as *bada* (great) *khayal*.

A *bada khayal* is generally followed by another short piece in the same *raga* but (in most cases) in a different *tala*. This is known as *chhota* (small) *khayal*. Sung in a faster tempo the *chhota khayal* affords more scope for *bol tan* and *tan*.

A less general and a somewhat atavistic practice is to sing *khayal* in *madhyalaya* (that is, medium tempo). From such a *khayal* accrues advantages of employing features of both *bada* and *chhota khayal*-s as it suits the musician.

A person who emphasizes the *tan*-phase in greater proportion is known as a *tanait* and his music is described as *tanaiti*.

1.5.39   *Khayalnuma/nama* (A H *khayal* + P *numa* = according to)

Numa is a suffix in Persian that points to something not directly presented in the word. Hence the form under discussion points to *khayal* (>) which in reality is not presented in the composition. *Khayal-numa* employs meaningless sound-clusters as in *tarana* but in a tempo which reminds one of a *khayal*. It is clear that the luxury to elaborate (because of the slow tempo) and the freedom from the constraints of language (because of the meaninglessness) constitute the special attractions of this form. The name sometimes includes *'nama'* — a clear distortion of *numa*, the original suffix.

1.5.40   *Kilbana* = see *Kaul*. The composition may be in Arabic, Persian or in Hindi.

Kilbana-Naksha is a subtype and it employs only one metre namely, *rubai*.

1.5.41   *Lachau thumri*

See *thumri*.

1.5.42   *Lakshangeet* (H < S *lakshan* = characteristic + *geet* = song)

Lakshangeet is a composition that versifies musicological features of a *raga* set to tune in the *raga* it describes. For example, it deals with the grammatical aspects such as notes included/excluded in a *particular   raga*, the time of its rendering etc. Obviously *lakshangeet* has more educational utility than musical potentiality.

Pandit V.N. Bhatkhande (1860-1937 AD) was the first major authority to take *lakshangeet* seriously. He not only composed them but varied the content. In his *lakshangeet* compositions, one finds three varieties. The first describes characteristics of a *raga* and it is composed in the same *raga*. The second kind of *lakshangeet* discusses theoretical issues in musicology and uses the question and answer structure. Finally there are some compositions that deal with characteristics of *tala*.

Pandit Govindrao Tembe (1881-1955 AD), a well known harmonium player, composer, playwright, writer on music and an actor-singer groomed in the Jaipur gharana composed *lakshangeet*-s which are poetic both in form and substance. As a consequence it is easier to render them in concert. In these compositions *raga*-characteristics are described but poetic craft is employed to diminish the effects of listening to a collection of bone-dry grammatical statements.

1.5.43   *Langda dhrupad* (H *langda* = lame + *dhrupad* (>)

Langda dhrupad constitutes a class of compositions that try to avoid rigidity of *dhrupad* as also the much acclaimed extreme flexibility of *khayal* (>). The most noticeable feature in *langda dhrupad* is free movement of words. They do not strictly follow the *tala*-beats though the tendency to recognise the main divisions of *tala* is still unmistakable. On the other hand a *khayal* moves with notable freedom in the *tala*-frame employed.

1.5.44   *Led*

A song-type sung mainly in Bundelkhand during the month of *Phalgun*, it concentrates on love themes. The compositions are mainly sung in *tala*-s such as *Ektal*, *Jhumra*, *Tilwada* as well as in fast *Dadra*, *Tritala* and *Keherawa*. *Raga*-s such as *Yamankalyan*, *Jungla*, *Jhinzoti* are employed. These features and the manner of presentation place the genre very much near to *khayal*.

1.5.45   *Le/ahra*

The corpus or a body of popular or widely accepted 'tunes' in Braj folk music is known as *Lehra*.

1.5.46   *Marsiya* = > *Soz*

1.5.47   *Phag* = (< H *Phagua* < S. *Phalgun*)

A song-type rendered to celebrate the advent of spring i.e. *Vasant ritu*. It is also called *Holigeet* after the well known festival *Holi*.

In its early manifestation it was regarded *Madanotsava* (festival of the God of love, i.e. Madan) or *Vasantotsava*, i.e. festival of Spring. This is the reason why early related literary references are about Shankar-Parvati as well as Radha and Krishna. King Udayana of the antiquity has been mentioned to celebrate it. It was probably designed to bring together the otherwise inaccessible monarch and his subjects.

Playing of instruments such as *dhol, manjira* and spraying of colour are important elements.

Today *Phag*-songs are folksongs often sung by both men and women together. On a cold winter night a fire is stoked and singers sit around to sing songs — sometimes the sessions continue whole night. Sometimes groups of singers go from house to house to sing the songs. In some cases these songs border on obscenity.

1.5.48 *Phagua* = see *Phag*

1.5.49 *Phataha* = see *Kajri*

1.5.50 *Phoolband/h (H.phool = flower, band.* H = pattern, structure)

It is a kind of *dhrupad* composition in which names of various flowers are included in a double-meaning manner. Obviously the general tone of the composition becomes less serious as contrasted with the conventionally graver content of *dhrupad* compositions.

1.5.51 *Phoolpad* = *Dhrupad, Phoolband* >

1.5.52 *Qawwali* (H A *kaul* = aphorism, saying)

Originally *qawwali* compositions were Islamic religious songs in praise of knowledge, God's attributes and saints, etc. It was also customary to pair together *qawwali* and *kalbana*; both being concerned with similar themes.

The word is derived from *kaul* (>). In *qawwali*, some aphoristic saying of the Prophet was combined with the process of *tarannum* (>) to enable and create musical elaboration. Khusro began the vogue of composing such songs in different *raga*-s such as *Bageshri, Basant, Sohoni* and *Yaman.*

Later the form came to include compositions in Persian.

In India *qawwali* stabilised around the thirteenth century and the *Sufi*-s employed the genre to spread their message. Amir Khusro, a *Sufi* and a music-innovator contributed to the vogue of the form.

In an earlier tradition, when the genre was more strictly treated as a *Sufi* expression three preconditions were to be fulfilled: (1) *Makan* = The place of the performance should be away from the general populace and such as would allow only *Sufi*-s and other devotees of Allah. (2) *Jaman* = Time should be such as not to interfere with Namaz and no other work be scheduled at that time. (3) *Akhwan* = Auditors should consist of *Sufi*-s alone.

Those who sang *kaul* and *tarana* (>) were known as *qawwal-bacche* (sons of *qawwali*-singers). A disputed tradition traces the performing dominance of *khayal* (>) to effective performances by the *qawwal-bacche*.

Contemporary practice suggests that *qawwali* is a mode of singing rather than a song-type or a variety of composition. A kind of *ghazal* (>) when treated in a particular mode becomes *qawwali*. With a little simplification it may be said that while a *ghazal* dealing with the theme of love is rendered in the *ghazal*-way that which centres on the love of God is presented as a *qawwali*.

In performance, *qawwali* presents a fascinating, interchanging use of the solo and the choral modalities. Usually, a party of singers sings *qawwali* (and two parties render it if the event is competitive). One or two of the singers are chief presenters and two or more from the others provide vocal support. In addition there are others who take care of contributing with rhythmic support (playing *dholak*, *tabla* and *khanjiri* and also prominently with handclaps) and melodic support (on harmonium and *bulbultarang* — the latter is a curious keyboard string instrument).

Qawwali developed as a popular and evocative form. Terminology related to this music is given below for making it easier to understand a standard performance:

Actions = Gestures/movements the lead singers employ to elicit proper response from the listeners and invoke a mood to support the major thrust of the text.

Alap = Introductory phrases of a *raga* sung without rhythm to create a background for the *raga* used in the composition.

Anga = Aspects of singing which bring out the main style followed by the singer (e.g. Punjab *ang* would mean use of a particular kind of cascading, fast *tan*-s etc.)

Baja = Instrument, chiefly refers to harmonium, the keyboard instrument , which is employed by musicians in spite of its being a 'foreign ' instrument — with no precedent in the traditions associated with Islamic music- making of the religious type.

Band = A verse of more than two lines — inserted from a longer poem.

Band sama = A closed or an exclusive performance in which a special song-repertoire is rendered without any instrumental accompaniment.

Badhana = To extend, or elaborate the melodic theme.

Bari ka gana = To sing by turns in an assembly of *Qawwal*-singers.

Basant = Spring festival and the related ritualistic performance of songs and *raga*-s associated with this festival at the Nizamuddin shrine.

Bol = Utterance, the repeatable part of the song-text sung by the chorus.

Bol samjhana = To convey the meaning of the text through musical variations, etc.

Chachar = Metric pattern of 14 beats frequently employed in the genre.

Chal = Gait, the specific melodic contour of the song.

Chalat phirat = Melodic improvisation mostly in a faster tempo and intricate in design.

Cheez = A complete, original song without additions etc.

Chaoki = A performing group of *qawwal* named after the leader or his ancestor.

Dhun = A tune which is satisfyingly complete and yet may not be in a codified *raga*.

Doha = A couplet making a complete, rhyming poetic statement in common metre employed by the singers at the beginning or as insertions.

Dohrana = To repeat.

Ghazal = As a poem it is the Pharsi/Urdu genre in which couplets are linked with rhymes and metricality.

Girah = A knot, i.e. inserted verse in a *qawwali*.

Hamd = Poem in Urdu/Pharsi in praise of God.

Hawa = Archaic *Sufi* song in Farsi said to be composed by Amir Khusro.

Khas tarz = Special tune.

Makhsus tarz = Special tune.

Manqabat = Poem in praise of a great religious personage, especially *Sufi* saints.

Masnavi = Extended Farsi poem with rhyming couplets

Matra = Durational unit in music making.

Misra = Verse line.

Misra kholna = 'to open the verse line'. A musical procedure in *qawwali*-singing. To set up the concluding statement contained in the second line of a couplet by effectively connecting the opening statement of the first line to the concluding statement of the second.

Misra ula = First verse line, especially the opening line of a couplet.

Mukhra = The opening refrain line of the song.

Murki = Melodic 'turn' — a specific musical embellishment.

Mushtar ka gana = Mixed i.e. communal singing.

Naghma = Melody, tune, played as a prelude to the *qawwali,* usually based on a tune derived from the *Zikr Allahu.*

Naghma-e-Quddusi = A traditional *Sufi naghma* reportedly originating in the shrine of Abdul Qudua Ganghoi.

Nat = Poem in praise of Prophet Muhammad.

Panchayati gana = communal singing.

Padhna = Recite, read or chant without instrumental accompaniment.

Phailav = Melodic spreading, expansion.

Qata = Four line aphoristic poetic form in Urdu/Pharsi used in introductory section of the *qawwali.*

Qaul = The basic ritual, obligatory song either as opening or closing hymn with the text based on sayings of the Prophet.

Rang = The second principal ritual, obligatory song after *Qaul* celebrating the saints (Nizamudin Auliya) spiritual guidance (colouring) of his disciple Amir Khusro.

Rubai = Aphoristic four-line poetic form in Farsi/Urdu in *qawwali.* It refers to the recitative preceding the *qawwali* often based on a *Rubai.*

Sany bolan = Saying it as second, singing a verse line to the tune section of the second concluding line of a couplet.

Sargam = *Sol-fa* passage.

Sher = Couplet, literally the strophic unit of the *ghazal* poem.

Takrar = Multiple repetition.

Tali = clapping.

Tarana = A genre of songs with meaningless auspicious words, often derived from *Sufi* invocations.

Tazmin = A poem incorporating famous verses around Sufi classics in Farsi.

Thap = An accented drum beat.

Tiyya = A triad of a rhythmic/melodic cadence.

Zamin = Poetic metre of the song-text.

Zarb = Accent, rhythmic stress.

1.5.53   *Ragasagar* (H.< S, *raga* + *sagar* (ocean)

Literally it means 'a sea of *raga*-s'. It is a genre in which many *raga*-s are consecutively taken up for a limited elaboration. The original composition is set in the desired specific *raga*-s and *tala*-s, and has words just as in *khayal*, etc. The exception obviously would be when it is rendered in melodic instrumental music of *sitar*, *sarangi*, etc., when it will exclude words or the literary expression in the usual sense.

1.5.54   *Raas* (H < S *ras* = to create a din)

1. Kind of dance practised by Krishna and his cowherd companions, but particularly by legendary *gopi*-s, the milkmaids of Vrindavan. It is a circular dance with an accompanying song.

2. A rare vocal classical form akin to *tarana*. Differs from the latter because *ras* employs meaningless sound-clusters used in the rhythm-language of dance: example, *ta thaiya*, *thun*, *thun*, etc.

1.5.55   *Reekhta / Rekhta*

Originally a genre of love songs in Persian describing the beloved in general. It was often composed in Urdu too. *Dhun-raga*-s were employed to sing it.

1.5.56   *Sadra*

A *dhrupad* (>) or a *hori* (>) composed specifically in *jhaptal*, a *tala* of ten beats, is called *sadra*. Tradition has it that two composer brothers, Shivamohan and Shivanath, followers of the style of the legendary Baiju Bawra, hailed from Shahadra and the genre derives its name from this place-name.

Alternatively it is said that *sadra* corresponds to *gurcha*, a song-type in Rajasthani language. The latter composition-type in praise of valorous deeds is characterised by long running lines. *Sadra* is in the *brij* dialect.

1.5.57   *Samaji Bhajan* = see *Bhajan*

1.5.58   *Samvadi Bhajan* = see *Bhajan*

1.5.59   *Sargamgeet* (H *sargam* = note names of the Indian musical scale + *geet* = song)

Even though taught and practised in traditional music teaching, it was rarely sung in concerts. However, *sargamgeet* enjoys the advantages of meaninglessness (*a la tarana*) and also presents the *raga*-image with fidelity. It remains a mystery why *sargamgeet* has not caught the fancy of enterprising vocalists, especially because *raga*-elaboration in varied tempi along with use of *sargam* has already become prevalent. This vogue is merely a step away from bestowing a full, concert status on *sargamgeet* as a genre.

Medieval performing tradition had a form named *swarartha* (notes with meaning): the term is a tribute to the terminological precision of medieval sensibility!

Possibly another synonymous term for the genre is 'Swaravarta'.

1.5.60   *Sawan* (H S *Shravan* = a month in the rainy season)

A form of semi-classical song sung in the rainy season. It describes rainy season and pangs of separation conventionally associated with this season in India.

Basically, *Sawan* uses varieties of *raga*-s such as *malhar*, *desh*, etc., and it employs *ardhatala*-s such as *keherawa*, *dadra*, etc.

A variety of *Sawan* songs sung while sitting on a swing is known as *Sawan-hindola*. Women sing it and the theme is love.

Kajri and *Jhoola* are other genres sung on similar occasions with a similar purpose.

There are evocative descriptions of how forms such as *Sawan* were rendered and how the coming of rains was celebrated in the princely states like Rampur!

1.5.61   *Sohar* = Folk songs from Rajasthan sung after a childbirth. *Jaccha* is a synonymous term.

1.5.62   *Sohila* = Reportedly it is a genre of marriage songs which Amir Khusro imported from the Persian music tradition.

1.5.63   *Soz* = Song of lament Muslim singers sing during the observance of Muharram (Also see *Marsiya*, *Mehfil*)

The *Shiya* sect of Islam observes Moharram to commemorate the memory of martyrdom of Hasan and Hussain. When Isna Asahri became the main national religion of Persia, this vogue received royal support. In India too wherever the *Shiya*-s became influential, the vogue struck roots and became strong. Unlike the Delhi dynasties, which were *Sunni,* those in Lucknow were *Shiya* and that meant increased importance of all cultural features associated with the *Shiya.* One such was *Marsiya-goi,* the presentation in which lament-poetry was recited. As would become clear later the musical parallel of the lament was the rise of *Sojkhwani.*

In Lucknow, both developed to such an extent that they came to be regarded 'arts' to be purposefully cultivated! In poetic meets known as *Mushayra,* poetic genre identified as *ghazal* is recited i.e. compositions are read aloud in a grave voice, appropriate cadence and gestures without 'singing' it. *Marsiya* compositions were also presented in a similar manner. *Soz,* however, moved further in musical direction and it consisted of singing of relevant compositions in a voice full of pathos. It appears that in the beginning *Marsiya* itself was singing of lament-compositions — at least wherever *Shiya*-s were in ascendance. It has been noted that during the period 1860-1926 AD in Lucknow, *Marsiya* compositions written 150 years before were also sung. The tradition of merely reading/reciting *Marsiya*-compositions, also originated in Lucknow. In Lucknow, singing of older *Marsiya*-compositions developed to such an extent, that music concerts of even professional singers appeared faded into insignificance when compared to gatherings arranged for *Marsiya*–singing. Khwaja Hasan Moududi, *guru* of the author of *Naghmat-ul-Asafi* is credited as one of the main originators of the art of *Sozkhwani*. Though he himself was a *Sunni*, he taught his original tunes to many disciples to shape the tradition to prominence. After him, came Haidarikhan who, in addition to giving a marked pathos to tunes, strengthened their structures. Haidarikhan's major disciple was Saiyyad Mir Ali. Nasir Khan, who hailed from Tansen's family, also made a name as a specialist singer of *soz*.

It has been specifically noted that women-folk from Lucknow were so impressed by the genre that they became the main propagators of the *Soz*-tunes. Even though the *Shiya* priests preferred *Hadiskhwani*, i.e. recitation of Koranic verses and reading of *Marsiya*-compositions, the singing of *soz* became a major musical tradition — such is the power of music in religion.

It can be stated that the entire vogue of making music to mourn the martyrdom of Hazrat Imam Hussain and his family members is collectively known as *Risai kalam* and this included *Marsiya* etc. *Shayar* (poet) Sayyad Abdul Wali Uzattan Soorti — contemporary of Mir and Sauda — was so expert in this art that he was called Amir Khusro Sani (the second Amir Khusro). He wrote and presented compositions in such a manner that moving away from mere recitation *Marsiya*-presentation soon became comparable to 'singing' in a classical concert and from the period of Nabab in Lucknow, Meer Ali's name was often eulogistically mentioned.

This kind of singing — in good voice and with a clear impress of *raga*, etc. — came to be generally described as *Khwanindgi*. Meer Jamir and Meer Anis, etc., however had also established a manner of recitation without musical tune (*tehtul lafz*) with its own rules and norms. This became so effective that in the initial stages the vogue was called

Marsiyakhwani. To avoid confusion tuneful presentation came to be known as *Sozkhwani*.

Gradually *raga*-music began gaining importance in *Sozkhwani* but the *soz* experts took care that the presentations were not transformed into *dhrupad, khayal* etc., from the classical traditions! Norms formulated to ensure this musical identity were so rigid and observed so meticulously that *soz*-singing could establish its own independent tradition and even classical vocalists of the caliber of Ustad Abdul Karim Khan, Ustad Rajab Ali , Ustad Faiyaz Khan and Ustad Bade Ghulam Ali used to regard singing of *soz* as a difficult task.

Some details of the *soz* presentation are worth noting. Sayyad Mohammad Nusrat Ali Dehelawi has given some details of the *soz* presentation. A person designated as *Saheb Basta* sits in the middle and two persons sit on two sides. The person on the right side is known as *Bazu* and one on the left is called *Jawabi*. They recite in coordination. It is to be noted that *'baju'* and *'javabi'* can be more than two. In their specific tasks *Baju* only intones one note in vowel *'aah'*- providing a vocal drone. This procedure is aptly known as *'aas dena'*. From time to time the *jawabi* repeats what the *Saheb basta* has sung. This is why Meer wrote one of his well known *'sher'*(couplet) in which the suggestion is that it is only the Bulbul which is feeling sorry that the flowers have disappeared!

An expert *soz*-singer can show his skill in many ways. Sometimes each 6 line-stanza (called *'band'*) of a *Marsiya* or on occasions each line (*misra*) from a stanza is composed in different *raga*-s. Such a presentation is rightfully described as *'raga-sagar'* (ocean of *raga*-s)! On another occasion Nadir Shah Sozkhawan declared to the audience, "I am going to

recite one stanza (*band*) of *Rajaj* (which is a name of a martial
compo-sition-type as well as that of a metre). If you like this
tuneless song then join by reciting *Darud* (a composition-
type centreing on Hazrat Mohammad). Actually *Soz* and
Rajaj differ as do East and the West! But Nadirshah was so
effectively forceful that the entire congregation joined in the
Darud!

Recently Sayyad Sikandar Aga has written a book titled,
Sozkhwani, Tarikh aur ... (1999). Anthologies of *soz* often
indicate the *raga* in which the composition was sung. Yet
another collection is titled, *Jakhir-e-Masood Hasan Adib*. From
it one can list names of 73 *raga*-s in which *soz* were composed.
The *raga*-s are: *Alhaiya, Alhaiya Mishra Dhanashri, Alhaiya
Bihag Mrig, Ahiri, Yaman, Yamankalyan, Bageshri, Bibhas,
Barjak, Basant, Bilawal, Brindavai, Bihag, Bihag Mriga, Bihagda,
Bhairavi, Bhairavi Subah, Bhairavi Makam, Bheem Palasi, Bheem
Sarang, Pat Manjari, Paraj, Pancham Raga, Todi, Janki, Jaunpuri,
Jaunpuri todi, Jhinhoti, Jayat, Chayanat, Deskar, Ramadaski
Mallar, Ramkali, Jhilaf, Savani, Shri Raga, Sindh, Sindh Bhairavi,
Sindhura, Sindhada, Sorath, Suha, Sohani, Shuddha Sarang, Kafi,
Kalingda, Kalindra, Kamod, Kanhra, Kedara, Kalbani, Khat Raga,
Khamaj, Khamaj Bahar Mishra (Murakkab), Khamaj Jhinjhoti
(Mishra), Gunkali, Gauhari, Gauri, Gaudsarang, Gaud, Lalit,
Malsri, Malkauns, Mriga Khamaj Jhinjhoti, Miyaki Mallar, Megh,
Nayaki, Nata, Nat Mallari, Hameer, Hindol, Hem Sarang.*

The *raga*-list is interesting for three reasons: (1) It
certainly indicates close connections of the *soz* music with
the classical *raga* lore of the Hindustani tradition. (2) It has
raga suggesting connections with Persian music. (3) Finally,
it is clear that the repertoire shows how musicological
codification of Hindustani *raga* that has been taking place
in the modern times had adequate and digested musical
material to work on! It was not operating in a scholastic

vacuum as the oral tradition was already working on a dynamic performing tradition that was taking neat cues from earlier codifications governing the actual practice of music.

The work also has included 13 illustrative *soz*-texts that employed the *raga*.

Obviously the *soz* corpus and the vogue of its renderings were gradually permeated by classical music. This was also apparent in the way *soz* renderings were often appreciated. For instance, in Wajid Ali's court Wajid Ali himself would respond to Mehendi Khan —an expert *soz-khwan* — by getting up and exclaiming — "O what a way to use the *Pancham* and *Nishad* notes, Wah Wah !" *Soz*-singers invariably received some intense training in classical singing. Very often some pious people who felt that they should not lend ears (to sensuous, seductive, technically boastful music) as a matter of religious observance, refused to listen to even *soz*! For this reason the *Soz-Ustad* laid down certain restrictions. For example, use of musical embellishments such as *tana, palta, gitki, murki,* etc., was a taboo. A story goes that once Sayyad Amir Haider Sozkhwan was to render *soz*, when the head priest who was to address the gathering later got up to leave. The Sozkhwan, seeing this, got up and requested with folded hands, "Sir I request you not to leave and to listen to me. If I sing against the law (*shara*) I am ready to accept the punishment!" The Maulana sat down, listened to the rendering and was moved to tears! Most of the older *soz*-compositions were simple but effective and were taught and learnt according to the accepted tenets of *guru-shishya parampara* — which has been one of the most characteristic feature of music education in India till recent times. The famous courtesan Umarao Jan used to refer to one feudal lord for his deep knowledge of the *soz*-music.

Soz-music has obviously flowed in two streams — one nearer to recitation, with minimal music but very evocative and the other closer to the art music mode as well as the corpus. For example Masood Hasan Rizvi Adib, (who himself had a good voice) had heard a simple, moving older *soz*.

It is significant to note that non-Muslims and females were also great contributors to the *soz*-art. Non-Muslims such as Lacchu Maharaj and Jyoti Pande are mentioned with great respect for their contribution.

Soz-performance: The *Aja* presentation is the larger framework of mourning-music and *soz* is to be placed in it. The *soz* performance takes place from a high platform as a preparatory or prefatory item but sometimes the entire event may be devoted to *soz* in which a particular highly valued expert (*ustad*) would specially be presented. This vogue is however now on the decline. The *kalam* (text) included in the *soz* is prescribed in the tradition and it is organised according to definite principles. In reality today *soz, salam* and *marsiya* together are known as *Sozkhwani*. The first in sequence is *soz* which consists of some stanzas (*band*) of *marsiya, rubai* (four lines) or *kata* (a group of four lines). Sometimes pieces composed with reference to some other poet's work with corresponding rhymes and metre may also be presented. (This is described as *tajmeen*). Pharsi *kalam* or a *duha* could also find a place. The *Khwanindgi* of one single *soz* does not include more than one stanza or *rubai* though in the entire performance, inclusion of more than one *soz* is allowed.

After *soz, salam* is presented. Singing of more than one *salam* in one performance is allowed.

Marsiya is the last item to be performed. It may include indefinite number of stanzas though they have to be in an identical tune. It is not mandatory to recite the selected *marsiya*-compositions in full — however there must be a thematic and descriptive coherence in whatever is chosen. The *soz-salam-marsiya* sequence is unalterable.

Examined as performances, the three differ notably. *Soz* is slower and in its renditions words may be held or prolonged for the musical requirement. In fact so slow is *soz* that three *marsiya*-compositions can easily be accommodated within the duration of a single *soz*! *Salam* is more flexible in respect of tempo of rendering and it can be rendered slow or fast as equired. *Marsiya* is slow in a dignified manner but invariably faster than the *soz*. Thematically, *soz* compositions are about God, Mohammad and his family — especially about Hazrat Imam Hussain and his martyrdom in *Karbala*.

It must be admitted that *soz* singing may have passed its heyday and in its place we have performances that appear to be addressed to the gallery (*Khitabat jakiri!*)

1.5.64 *Stuti* = A composition in praise of a higher authority.

1.5.65 *Sumirani* = see *Kajri*

1.5.66 *Suravarta* = see *Sargam*

1.5.67 *Swaravarta* = < S. *Swara* (note + *avarta* (circle, circular, repetitious pattern). See *sargamgeet*.

1.5.68 *Tarana*. See also *trivat, raas* and *khayal-numa / nama.*

The repertoire of Hindustani art music boasts of a number of genres that purposefully combine meaningful words and meaningless sound-clusters, the latter usually borrowed from the 'language' of rhythm and string instruments. A contributory convention is to regard specific (otherwise meaningless) sound-clusters as specially and mystically auspicious.

It is against this background that the four forms grouped together in the entry need to be understood.

Tarana (H *taranah*):

In essence it is a composition-type in vocal music that consists of onomatopoetically identified sound-syllables of rhythm and string instruments (excluding those of the *pakhawaj*). Sung in medium or fast tempo, *tarana* mostly relies on fast elaborations known as *tan* (>), and perceptibly fast rendering of the composition itself for its overall impact. Ordinarily, it has two parts known as *sthayi* (>) and *antara* (>). The form does not restrict itself to any particular *tala* and it is also found in almost all *raga*-s.

As has been noted, the *Razakhani gat* (>) in *sitar* music has been inspired by this genre.

Tradition credits Amir Khusro (1253-1325 AD) for having combined the Pharsi *rubai* (a poetic form of aphoristic couplets) with elaboration of the then prevailing modes of employing meaningless sound-clusters, especially '*dir dir*' to shape and structure the song-type. These compositions were therefore developed according to the melodic logic related to playing of *vina*, a lute regarded fundamental in many musical contexts. It is also suggested that he was able to innovate two musical genres, respectively *tarana* and *kaul*, because he received help from two music-making institutions of his times, namely *Samiti* and *Tatar*. The former is explained as a coming together of indigenous artists hailing from India of his times and the latter as a similar gathering of artists hailing from Turkastan — artists who had become a feature of the Indian society then. Amir Khusro's total outlook towards a re-construing of the then existing musical behaviour in India was later claimed to culminate into a comprehensive philosophy of music described as Hanuman Mata.

The usual sound-clusters encountered in a *tarana* are *dir dir, ta na, na na, yalali, lom, ni, tom,* etc. In this context the medieval tradition of combining *tena-shabda* (meaningless syllables regarded auspicious) and the *patashabda* (the instrumental sounds) needs to be remembered. Such sound-syllables were called *shushkakshara* or *stobhakshara* in ancient musicological texts. They had three basic characteristics: (1) They were based on or inspired by patterns of instrumental sounds. (2) They were onomatopoetically identified. (3) They could be pronounced. To an extent *tarana* is a resultant version of ancient instrumental genres.

1.5.69 *Trivat*

Similar to the *tarana* in most respects, except that it employs sound-clusters of the *pakhawaj* (>). The latter are more rotund and sonorous compared to those used in *tarana*. For example, *tak ghidan, dhir dhir kidtak, didnag, ghidnag, tak kadan,* etc., are noteworthy.

Also see *raas* and *khayalnuma*.

1.5.70 *Tapkhayal* (H *tap* = sudden, or P *tappa* = to jump + *khayal*)

The genre is a result of resourceful combination of characteristics of two otherwise independent genres namely, *tappa* (>) and some features of *khayal* (>).

In dynamics, clustering of notes as well as the language selected for compositions in the genre, a *tapkhayal* is clearly mapped on *tappa* (>). It has *sthayi* (>) and *antara* (>) as its parts. It is not restricted to 'lighter' *raga*-s. These latter features are borrowed from *khayal*.

Alternatively the genre is also known as '*tappa-khayal*'. Also see *tappa* (>)

1.5.71   *Tappa* (H *tap* = unexpected, sudden. P *tappa* = jump)

In Punjabi the term '*tappa*' means 'to jump over'. The genre indeed repeatedly employs melodic and/or rhythmic jumping movements and hence the term '*tappa*' is an apt and colourful description of the genre!

It is a genre of semi-art music reportedly inspired by folk songs of camel-drivers in the Punjab area and Ghulam Nabi from Ayodhya (U.P.) is credited to be the main originator. Another tradition has it that Ghulam Nabi was known as Shourimiya and his wife's name was Shouri. Incidentally, Shourimiya is also credited as an originating proponent of *thumri* — another major genre of Hindustani semi-art music discussed under the relevant head.

Yet another variation on the theme of the origin of the genre needs to be noted. According to it, Ghulam Nabi (Shouri) was a son of Ghulam Rasool, a singer of *khayal* in *qawwal* tradition. Initially Ghulam Nabi was a follower of the '*makam*' system but after settling in Punjab he combined embellishments such as '*tehreer*' (>), and '*Jamjama*' with the folk singing styles of the region to crystallise the *tappa* genre.

Couched in Punjabi and Pushtu languages, and set in *raga*-s generally used for the semi-classical forms, *tappa* displays tonal movements that are jumpy and flashy.

Compositions in the genre consist of two sections, namely, *sthayi* and *antara* as in *khayal*. As is to be expected from its nearness to *khayal* in many matters the genre employs many *tala*-s of 16 beats. Punjabi, *Ekwai*, *Adhha* and *Trital* would easily come to mind. In addition, it also employs *tala*-s such as *tevra*, *jhumra*, Pashto (of seven beats). The genre recurrently employs embellishments such as *jamjama (>)*, *gittakadi/ri (>)*, *khatka (>)* and *murki (>)*. All these embellishments exhibit notably quick melodic movement and an equally quick imagination on the artists' part because almost every word of the composition is to be embellished. The genre displays complexity of structure and brings about a dazzling impact on listeners who are surprised more than anything else! In keeping with the folk idiom and the Punjab-origin, a number of compositions are thematically related to the folk love-story — with Heer and Ranjha respectively as its hero and heroine. The form proves so attractive that it was combined with *khayal (>)* to produce *tapkhayal (>)*.

During Wajid Ali Shah's reign a person called Sarshar, of the Dholi caste also reportedly composed in a similar manner.

It was during Asafuddaula's times that the genre was recognised in the art stream of music. Till then it was mostly confined to folk category of music.

It must however be mentioned that a folk song-type of the same name in contemporary Punjab differs from the genre under discussion. It is held that the genre reached Benaras through Ghulam Nabi's disciples, Miyan Gammu and Tarachand who were in the employ of the Benaras king Udit Narayan. The *tappa* then reached such a level of development and acceptance that during Wajid Ali's times even *khayal*-s were presented in *tappa*-style — thus inspiring 'tap/

tappa-khayal'— a sub-genre borrowing its features from both *khayal* and *tappa*.

There are no *gharana*-s associated with the genre but Gwaliyar *khayal* and Benaras *thumri* and folk songs of the area are mentioned as major influencing agents.

Chiefly Ramnidhi Gupta 'Nidhubabu' (1148-1235 Bengali samvat) developed a very interesting and engaging variation of the genre in Bengal. It is known as Bengali *tappa* as it is in Bengali language, because it is specific to Bengal and also because it is very much different from the *tappa* in Hindustani semi art music.

1.5.72   *Thumri* (H A *thumakna* = to walk with dancing steps so as to make the ankle-bells tinkle)

A simple definition of this popular form would be "*Thumri* is a semi-classical genre of Hindustani art-music, rendered primarily in vocal mode. It has close and inherent connection with evocative movements, or dance, dramatic gestures, mild eroticism, suggestive love poetry and it is said to have originated from folk songs of Uttar Pradesh. It also has instrumental renderings — of course without words."

History:

It is not farfetched to regard *thumri* as a modern manifestation of the ancient *Kaishiki* mode/style, which Bharata referred to in his *Natyashastra*. An identifiable prototype of *thumri*, and a manifestation of the *Kaishiki* have been traced to *Harivamsha* (400 AD). This ancient work, describes a musical presentation called *chalikya*. The ancient genre combined song with dramatic gestures and dancing movements. Samba and Pradyumna, sons to Lord Krishna, are described to have presented it. Melodic speech, singing and *abhinaya*, which employed body-movements, marked it. In the later period, Kalidasa, the famous playwright in the Sanskrit theatre, depicted Malavika, the heroine of *Malavikagnimitra* (600 AD) — rendering it. The *Deshi* (as opposed to *Margi*) mode of music making could be said to have processed *Chalikya* to result in *thumri*.

The next historically important reference is in *Rajtarangini* (1070-1072 AD) of Kalhana who deals in great detail with a genre called *dombika gayan*. (The genre also displays striking similarity with a song-type called *jhumri* in later times.)

In the medieval *Manasollasa* (1131 AD), *tripadi*, a musical form, though proscribed from concert-repertoire, is described as: 'treating themes of love and separation, the three-line composition is sung by women who embellish the song to bring out shades of meaning'.

Further on, *Sangeet Damodara* (1500 AD) refers to a compositional genre called *jhumri*. The description runs thus: 'replete with love-sentiment, not bound by the constraints of prosodic rules, sweet as a wine, the rhythm-oriented *jhumri* is sung by dancing females'.

As one enters the modern period it is often argued that Wajid Ali Shah of Lucknow (1822-1887 AD), should be credited to have invented *thumri*. However, this flies in the face of history. Capt. Willard in his *Music of India* (1838 AD) mentions well-known *thumri* singers and Wajid Ali Shah was born in 1822 AD. Obviously the genre has crystallised over a long period with many practitioners contributing to its development in many ways. Many of them could be expected to have left marks of their inputs in *thumri* presented today.

In a way *dhrupad, khayal, tappa* and *thumri* are all modern derivations of the generic, ancient genre *Geet*. It is surmised that *thumri* came into vogue after *khayal* and *tappa*, and hence earlier traditional compositions in the genre bear imprint of *tappa* and *khayal*.

On examination, texts of *thumri* compositions in *Ragakalpadruma* of Krishnanand Vyas reveal that erotic import was not without numerous exceptions in the genre corpus. Under the title *thumri*, Vyas has in fact included some *bhajan*-s. It is also interesting to note that even today '*thumri-ang*' is a current descriptive/technical term in musicology; obviously suggesting that *thumri* can also be understood as a particular way of shaping musical material, which may not contain specifically erotic texts, etc. On the other hand, majority of compositions in the genre certainly are lovesongs of one kind of the other. Further, Muhammad Karam Imam's complaint about obscenity of *thumri*-s also serves as pointer to the generally erotic content (though many *khayal* compositions — it must be admitted — have an equally erotic content!).

One may therefore conclude that the genre passed through many stages of development before reaching the present state and status. Of essence is the fact that all historical predecessors and musical ancestors of *thumri* consisted of moderate and suggestive dance-movements, mostly restrained *abhinaya* (acting), and music as controlling components while gentle and feminine eroticism constituted its moving spirit. The contemporary *thumri* is obviously a logical and gradual culmination of a natural process of growth of musico-dramatic forces, which moved in combination to crystallise into to an appealing genre.

Some details about factors that helped in developing the genre are identifiable.

Firstly, the reigning dynasty in Avadh (with Lucknow as its capital) was *Shiya* by faith. Hence, rulers in the dynasty were not inclined to encourage musical forms such as the *qawwali* (>) that has strong *Sufi* associations of the Chishti tradition. Rulers like Sujauddaula, Asafuddaula and finally Wajid Ali in the Lucknow dynasty were, on the whole partial to Avadhi folk songs in general and to *chaiti, kajri* in particular. These were consequently offered generous court patronage. However, during Wajid Ali's times, *dadra* and *ghazal* were more popular genres. Muhammad Karam Imam, the author of *Naghmat-e-Asafi* (1813 AD) pointedly stated that Vazir Mirza 'Kadarpiya', grandson of Emperor Nasiruddin Haider, was the originator of *thumri*, Katthak dancers performed to the accompaniment of these compositions and added that it is incorrect to render them as *chhota khayal*. It is significant that the same author dos not mention the Benaras variety of *thumri*, which is explained later.

These compositions that prospered in Lucknow can be classified as *bol bant ki thumri*. Further, in the present context it is to be noted that Muhammad Raza, who was in the employ of Asafuddaula (d. 1797 AD), composed compositions for *sitar*-music and they are known today as *Razakhani gat*-s. These gat compositions were originally inspired by thumri. As these instrumental compositions were intended for an audience consisting of *Nabob*-s and *Amir*-s, — who perhaps appreciated rhythmic qualities better — *Razakhani gat*-s excluded phases known in contemporary *sitar*-music as *thok* and *jhala*.

Secondly, as with many other genres of music, *thumri* also presents a case of successful compromise between monochrome 'devotionalism' and inescapable secular pulls of ordinary life felt by people. Life of the senses, which can easily permeate secular behaviour, always found an outlet through numerous devotional cults in India — Krishna-cult being the major channel. There are, for example, very few *thumri*-compositions about Rama and Seeta! The Krishna cult and associated rituals, etc., dominated the musical hinterland of *thumri*. Presentation and content of *thumri* were thereby notably influenced.

Thirdly, it is reported that Sadiq Ali Rahatulla (son of Jafar Khan and grandson to Pyarkhan — who hailed from the family of Sadarang, the famous composer of *khayal*) introduced the practice of changing the key note in *thumri*-singing and thus made it musically more varied, brighter and hence attractive.

Professional entertainers such as Courtesans, Katthak dancers and *Bhand*-s used to rely in a major way on *thumri*-s before the genre gained a more general acceptance and currency. Some experts are of the opinion that *thumri* resembles the genre known as *Padam* in the Carnatic system of art music.

Structure:

Thumri has two parts: *sthayi* and *antara*, as in *khayal* (>). It is usually sung in *tala*-s such as *deepchandi, roopak, addha* and *Punjabi*. It is a general experience that these specific *tala*-s display a characteristic lilt, absent in *tala*-s employed in *khayal*-s.

Depending on the individual temperament of the artiste, thematic thrust and the type of particular composition artist selects, three strategies of elaboration are followed though in varying proportions to present *thumri*. The strategies are:

1.   Distributing words in the employed rhythmic framework to create lilting patterns.
     This technique is known as *bol-bant*.

2. Evoking subtle shades of mood/emotion through devising combinations of words and melodic phrasings. This technique is known as *bol-banav*. It abundantly uses the strategy of *bol alap* as in *khayal*-singing.

3. Interchangeably using different non-verbal modalities to express the same mood or its shades in varying intensity. This is achieved by creating emotion through gestures that approximate graceful dancing. Inversely the performer may fall back on words to evoke gesture-situations of dramatic significance. These two procedures are respectively known as *'bolme bat'* and *'batme bol'*.

A *thumri* singer employing all or some of these strategies creates an impact entirely and qualitatively different from presentation of *khayal*-s, which noticeably are often similar to *thumri* in other structural features.

Generally speaking, musical embellishments such as the following prominently figure in presentations of the genre: *Kaku, murki, khatka, jhatka, meend, dard* and *pukar.* These embellishments clearly indicate decorative, tender and delicate elements in musical expression. It is no wonder that the genre was often and rather mockingly described as *janani* (feminine).

The last phase of *thumri*-singing usually consists of doubling of the tempo employed in the earlier phases and this allows greater scope to the *tabla*-player to weave rhythm-patterns characterised by sprightly movement and delicate touch. These kinds of *tabla*-compositions are known as *laggi*-s. As popular etymology would have it, *laggi* is a shortened impressionist version of the Hindi phrase *'lag gai'* meaning 'it hits'! Singing in double-tempo is known as *dugun*. It appears that many performers do not regard the last phase mandatory for *thumri* — at least in call cases.

Types:

It may be safely stated that *thumri* can be classified according to the basic orientation it displays either in favour of dance, *abhinaya* or music. Some types emerging from these basic performance-orientations are:

Lachau: (> H. *lachana* = to bend). Movements approximating dance characterise this type. Employing the Braj dialect, compositions in this sub-genre depict self-surrender by the heroine as well as a dance-oriented and erotic content.

Punjabi: Sung in expansive *tala* of the same name, it is nearly a *khayal* steeped in an evocative mood.

Bandish ki thumri: It is sung in faster tempo and displays a greater word-density than other types of *thumri*. Widely sung in Lucknow and Rampur *gharana*-s, compositions of this kind consist of syllabic units that perceptibly match rhythmic units of the *tala* (mostly in *teental*) in a manner conducive to create mutual rhythmic reinforcement. Sung in a wide variety of *raga*-s, it consists of 'easy-to-pronounce' text and musical movement closely resembling instrumental music. This variety of *thumri* is also described as *Bol bant ki thumri* as in it musical elaboration is prominently achieved through purposeful distribution of words/syllabic units.

Names of some of the well-known composers in the genre are: Sugharpiya, Kadarpiya, Akhtarpiya, Lalanpiya, Nasirpiya, Madho, Naat, Sanadpiya, Najarpiya, Krsihnakanha, Meherban, and Bindadin. At one point of time, a general convention followed in naming of composers was to suffix *'piya'* after the name in case of *thumri* and *'rang'* in case of composers of *khayal*.

The modes of thumri-singing outlined above are in a manner of speaking comprehensive strategies of treating or developing musical ideas/material. Their methodical application in different degrees has predictably led to musical ideologies or *gharana*-s. As a consequence, contemporary *thumri*-singing reflects adequate maturity, variety of idiom, as well as richness of repertoire. Some of the easily identifiable *gharana*-s in *thumri* are:

Gharana	*Main features*
Benaras	*Thumri* of this *gharana* is dignified in rhythmic movement and tonal contours, expansive in thematic treatment and notably controlled in emotive utterance. It is no exaggeration to say that it exhibits an approach similar to that of *khayal*-singing.
Lucknow	*Thumri* of this *gharana* is decorative and markedly explicit in expressing emotions. To some extent it is closer to dance and also shows affinity to *ghazal*.
Patiala	*Thumri* of this *gharana* is perceptibly flashy and yet it is full of emotive appeal. Moving in a special way, it is melodically less expansive and can easily be placed nearer to *tappa* than *thumri*.

Paradoxically *thumri* is also rendered on melodic instruments such as *sitar*, *violin* even though a direct use of words and literary expressions are obviously ruled out! Considering the premium placed on language and meaning in the Thumri-genre, it may be appropriate to describe instrumental *avatar* of *thumri* as *dhun*.

1.5.73   *Vishnupada*

It is a special variety of *dhrupad* (>) in Braj dialect. Saint-poet Surdas (1478-1583 AD) brought *Vishnupada* into vogue and Mansinha Tomar (1486-1516 AD), king of Gwaliyar gave it royal encouragement. However, while Mansinha's accent was on devotional content, the Braj variety introduced love sentiment in it and the Braj *dhrupad* was thereby enriched. The kind of semi-erotic import, which Jayadeva and Vidyapati had supported earlier, consequently entered the *pushtimarga* (also known as *Ashtachhap*) corpus through *Vishnupada*. In the opinion of Abul Fazl (1551–1595-96 AD) *Vishnupada* was characterised by a stanza of four to six lines and centered on the theme of the praise of Lord Krishna. *Tala* was selected according to the metre employed. It is also argued that thematically speaking *Vishnupada* was a Hindu response to the vogue of Islamic *qawwali*. Popularity of the *Vishnupada* was more or less confined to the religious cenres and hence it does not seem to have enjoyed high concert profile in general.

1.5.74   *Yugal* (H. *Yugal /Yugul* = pair, couple)

It is a subtype of *dhrupad* genre in which a composition is modeled in all respects on another *dhrupad* composition already in existence — except of course in respect of the text of the song. Apart from bringing in poetic variety, the sub-type may have an educational value as these marginally varying compositions may help students in consolidating their understanding of *raga, tala* and such other aspects in-volved.

In contemporary music *jod* (pair) is a term used to refer to compositions in *khayal* as well as in rhythm-music. The two compositions in the pair are identical to existing compositions in every respect except the text. The conceptual parallel between *jod* and *yugul* is unmistakable.

1.6 Forms of Music (Instrumental)

It is not an exaggeration to say that a majority of instrumental musical forms in India are restricted to instruments normally used to provide rhythm in music. This important orientation has some valid reasons:

Firstly, a great number of instruments cannot but function as accompanying instruments. This is so because no instrument could be expected to develop a vocabulary, language, idiom and repertoire of its own unless it commands an innate capacity to produce a considerable variety of identifiable, typical and attractive individual sounds. Instruments lacking in this respect are greater in number and they are automatically eliminated when instrumental musical genres are attempted or discussed.

Secondly, instruments capable of producing sustained sounds naturally turn to voice and vocal music to emulate the latter and concentrate on exploring melodic dimension. As a consequence, musical forms that they develop are modelled on the dominant forms of vocal music. These instruments naturally have to clear the handicap of unavailability of linguistic and literary resources — an area vocal music can explore and exploit so freely. On the other hand, instruments can bring in a greater tonal range as also a marked variety of tonal colour. Together these features appear to adequately compensate for the lack of language and literary resources.

Thirdly, it is also noticed that instruments generally prove more useful in forming unambiguously perceivable rhythmic units and therefore individual instruments tend to evolve playing techniques particular to them.

In the final analysis, evolution of instrumental musical genres depends on the cumulative effect of all three features referred to.

It is reasonably correct to say that we may be able to guess relative antiquity or modernity of an instrument by examining variety as also multiplicity of forms the instrument manages to develop. Other circumstances being equal, an older instrument could be expected to display a more impressive array of forms because, by virtue of its long life, it gets time to interact with other musical forces and develop as well as enjoy the luxury of having a mature language and idiom.

A kind of 'survival of the fittest' principle also seems to prevail in music! If a new instrument proves capable of doing what an old one has already been doing, and in the process also guarantees a bonus of its own specific contribution, the instrument tends to take over musical forms already in circulation. The older instrument is consequently forced to move back, however grudgingly!

Against this background, it is not difficult to understand reasons why major forms of instrumental music have evolved mainly in case of two instrumental categories, namely *avanaddha* and *tata*, and there are specific instruments exemplifying this truth namely, *pakhawaj*, *tabla* in the *avanaddha* category, and *been* and *sitar* in the *tata* category.

What does traditional musicology tell us about instrumental musical forms?

The medieval scene was extremely rich. It is significant that solo playing of instruments was described as *shushka* (dry)! Admittedly instrumental music-making not accom-

panying dance or singing was viewed rather condescendingly! Yet, instruments certainly enjoyed an abundance of
musical forms. In respect of medieval instrumental musical
forms the following points are worth noting:

1. There were *vina*-s of many types and they explored
    raga-music following in the steps of vocal music.
2. At least fifteen types of flutes existed. Flute-music
    was also modelled on vocal music.
3. On the other hand, rhythm instruments, taken as a
    class, presented a different picture because they *did*
    have their own forms of music. With reference to
    membranophonic (*avanaddha*) instruments the basic
    'alphabet' of sounds producible (sixteen in case of
    pataha and thirty-two in case of the more developed
    mridang), prominent phrase-moulds resulting from
    them and forty-three resulting genres are discussed
    in detail.
4. As is to be expected, separate genres for instruments
    of the idiophonic variety (*Ghana*) are not described
    because such instruments were clearly regarded as
    the least conducive for developing an independent
    array of forms and repertoire.

This is the challenging backdrop against which contemporary instrumental musical forms may be discussed.

1.6.1   *Bajant* = See *Padhant*

1.6.2   *Bol* (v. H *bolna* = to speak)

It means 'something that is said or uttered'. The term
enjoys a wide connotation with varied applications both in

vocal and instrumental music. In the latter it is used at two levels: At a lower level *bol* refers to all those sound-syllables producible and useable in diverse ways to formulate meaningful patterns/arrangements during musical elaboration on all instruments except *pakhawaj*.

Each instrument has its own identifiable and perceivable sounds. These sounds are assigned specific linguistic syllables determined according to operation of the principle of onomatopoeia. These are collectively known as '*bol*' and obviously they differ as per the class of instrument involved.

For example, in *tata* class (i.e. string instruments described as chordophones) inward stroke is identified as '*da*' and the outward as '*ra*'. In *Ratnakara* the same are respectively described as '*sanlekha*' and '*avalekha*'. Some hold that in the Sarod-music, an inward stroke is '*ra*' and the outward as '*da*'. It is also stated that in bowed instruments such as *Israj* the situation is similar. In *vina* both the '*da*' and '*ra*' are inward. All strokes on the '*chikari*' (the high pitched string placed last on the finger board) are upward while all other strokes are downward. For instruments such as *rabab*, *surbahar*, *sitar*, *sarod* the main *bol* are '*da*' and '*ra*'. All other letters in their respective alphabets result from permutation and combination of these two.

The same strategy is used for identifying '*bol*' for the *avanaddha* (membranophonic) class of instruments. *Ratnakara* uses the term '*pata*' (< S. *pataha*=drum) for sound syllables of *avanaddha* instruments. Hence '*patakshara*' is the term used for sound-syllables in the instrumental 'language' of instruments from this class.

However in *pakhawaj*-music the term '*bol*' refers to a class of compositions consisting of sound-syllables that faithfully reflect structure of a particular *tala*. Naturally this composition covers one full cycle of the *tala* concerned and employs simple progressions.

1.6.3   *Chhed* (v. H *chhedna* = to begin, to initiate activity)

It generally means to produce sound by strumming strings of chordophones.

However the term also has a specific connotation. In its narrower connotation the term indicates a phrase or a minor composition in *pakhawaj*-music. It is customarily played as the first piece at the commencement of a solo concert. It is also the piece taught to disciples on the occasion of their initiation into *talim* (serious training under a *guru*).

1.6.4   *Dhun* (H < S *dhu* = to sound, to be agitated, or < S *Dhvani* = a sound)

The term is used in the context of music made on melodic instruments capable of solo expression, e.g. *sitar, sarod, sarangi.*

It is a basic melodic framework with both *raga* and *tala* being treated as optional. As a genre in instrumental music, *dhun* fulfills the precondition of creating flexible, and evocative and generative moulds similar to those provided by *thumri, geet* or *bhajan,* etc., in vocal music. Composer's imagination enjoys a free play in a *dhun* due to comparative absence of grammatical restrictions.

Usually a *dhun* consists of two sections respectively functioning as *sthayi* and *antara*. However, employing a *mukhada* with some improvisations may also be described as a *dhun*. It is significant that as a rule *dhun*-s are composed in nonmajor *raga*-s or in *raga*-s used in semi-classical forms of music. Combining *raga*-s at will is a much-used device in presenting *dhun*.

1.6.5   *Gat* (H *gati* S *gam* = to go)

A term widely prevalent in instrumental music, it has regular applications in case of music produced on instruments such as *tabla, pakhawaj, sitar, sarod* and *bansuri.* In other words the compositions figure prominently in music of chordophones, aerophones and membranophones. While in case of melodic music they are based on *raga / dhun* in case of rhythm music they rely on tempo and *tala* (which is a distinctive framework   resulting from processing of the phenomenon of rhythm).

In case of *tabla* and other such membranophones the term also has a narrower connotation related to playing technique in which *bol* with distinctive timbre is produced by stroking on edge (known as *kinari*) of the membrane of the instrument.

Pakhawaj:

Some authorities hold that *gat* has no place in the *pakhawaj*-repertoire. On the other hand, some maintain that any composition without a *tihai* (>), and lasting one cycle in *pakhawaj* music is a *gat.*

However another and an older tradition has it that *gat* in *pakhawaj*-music actually refers to a specific *theka* (>) employed to provide accompaniment in a particular form of vocal music. For example, a *gat* composition described as *khayal ki gat* indicates *tala tilwada,* which is abundantly employed in *khayal*-singing. According to this tradition similar usage points to use of definite *theka*-s conventionally employed to accompany compositions in genres such as *tappa, dadra, dhamar* and *ghazal.*

Tabla:

In *tabla*-music *gat* constitutes a major compositional genre. Some important features of *tabla gat* are:

1. Generally it is speedy in movement.
2. It usually runs over many *tala*-cycles.
3. A *gat* enjoys a structure that does not necessarily and closely follow segmentation of the *tala* in which it is composed.
4. Compared to other genres in tabla music, *gat* is remarkably rich in degrees of sonority, and its syllabic density varies considerably. In addition, in it *tempi* may frequently be changed. In fact, in this genre no aesthetic strategy of treating rhythmic material is left unexplored.
5. Compositional sections of *gat* immediately preceding the *sam* often consist of 'weak' syllables so that the composition as a whole lends itself easily to successive repetitions.
6. Structurally, a *gat* may or may not include *tihai*-s and/or *rela*-passages to enhance appeal based on dynamics, i.e. changes in volume and movement.
7. Unlike genres such as *peshkar* (>) or *qayada* (>), etc., a *gat* is complete in itself and is not further elaborated.

On account of their perceivable accommodative stance and notably flexible aesthetic policies *gat*-s have become major indication of a performer's mastery over his instrument as also a pointer to the depth of his knowledge. In view of the great numbers and variety of *gat* in circulation it is difficult to classify them exhaustively. However, some important types are briefly described below:

a. *Seedhi gat* (a. H straight, simple): In a four-four measure, the *gat* is initially played in medium tempo to be immediately repeated in double tempo.

b. *Rela gat*: A *gat*, which includes a *rela* (>) in its final segment.

c. *Manjhadhar gat*: (H a. 'in midstream'). It is a *gat* characterised by highly unpredictable changes in *tempi*.

d. *Tihai gat*: As suggested by the name, it ends with a portion successively repeated thrice. There are three sub-types of this type:

  i. *Seedhi tihai*: simple.

  ii. *Akal tihai*: the beginnings of the *tihai*-sections remain unstressed.

  iii. *Sab akal tihai*: all the 'stressable' points (that is, beginnings and ends) of the *tihai are* unstressed.

e. *Barabari* (equalised) *gat*: Characterised by medium tempo and even distribution of *tempi* throughout the composition.

f. *Tipalli gat*: *Gat* with its three successive sections set respectively in medium, one-and-a-half, and double tempo.

g. *Dumukhi gat*: *Gat* employing identical sound-clusters in initial and final sections.

h. *Farad gat*: *Gat* discouragingly difficult in its initial and final section is called *farad* because it cannot be easily played successively. According to a tradition such compositions invariably include syllables *katta dhete kate tak dha* in the last segment, which in addition, are to be played in double the tempo.

i.   *Gat-paran*: It is claimed that the term is derivable, at least partially from *parna* S. meaning 'a leaf'. Expectably, identical constructional sections placed before and after *khali* identify the composition.

j.   *Jod/a gat*: (of a pair or couple, a double) Composition inspired by an existing *gat* and very similar to it. Often it is also known as *jawab* (answer).

k.   *Gat-toda*: The composition borrows complexity of construction from the genre *gat* and flashy and attractive movement in approach to *sam* from genre of *toda*. However *gat-toda* is less ambitious in scope than a full-fledged *gat*. (See *tukada* for *toda*).

Sitar, sarod etc.:

Major compositional genres in music designed for *tata* (string) instruments that have attained concert stature, are called *gat*-s. In fact, *sushira* (blown or wind) instruments (such as *bansuri, shahnai*) or bowed string instruments (such as *sarangi, violin*) also mostly use *gat*-s as basis of their music-making. In solo music-making, these instruments aim at *raga*-elaboration and they also need forms suitable for exploration of their individual technical resources. Unable to sustain the tones to any considerable length, *sitar*, etc., cannot hope to compete with *been* and other varieties of *vina*. As a consequence, use of *dhrupad*, as a form to be exploited, is nearly ruled out. Further, *sitar*, etc., possess different timbre-personalities and cultural associations which in a way influenced their choice of genres. For example, both *sitar* and *sarangi* had strong connections with music-making practiced by courtesans. The cumulative result of these factors has led to an evolution of a sparkling and quick-stepped instrumental idiom, which is also determined to emulate *khayal* music! Under these circumstances *sitar* has gradually emerged as a solo instrument during the last century and a half, evolving in the process *gat* as its major compositional type.

Sitar has developed two types of *gat*-s to achieve, and in reality to add to, what *bada khayal* (>) and *chhota khayal* (>) respectively accomplish in vocal music. The two types of *gat* are known as *Masitkhani* and *Razakhani*.

Till about the middle of the nineteenth century, *sitar*-soloists relied on successive renderings of compositions of the type of *suravarta* (>) followed by presentation of pre-composed *toda* (>). Performances of *sitar*-music were therefore notably short in duration and restricted in scope. The general tempo of music ranged from medium to fast, a feature inevitable in view of the intrinsic capacity of the instrument. Two corroborative facts need to be noted: (1) To do justice to the valued musical strategy of improvisation and highly desired musical elaboration, it was customary to play slow-tempo elaboration on *surbahar* before a switch-over was made to *sitar* to play the faster music. (2) *Sitar* was in fact often regarded and described as a stepping stone for a student aspiring to graduate to *been* or other *vina*. A number of factors changed the situation and enabled the *sitar* to nudge out *been*, *surbahar* and *vina*. Even though it is difficult to establish a clear chronology of events, their musical consequences prove their logic.

Masitkhan thought of evolving a musical genre with an in-built provision for slower musical statements and elaboration as in *khayal* to allow greater scope for improvising techniques developed to maturity in vocal music as well as in the earlier pre-*sitar* string instruments.

To facilitate sustained production of notes — so necessary to emulate voice and vocal music — more playing
strings were added, increasing their number from three to
five. This also led to a greater tonal range.

Masitkhan also arrived at the concept of a graver music
import and hence created a type of *gat* that deliberately es-
chewed use of *chikari* (high-pitched side-strings) and *taraf*
(high-pitched sympathetic strings). With the same purpose
was ruled out employment of comparatively flippant-sound-
ing joint sound-syllables. In sum, tempo, vocabulary and
techniques were collectively harnessed to create music,
which is essentially continuous, serious and challenging.

Thus emerged the *Masitkhani gat* — as it is known today. It has a *mukhada* (>) of the duration of about four beats.
Usually set to *teentala* and played in slow tempo, improvisations and *mukhada* of this *gat* are employed as in *khayal-
music*. Accompanied by *tabla*, the *Masitkhani gat* has two sections respectively functioning as *sthayi* and *antara*. Sometimes an intervening stanza is composed and it is aptly described as *manjha* (< S. *madhya* = middle, intervening). There
are obvious parallels to *khayal* even in the structure of the
Masitkhani gat.

The *Masitkhani gat* is followed by a *gat* called *Razakhani*.
The latter is a fast-paced composition set in *raga* and *tala*.
This *gat* may begin from any beat and, during elaboration it
generously uses *tihai*, fast-paced *toda* as well as the *jhala* (>).
The *Razakhani gat* also has two sections called *sthayi* and
antara and the similarity to the *druta/chhota khayal* in matters
of structure and import are easily perceived. Very aptly the
Razakhani gat has been described as *duguni gat* (a *gat* in double
the tempo).

1.6.6   *Jhala* (H)

A term employed in different senses in the music-making of *pakhawaj, sitar, sarod,* etc. It is only in case of *pakhawaj* that *jhala* refers to a form of music; hence it finds a place here. In case of other instruments *jhala* refers to a particular mode of technique of playing instrument as well as a specific phase in their musical mapping. It would therefore be discussed in their respective contexts at appropriate places.

In *pakhawaj*-music, *jhala* is a composition basically designed to provide accompaniment to the final and faster phases of music made by string instruments.

The distinguishable structure of *jhala* consists of individual units of three, four or more beats. Due to this manageable duration of individual units, the *jhala* composition can easily be fitted into any desired *tala*. While rendering *jhala* to match elaboration on string-instruments, these units are accentuated as and when required but reasonable care is taken to keep a continuous stream of music. It may be said that *jhala* thus constitutes a rhythmic and membranophonic response to a specific stimulus-situation created by melodic aspect of music of string instruments.

In *pakhawaj, jhala* that uses sound-syllables in abundance is known as *kattar jhala.*

1.6.7   *Ladi* (H series, garland)

It is a genre in *pakhawaj* music. *Ladi* is a composition relying on close and repeated entwinements of sonorous sound-clusters such as *'dhum kit tak tak'* employed in various permutations and combinations.

In string-music (especially *sitar* etc.), *ladi* is a technique of binding together the tonal material.

A *ladi* composition in *pakhawaj* and tabla that employs the syllabic structure *kattar* is known as *kattar ladi*.

1.6.8   *Lad-gutthi* (H *lad* + *gutthi* = knot)

It is a composition in which sound-cluster designed to introduce a 'knot'-effect within the composition is added to *ladi* (>) composition. For example, in a *ladi* of *dhumkit*, a cluster of *kdadhan* would be introduced to momentarily arrest or 'entangle' flow of the concerned composition to create a complexity in the total pattern thus obtained. As a composition in *pakhawaj*-music, *lad-gutthi* points to a technique of organising rhythmic material in response to tonal material produced by string instruments such as *sitar*, etc.

Lad-guthav appears to be synonymous with *Lad-gutthi*.
Also see *alap*.

1.6.9   *Lad-lapet* (H *lad* = series, garland + *lapet* = to wrap around)

Essentially, *lad-lapet* is a term indicating a playing technique in string instruments such as *sitar*, etc. *Lad-lapet* also presents a minor composition in membranophonic rhythm instruments. In *lad-lapet*, passages of the *lad* (>) type are interspersed with places wherein an effect of a *meend* (legato), i.e. essentially of continuity, or unbroken sound is created by a skillful rubbing and change in wrist pressure on the skin of drum-face of membranophonic instruments.

Also see *alap*.

1.6.10   *Laggi* (v H *lagana* = to use, to apply)

Essentially the term refers to any attractive sound-patterns or syllables played in double tempo in *tala keherawa* (eight beats) and *dadra* (six beats). Conventionally *laggi* is employed to accompany renderings of *thumri, dadra* and other similar semi-classical musical genres.

Normally laggi is composed/constructed by taking up small portions from other major genres such as *tukada, qayada, rela,* and *gat.* A reverberating use of the *bayan* and slight rubbing on its membrane, delicate though sharp tapping on the edges of the *tabla*-membrane, skilful use of wrist-pressures, and such other special effects are abundantly employed in the genre.

1.6.11   *Mohra* (H *muha* S *mukha* = mouth)

It is a minor genre in *tabla*-music. In one completed cycle of a *tala* if the last segment includes three *dha*-sounds, the variation is known as *mohra.* In fact, a wider interpretation of the term suggests that any rhythmic, *tabla*-phrasing that employs open sounds in a *mukhada* (>) used in accompaniment is known as *mohra.*

1.6.12   *Mukhada* (H S *mukh* = mouth)

Very often *mukhada, mohra* and *mukh* are used as synonyms in discussions of melodic as well as rhythmic music.

It is a minor genre in music of rhythm instruments such as tabla. Similar to *tukada* (>) in intent and construction, *mukhada* however may have a longer span of about eight beats. According to some authorities *tukada* ranges from *khali* to *sam* and the *mukhada* covers the complete span of *tala* cycle from *sam* to *sam.* Alternatively, *mukhada* begins at *khali/kala* (>).

In melodic music *mukhada* is synonymous with *mukha* (>).

1.6.13 *Padar*

It is a term in *pakhawaj*-music (see *rela*). *Padar* is a genre in which the composition consists of a sound-cluster for each of its beats. Some maintain that *padar* is derivable from *prastar* (S), which generally means elaboration of a phrase or an idea etc.

There are others who maintain that in *padar* some sound syllables generated by *avanaddha* instruments such as *pakhawaj* specific sound syllables are identified as exact correspondences of meaningful words and the composition is created. The result is *padar*. For example, *'tat deha bhooshit'* — a phrase from a Sanskrit *sloka* — is represented by *'dhet dhere ketetaak'* in *pakhawaj* music to create *padar*.

1.6.14 *Padhant* = (H. *padhana* = to say aloud, recite)

This term — employed with a special significance in *pakhawaj* music — means 'to recite *bol* of compositions aloud in order to bring out literary value, structural peculiarity, and complexity/skill of the required playing technique'. *Padhant* thus involves a three-phased process: selection of *pakhawaj* syllables, identification of matching literary text and finally a reciting aloud that brings out structural qualities of the composition. An example of *padhant* composition may strike equivalences such as *Ganapati* = *gadikata*, *Jagat* = *digat*, *Shankar* = *dingan*. Actual performance of such a composition is known as *Bajant*.

Also see *bol paran*.

1.6.15 *Paran* (H S *parna* = leaf)

Paran is undoubtedly the most important genre of composition in *pakhawaj*-repertoire. The analogy with a leaf is perhaps intended to bring out the 'regular irregularity or symmetrical asymmetry' of the compositions included in the class! Some have suggested that the term *paran* is derived from the medieval *'tala pooran'* which was cluster of rhythmic, instrumental syllables employed to fill gaps in structural sections of a *tala*-frame. Others hold it to be derived from *'prakramanika'*.

From various definitions some major characteristics emerge clearly:

1. As a composition, *paran* moves precisely in response to the tempo of *tala* concerned.
2. It employs sound clusters other than those used in *tala* it is played in.
3. Both open and closed syllables of the *pakhawaj* are skillfully and flexibly woven in the *paran*. The selected sound-syllables may be one-fourth, one-half, three-fourth of a beat in duration or they may range from one to four beats in duration.
4. Being a major compositional genre, *paran* unhesitatingly borrows readymade formats from repertoires and tried out modalities of other instruments to enrich its own set of moulds. As a consequence, it can boast of innumerable varieties warranting a major classificatory exercise if justice is to be done to its contribution to *pakhawaj*-repertoire and rhythm music it creates.
5. Usually *paran* needs two or more *tala*-cycles for a complete rendering.
6. A *paran* may or may not include *tihai*.

Some major types of *paran* and criteria relevant to place them in the perspective of rhythm music in general and *pakhawaj* music in particular are briefly described below:

a.   Structural pauses within the composition are used in different ways and *paran* compositions are accordingly brought together in a class. For example:

Bedam paran = without pause. A *paran* with successive *tihai*-sections is called *bedam* while one, which allows pause, is known as *damdar* (with a pause).

Atit: A *paran*, which is completed a beat beyond the *sam* of a *tala*.

Anagat: A *paran*, which is completed a beat prior to the *sam* of a *tala*.

b.   Association with a descriptive content distinguishes a class of *paran*. These are often described as *bol paran*. An ideal presentation of such *paran*-s is likely to make varied demands on performers. In a prototype performance of these *paran*-s the artist initially explains the marked relationship between literature, rhythm music and (in some cases) intended movement-orientation. Then he deals with the literary nuances and compares aptness of correspondence between literary and rhythm 'text's. Very frequently *Katthak* dancers make use of these kind of *paran*-s:

Chhavi paran: It draws a portrait of God with words, which lend easily to rhythmic arrangements analogous to sound-syllables particular to *pakhawaj*.

Madandahan paran or such other compositions describe some mythological event in a language corresponding to *pakhawaj*-syllables arranged in rhythmic groupings.

The same criterion applies to *paran*-s regarded auspicious because they are in praise of deities. For example *Ganesh paran, Maruti paran, Shiva paran, Guru paran* are noteworthy in this respect. Unless one wants to create another separate class, *ashirwad* (blessings) and *salami* (salutation) *paran* may also be considered descriptive and auspicious.

c. **Affinity to a particular *tala* in which the *paran* is actually not played creates a type! For example *jhampangi paran* would be played in *adital*, etc., but it would be characterised by progressions that recall *jhampatala*.**
d. *Paran*s may be inspired by specific **movements, etc., that have nonmusical origin and rhythmic** mapping of the composition thus created may reflect their non-musical origin, e.g. *jhoolna* (swing-movements), or *kanduk-krida* (playing with a ball) *paran*.
e. Some *paran*-s have a declared thematic as well as movement-related dance orientation with appropriate names, e.g. *raas paran, maharaas paran, nrittyangi paran, nach ka paran*.
f. Some *paran*-s are characterised by special sound-effects they are designed to create. Sound-syllables in them are accordingly selected, prefatory legends are fittingly narrated and required movements are precisely executed. The way some *paran*-s of this class are composed, one is almost

tempted to conclude that the concept of programme music is hardly alien to Hindustani music! For instance the following traditional *paran*-s may be noted:

Karne ka paran, tashe ka paran, and *nagare ka paran*: Respectively imitate playing of *karna* (a type of horn), *tasha* (bowl-shaped small pair of drums used in processions) and *nagara* (a big drum employed in marching music).

Titodi paran: Onomatopoeic imitation of calls etc. of the common Indian bird *titodi* (lapwing).

Hathi ko rokna paran: The legendary *paran* which, when effectively played is expected to stop an elephant in its tracks!

Hathi ko nachana paran: The legendary *paran* that is expected to make an elephant dance!

Rail ki dhvani paran: An obvious rhythmic response to a modern situation, the *paran* onomatopoeically creates dynamics of railway engine steaming ahead.

Kadak bijli paran: Suggestive of 'thunder and lightening" effect.

Top ki paran: The event represented is firing of cannon. What is remarkable is that a detailed presentation is attempted and equally detailed directions are given. An assiduous attempt is made to imitate the act of firing cannon by closely following movements, rhythms and sound-dynamics involved in the act. For example a break-up of the successive stages would reveal following parallels:

Action	Meaning
Playing in the triple tempo	Movement of the canon wheels
Playing in one-and-half tempo	Cleaning the canon barrel with the iron bar
Playing in one-and-half tempo	Initial explosion of the gun powder
Playing in triple tempo	The dying out of the explosion

g. Some *paran*-s employ special playing techniques and their names carry a clear suggestion of their playing action.

Ek-hatthi paran: To be played with one hand.

Du-hatthi paran: To be played with both hands.

Tali-ki paran: That which has gaps to be filled with hand-claps.

Jai shabda ki paran: (*Jai* = hail, victory): This composition includes utterance of the word *jai* while hitting leather straps of the instrument in addition to normal playing on the membranes.

h. Some *paran*-s are inspired by other *paran*-s already in existence and as such allude to them. Hence they are described as *jawabi* (answer) or *jodka* (in couple or a double).

i. Variation in *tempi* characterises some *paran*-s: hence they constitute a class by themselves. Examples are:

Aad paran: It is in one and half times the tempo of the *tala* concerned.

Gopuccha: The name (cow's tail) suggests a progressive thickening followed by a tapering off. In rhythm this is translated in terms of *tempi* used. Beginning with a fast tempo, the composition moves to medium and then to slow tempo and further on to fast, etc.

j. A very important class of *paran* is constituted by those featuring some kind of structural complexity, a feature that also makes special demands on the technical virtuosity of the player.

    i) *Bina-dha* or *bina-kiti paran*: Omitting certain important sound syllables through a composition is one way of composing an especially effective *paran*.

    ii) *Tehttis-dha paran*: Going to the other extreme and repeatedly using particular sound-syllables also makes interesting *paran*-s. One such is the *paran tehttis-dha*, which as the name suggests includes the letter *dha* thirty-three times within one, single composition!

    iii) *Ulti paran*: As the name suggests, the progression entirely reverses itself to complete the composition in the manner of 'abcd-dcba'.

    iv) *Sundar-singar* (beautiful decoration): Compositions thus classified are reputedly 'the complete' compositions because they include every important sound-syllable producible on *pakhawaj*. Such *paran*-s are also regarded educationally significant and mastery over them is considered equivalent to mastery over the total range of instrumental potentiality.

v) *Jagah ki paran* (place): In compositions of this class, the same composition is played in succession from first, second, third beat etc. of the *tala*. Obviously, the rendering results in very remarkable compositional intricacy. Each new stating-point is described as *jagah* (location)

vi) *Farmaishi paran* (adj. H P *farmaish* = special polite request)

vii) *Kamal paran* (adj. H, *Ara.* 'Involving extreme skill). According to a tradition the composition has three *dha* sounds in its *tihai* and none of them come on the *sam*.

k.   Some *paran*-s are specially designed to provide accompaniment and are therefore known as *sath paran*. There are various ways in which meaningful words are employed in composing *paran*. For example:

Birudavali paran: It is composed of names, adjectives in praise of king, god, etc. Expectably praise-words in the composition often alternate with sound-syllables of the instrument.

Sarthak paran: The composition uses meaningful words and sound-syllables of the instrument in such a way that even though both appear alternately, taken separately each forms a coherent sentence.

1. Some *paran*-s are minor in scope and intention thus nearly amounting to casual utterances as *chhutkar* or *chhutput paran*.

1.6.16 *Peshkar* (H *pesh* = to present respectfully)

A composition-type in solo-*tabla* music customarily presented at the commencement, i.e. as the first item, of a performance. Played in a perceptibly slow tempo, the *peshkar*, as a composition, displays a purposefully balanced distribution of sound-syllables producible on *bayan* (>) and *dayan* (>) of the paired drum that *tabla is*. After initial presentation of the composition, *peshkar* is elaborated through various permutations and combinations of sound-syllables, *tempi*-variations, etc. Employment of sound-syllables other than those in the composition presented is not prohibited in a *peshkar*. Hence the choice is wide. This is unlike *qayada* (>) — another major genre in rhythm music. In fact *peshkar*, it is often argued, is designed to allow performers to warm up by extensively exploring possibilities of the sonar spectrum of the instrument. It also provides an idea of performer's depth of knowledge and rhythmic creativity.

1.6.17 *Qayada* (H U = law)

It is an important composition-type in solo repertoire of *tabla*. *Qayada* is more tightly structured than *peshkar* (>) and it is customarily played after the former. *Qayada* is characterised by its notably close relationship with the basic design of *tala* in which it is played. *Qayada* is a deliberate minimal arrangement/design of sound syllables of *tabla* set in a particular *tala* expected to be elaborated further through permutations-combinations, *tempi*-changes, etc. The one distinguishing precondition *qayada* has to fulfill is to use in elaboration only those sound-syllables which the original *qayada* text has selected. To that extent *qayada* is a seed-form. Further, a *qayada* is so structured that patterns and sound-syllables in *khali* (>) segment are matched by those used in the *bhari* (>) segment of the *tala* — thus creating a larger symmetry.

Qayada is elaborated in four well-defined phases appearing in sequence and respectively known as *mukh, dora, bal* and *tihai*. The first phase is *mukh* (mouth) in which an unelaborated and unadorned *qayada* is presented in equal time.

The second phase called *dora* (thread) divides composition presented in the *mukh*-phase into smaller units to facilitate patterning during the elaboration.

Bal (twist), also called *palta* (reversal), constitutes the third phase. In it, patterns created out of the sound-syllables of *qayada* are rendered in close adherence to the structure of *tala* in which the *qayada* is composed.

The final phase employs *tihai*-s (>) to round off the elaborations of a particular *qayada*.

1.6.18   *Rela* (H= heavy rain)

Rela is an impressive genre in *pakhawaj* and *tabla* music.

Pakhawaj: From amongst the sound-syllables used in *sath* (>) composition, those conducive to rendering in four-fold or eight-fold tempo are woven into a coherent pattern called *rela*.

A special variety of the *rela* in *pakhawaj* is known as *padar*. More extensive than an ordinary *rela*, it employs sound-syllables of the shorter duration and usually eschews the use of *tihai* (>).

Tabla: A *rela* in *tabla*-music is structured to consist of initial sonorous sound-syllables, followed by short medial sound-syllables and a consonantal final sound-syllable.

This constructional mode results into a near fusion of successive sound-syllables to create a near-continuous sonar movement. However, what is remarkable is that the rhythmic framework of the original *tala* is hardly obliterated. All elaboration in *rela* is rendered without allowing noticeable breaks because speed and near-continuous stream of patterns constitute the essence of a *rela*.

1.6.19 *Sath* (H S *sahit* = with)

Sath is a genre in *pakhawaj*-music. As is known, in other contexts the term means 'accompaniment'.

In the former context *sath* is a pattern of rhythmic sound-syllables running full distance of a *tala*-cycle from *sam* to *sam*. It may or may not have *tihai*.

It is helpful to remember that unlike *theka* (>) *sath* does not strictly follow the *tala*-pattern — mainly because it is, qualitatively speaking more than a nominal variation of the *tala* concerned.

1.6.20 *Suravarta* (S *sur* = note + *avarta* = cycle)

Suravarta is a genre in *sitar*-music. It is an introductory composition set in *raga* and *tala* for a *sitar*-solo. In the early phases of evolution of *sitar*-music, the customary order of performance was to present a *suravarta* followed by *toda* (>).

In addition to being a form of music, *suravarta* has a clear educational significance. When composed in terms of names of the notes themselves and not in sound-syllables of the *sitar*, *suravarta*-s become useful exercises or practice-lessons designed to provide a sound introduction to *raga*-grammar. It is obvious that this aspect of *suravarta* and a similar thrust in *sargamgeet* (>) in vocal music suggest that they are cognate musical entities.

1.6.21   *Talamala* (*tala* + *mala* = garland, series of *tala*-s)

Talamala is an extended composition in *pakhawaj* music. In it various *tala*-patterns are successively brought together to form one single larger pattern, which is expected to be further elaborated by employing usual strategies of rhythm music. In the known traditional repertoire *talamala* with a span of ninety to one hundred and forty beats in one cycle exists — indeed a tribute to compositional craftsmanship!

In a known *talamala* in *pakhawaj* music following *tala*-s are successively introduced: *Shakti, Ada Choutala, Teentala, Do bahar, Savari, Choutala, Rudra, Jhaptala, Chandrakrida, Manoj* and *Patatala*.

1.6.22   *Tar paran*

Tar paran is a minor genre in instrumental melodic music of *sitar*, etc., registering an imaginative response on the melodic instrument to rhythm music of *pakhawaj*, etc. Composition in the genre is a result of creating a piece in *sitar* music in response to existing *paran* composition in *pakhawaj*.

1.6.23   *Theka* (v. H *thekana* = to support)

Theka is an arrangement of sound-syllables employed in *pakhawaj*, *tabla*, etc. It is designed to reflect structural features of the *tala* concerned.

In *pakhawaj*-music especially, *theka* may be described as a minor genre played as a variation on the *tala*-pattern concerned. It covers the entire cycle of the *tala*, and one single *tala* might have many *theka*-s. However, *theka* is not elaborated and, as such, it is not regarded a generative rhythmic genre. In *pakhawaj* lore the instrument is often described as 'thapiya' obviously because of the importance it gives to 'thap' — the open palm stroke — so characteristic of *pakhawaj*-music.

1.6.24 *Tihai* (H = one third < S *tri* = three)

Basically any three-time repetition of a pattern of rhythmic sound-syllables is known as *tihai*. Hence often the term employed is '*teen-tihai*' — as three equal sections make one complete design. A *tihai* in which two inbuilt terminations are followed by a pause is called *damdar tihai*, while a *tihai* without such pauses is called *bedam tihai*. When the last syllable of the *tihai* comes on the *sam*, it is called *sam ki tihai*. When the last syllable comes on the beat next to the *sam*, the *tihai* is described as *atit ki tihai*. Finally, if the last syllable of the *tihai* comes on the penultimate beat of the *tala*, the *tihai* is identified as *anagat ki tihai*.

A very important variety of the *tihai* mode of organising rhythmic material is called *chakradar* ('one with a circle' or circular). Such a *tihai* contains smaller *tihai*-s within each of its three sections making special demands on the composing as well as performing skills. According to some experts this type of *tihai* has been taken from the dance repertoire to be incorporated in *tabla* music.

Actions/gestures such as greeting, salutation, etc., are often interwoven in a performance of certain *tihai*-s. They are therefore known as *salami ki tihai*, *namaskar ki tihai*, etc.

Tiyya is a synonymous term.

1.6.25   *Toda* (H *trut* = to cut away), *Tukada* (>)

It is a minor compositional format employed in *sitar*-music. The chief features are: (1) A short piece is made out of *sitar* sound-syllables such as *da, ra,* (2) their different combinations and permutations are also used, (3) they proceed in fast tempo. This makes a *toda*. In the early phase of the evolution of the instrument, *toda*-s formed an important item in *sitar* repertoire. These highly pre-composed expressions expectably do not allow improvisation.

Toda-s also exist in the repertoire of *avanadhha* instruments such as *tabla*, but in their context *toda* is better known as *tukada*.

1.6.26   *Tukada* (H S *trotak* = piece)

Tukada is an attractive though a minor pattern of sound-syllables played prior to *sam* in *pakhawaj* and *tabla* music. Generally it covers a short span of two to four beats and it is mainly designed to cover space between two claps. A longer *tukada* may include a *tihai*.

A special variety of *tukada*, composed in one and half times the tempo of tala played, is called *aad tukada*.

In *tabla*-music, *tukada* is also called *toda*. It is significant that *toda* also denotes a compositional format in dance (*Katthak*). A *tukada* in *tabla* invariably ends with the sound-syllable *dha* (irrespective of the use of *dha* in the *sam* of tala) — a clear indication of its function to make immediate impact (*Gat-toda* (>)).

2

TECHNICAL AND QUALITATIVE TERMS

Term is a word that conveys ideas or concepts. Technical terms are terms particular in application to a specialised field of knowledge. In the present context, names of instruments or their parts; *raga*-s, *tala*-s and their components; musical forms and parts thereof; words pertaining to playing/singing techniques; styles of presentation as also those words referring to relationships between various musical phenomena can be described as technical terms.

Technical terms form the warp and woof of all theoretical material in music. Misuse or misunderstanding of technical terms leads to inappropriate response to any musical situation. Teaching and learning, propagation, reception, appreciation, evaluation and all such acts suffer in the absence of appropriate technical terms.

Technical terms have certain characteristic features. Some of them are:

1. They are, relatively speaking, 'objective'. They are in a way 'outside the mind' and do not vary according to persons, occasions or places.

2. An offshoot of their stability is their durability. Technical terms operate with the same or similar meanings over long periods and in the process prepare a strong basis for scholastic as contrasted with performing tradition.

3. Scholastic traditions are mainly expressed through codified technical terms, which in initial stages may or may not be written down. However, sooner or later the written mode of their existence gains ascendancy. Thus the entire apparatus relying on etymology, chronology, genealogy, lexicography, construing, notation, etc., assumes important roles.

4. Mainly because they deal with the same larger theme, namely music, technical terms often form clusters. However, in addition to thematic commonality, use of language and grammar also play an important part in formation of terminological clusters. Consequently, a term originally coming into circulation as a verb may clear the way for related adverbs, adjectives, etc.

5. Technical terms are units in the grammar of music; hence they always remain a step behind performing traditions. In other words, concepts actually used in musical practice may have to wait before they acquire a suitable technical term.

On the other hand, qualitative terms are words that refer to the value-aspect of things, events and processes. For one thing, this aspect brings comparison into action. Therefore value-based preferences are expressed and hierarchies are established. In other words, interpretation (and not subjectivity!) is recognised to be a legitimate tool for investigation into music. Thus, actual performance and performing tradition in which it is placed, become the prime movers. Quality-oriented concepts emerge in performance and live in it. However, even though it is in circulation in actual practice, a concept may have to wait before it is verbalised. Compared to the technical aspect, a greater flux also characterises the qualitative aspect because values and, with them the corresponding terminology, are subject to change.

2.1 *Abhijata* (a. S = of legitimate, acceptable birth)

This is a term often employed to indicate art, i.e., 'classical' music as opposed to folk or primitive music.

The term obviously carries snobbish overtones not necessarily acceptable to musicians. Instead it is better to employ the term *'shastrokta'* (spelled out by *shastra*, i.e. science, scientific), thereby indicating existence and use of codified criteria and rules related to it. Further, it is advisable to use the term *'shastriya'* ('one which has *shastra'*) for all music that exhibits rule-structure even if the music may not be consciously and systematically codified.

According to the dictionary the term *'abhijata'* means 'of legitimate birth, lineage'. Art music in India, which is mainly identified with presence and use of concepts of *raga-tala* and *prabandha*, is generally described as *Abhijata*. It is clear that the term came into vogue during the nineteenth century, following the Occidental (mainly British) way of thinking, as an equivalent of the term 'classical'.

2.2 *Achala* (a. S *a* (non) + *chala* (moving, mobile) = invariable, constant

The term *achala* lights up an interesting and instructive lexicographic field. Three related and relevant meanings of *achala* are:

1. immovable, constant
2. seven
3. one name of the Indian cuckoo is *achala tvish* (*tvish* = speech).

Achala swara: Notes that do not admit *komal, tivra,* (flat, sharp) states or degrees are described thus. In Indian musicology and music-practice notes *'sa'* and *'pa'* (*shadja* and *pancham,* i.e. fundamental and the fifth) are accorded the status of being *achala* at least for the last four hundred years or so.

Achala thata: In instrumental music, the term indicates a particular kind of arrangement of frets in string instruments. An instrument with separate frets for each note is described as having an *achala thata*. Consequently in such instruments (e.g. *been*), shifting or moving of frets is rendered unnecessary.

The genesis of this phenomenon is worth noting. Functionally, accompaniment has always been an important task of fretted string instruments. As vocalists — singing solo — shift keynotes at will to create shadows of *raga*-s not directly being elaborated, accompanying instrumentalists naturally face technical difficulties (as frets could not be repeatedly and immediately shifted). The latter, therefore, established the *achala thata* which would accommodate all notes in one octave.

A type of *vina* was also called *achala* or equally aptly, *dhruva* (constant) in *Sangeet Ratnakara* and it was tuned to provide a constant reference.

Achala is also known as *avikrita* (undistorted, unchanged). *Chala is* the obvious antonym.

Interestingly, the term also means 'seven', and the basic notes in the Indian tonal framework also number seven!

Further, one name of the Indian cuckoo is *'achala tvish'* (= 'to speak, talk immovably, unchangeably'). In Indian lore, the bird is specifically said to invariably speak in a note identified as *'pancham'*, i.e. the fifth. Significantly, this note, along with *'shadja'*, *i.e.* the fundamental, is regarded to be immovable. It is obvious that the term suggests an intermingling of musico-cultural beliefs.

2.3   *Acchop* (a. H S *a* = not + *chhup* = to conceal, cover)

The actual meaning in circulation is however contrary to the one suggested by the term 'acchop' which actually refers to *'raga'*-s not so well known!

A rare *raga*, that is, one that is not in general circulation, is described as *acchop*. A more technical term with similar import is *aprachalita* (not in circulation). *Raga*-s befitting this description are complex in construction and usually convoluted in movement. They often consist of phrases characteristic of various other *raga*-s established in their own right. *Apoorva* (not before) is sometimes regarded to be a synonym.

2.4   *Aad* (a. H S *ati* = something which can conceal or H *ad* = horizontal, oblong)

The term *'aad'* in itself means convoluted.

The term indicates an important mode of organising rhythmic material and a way of organising tempo.

The process of converting a four-four measure into a four-three is known as *aad*. To convert a three-three measure into a three-two is called *ku-aad*. There is no example of *aad* in a pattern consisting of 5 units.

The basic feature is that the *'aad'* procedure shifts all existing accents of a rhythmic pattern precisely in the middle of the existing accents. In other words, the process redistributes duration of the original pattern in such a way that all original points of accent are rendered unaccented.

Customarily the one-and-a-half times of the medium tempo is called *aad*, which is thrice the slow (*'vilambit'*) tempo. Consequently, in a space of one beat, i.e. *matra*, three syllables are uttered or played and the *'aad'* is the result.

2.5 *Adhama* (a. S = the lowest)

In Hindustani music three terms are used to indicate overall qualitative levels of many musical phenomena. The terms are: *adhama* = the lowest, *madhyama* = the medium, and *uttama* = the best.

With diminishing severity of tone the terms also indicate lower, medium and the top portions of the human body and those of musical instruments.

The triad is additionally employed in respect of *raga*, *tala*, material of instruments, composers, etc., thus evincing a wide application.

For example, *'adhama' raga* is a *raga* not very useful in which to compose music. According to the more or less conducing nature of *raga*-s, Ramamatya classified them in *Swaramelakalanidhi* with these three terms. Somanath followed suit in *Manasollasa*. Today the term seems to have fallen into disuse.

Adhama vaggeyakara (composer) is one who composes the text of the song but gets the tune from others.

2.6 *Ahata* (a. S struck, beaten)

This is the generic term to describe all sound used in music. The other kind of sound, namely *anahata* (not struck), is only perceived by *yogi*-s.

2.7 *Alankara* (S *alam* + *kru* = to adorn, decorate, grace)

Musical embellishment or *alankara* is *a* very important concept with extensive aesthetic and musicological implications.

Basically *alankara* is a pattern resulting from various permutations and combinations of different fundamental musical components. Though it exists in both *raga* and *tala*-dimensions of Hindustani classical music, a detailed statement about *alankara*-s is chiefly available in vocal music. As a consequence, it is melodic aspect, which is more prominently explored in formulation of *alankara*-s.

Two fundamental categories of *alankara*-s are: *varna*-oriented and *shabda*-oriented. The former class of *alankara*-s explores and exploits sequence of notes (as also their pitch-levels) while the latter concentrates on quality of intonation. The *varnalankar*-s explore four sequential modes:

Sthayi = same, single note appears in a series of individual units.
Arohi = notes appear in ascending order.
Avarohi= notes appear in descending order.
Sanchari = notes appear in a mixture of all the earlier three modes such as *sthayi*, etc.

The main benefits of employing *alankara*-s are stated to be: (a) generation of delight or colourfulness in music, in making and listening too, (b) comprehension of the real nature of notes, and (3) thirdly comprehension of possible or potential variety in the components of four *varna*-s.

Traditionally sixty-three *alankara*-s of the *varna* category are listed.

In the *shabda*-oriented category it is obvious that infinite number of *alankara* is possible. The conventional listing of fifteen varieties of *gamak*-s is relevant in this context. Unfortunately all of them are not unambiguously identifiable.

Khatka, murki, behelava, meend and other *alankara*-s are known and employed today. They are apparently of modern origin and are discussed separately under appropriate headings.

2.8 *Alap* (S *alap* = narration, talk. a = near, towards, from, all sides, all round + *lap* = to cause to talk, to narrate)

It is a generic term which connotes elaboration of musical ideas, on melodic as distinct from rhythmic axis, in or out of *raga*, with or without *tala*, in vocal or instrumental music. Elaborations on rhythmic dimensions would be usually and preferably described by the term *prastara* (>). However the usage is fluid.

A phase of music making exists in which a melodic idea is musically elaborated without the aid of syllables or words. Obviously *alap* is a not a concept which has no past. Yet the contemporary *alap* is different from its earlier manifestations. Hence the interesting phenomenon of terms that differ even if they deal with similar   phenomenon, and yet there is a kind of continuity of performing vision!

According to *Ratnakara*, to do *alapana* of a *raga* meant to put forward the *alapti* of it. *Alapti* is to express or elaborate *raga*. By expanding or explaining a *raga* through elaboration of ideas constructed with notes is *alap*.

According to the present wider concept, the way the concept is dealt with by Sanskrit and regional writers on music, as also its actual *avatar* in vocal and instrumental music, *alap* mainly seems to have two types: first, according to nature of tonal elaboration and secondly according to its kind.

For example, in *alap*, two features are generally important — tempo and weightage given to various embellishments. To a great extent the intended form of music and selected modality (i.e., vocal, instrumental, etc.) determine the proportion of both these features. In the opinion of some of the authorities, *alap* is also divided in four or five parts, as is the genre *dhrupad*. Each part is further subdivided into four subtypes according to development and nature/ kind.

In spite of these and other such qualifications, some general features of *alap* can be noted:

Irrespective of the musical modality, *alap*-s usually proceed from slower to faster *tempi*. Three kinds of *tempi* are normally distinguished: *vilambita* (slow), *madhya* (medium) and *druta* (fast). No absolute standards are prescribed for these basic *tempi*. The tradition is to hold *vilambita* to be half of the *madhya*, and *druta* the double of the latter. However, in instrumental music, especially in string-music (*tata*, e.g. *sitar* etc.), *alap*-s in specific *tempi* (with certain accompanying features) carry special names. This is not so in vocal music.

In vocal music it is popular to connect *alap* with the vowel-sound *'a'* (as in father) and argue that it is mandatory for *alap*-s to employ vowel-sounds. The advocacy is strong in *khayal*-music. This has some justification because the actual practice does indicate *'a'* to be the vowel employed to a great extent. However, exigencies of performance rather than musicological and etymological prescriptions appear to be responsible for the norm. Not only that vowel *'a'* in general allows sustained sound-production (which is an essential melodic requirement) but it also encourages quicker movement over available pitch-ranges.

In reality vowels are found to 'eat out' singers' breath! Hence *alap*-s in *dhrupad-dhamar* (as also often in *khayal*-singing) rely on combinations of vowels and consonants. An example is available in *dhrupad-dhamar* renderings. In this genre *nom-tom,* i.e. *alap* presented through combination of meaningless syllables and vowels, e.g. as *nom, tom, ri, da, na, tana,* etc., have an important place. In *khayal*-singing, the same strategy of combining vowel-consonants with musical elaboration results into a combining of words of the composition with vocalisation. This is known as *bol-alap*.

Sometimes a term such as *madhyalaya alap* (medium tempo *alap*) is used — suggesting thereby that the term *alap* in itself is not an indicative of a specific tempo. However, *alap* is mostly understood to be in a slow tempo. In vocal music *alap*-s in *druta* tempo are often identified as *tan*-s though, strictly speaking, this is a musicological mistake. In fact this usage is yet another indicator of association of slow tempo with *alap*-s. (*Bol-alap, bol-tan,* etc. being special phases of *khayal*-singing are separately discussed.)

Thumri (>), a major form of semi-art music evinces a different approach to musical elaboration, though *bol*-s play an important role in it. A detailed discussion of *thumri* is found in a separate entry.

In string-instruments (especially in music of *been, sitar* and analogous instruments) there exists a well-developed system of musical elaboration, which, in all probability, evolved in close correspondence to singing of *dhrupad* (>). The basic features are:

There are four types of elaboration dependent on the development or expansion: (1) *Auchar*, (2) *Bandhan*, (3) *Qaid*, (4) *Vistara*. Their combinations give six subtypes: *Auchar+ Bandhan, Auchar+Qaid, Auchar+Vistara, Bandhan+Qaid, Bandhan+Vistara , Qaid+Vistara*. The original four types need to be understood:

1. *Auchar* (S *utchar* = articulation): Initial rendering of notes regarded sufficient for an unambiguous indica- tion of *raga*-identity. This may be elementary but enough to indicate basic identity of *raga*.
2. *Bandhan* (S *bandhan* = binding): Short but emphatic phrases characteristic of *raga*. This phase is actualised when phrases in accordance of the rules, etc., followed by different *gharana*-s are presented. *Auchar* is related to basic identity of a *raga* while *bandhan* is related to *raga*-identity which a particular *gharana* believes in.
3. *Qaid* (A restraint, constraint): Elaboration in which one note is given central importance. It is to keep a particu- lar note at the centre (as if imprisoning it) to elaborate a *raga* (for example 'sa' is often treated in this way)
4. *Vistara* (S *vi* + *stru* = to spread, to cover): The term in- dicates free and uninhibited exploration of an idea for which preceding phases are a preparation. It means to go beyond first three phases in order to depict a fairly detailed picture of a *raga*.

The second kind of the distinction, i.e., according to the *prakriti* (kind or nature) is based on the concept of four *vani*-s (*bani*-s). Depending on their overall use of embel- lishment and *tempi* four kinds of *alap*-s are distinguished in *dhrupad*-music. These types of *alap*-s are described as *bani* (S *vani* = voice).

Major features of the four *bani*-s are noted below:

a. *Gaudhar/Gaud*: *Gaurhar* or *gobarhar* must be distortions. Most probably the term is derived from the practice current in the Gaud region. Sometimes, this *bani* is alternatively described as the *shuddha*. It does not give importance to embellishments; emphasizes clear pronunciation; uses *meend, aas* and *syunt*. Calm and grave in effect, it is austere and is characterised by sustained and slow progressions.

b. *Dagur*: The term is probably derived from 'Dagar' a place-name. This *bani* has more embellishments than *Gaud*. It is also more intricate. From among the embellishments, it prefers *jamjama*. Comparatively more decorative it also employs more cross rhythms.

c. *Nauhar*: abundance of embellishments to the point of dazzling listeners into submission.

d. *Khandar*: *Khandar* (has it any connection with Kandahar one wonders!) It relies on *gamak-s*. Broadly speaking it may be said that features of *Gaud* and *Dagar* are employed in *vilambit* tempo and of the other *bani*-s in the medium and *drut tempi* in music-making.

It is obvious that the *bani*-s cannot be expected to be more than broad stylistic classifications. Interchange of their characteristics would be detected in performances according to the employed tempo as well as the musical temperament of the concerned artist.

A more systematic phasing of *alap*-s is put forward in context of string-music. The phasing clearly reflects care taken to allow greater role to technical resources of instruments concerned. In this context the following phases are worth noting:

Vilambit alap: Chiefly it consists of slow-tempo, *tala*-less elaboration of musical ideas implicit in a *raga*. A *mukhada* (>) characteristic of the *raga* is introduced after each completed statement of an idea. The tempo increases gradually and in place of sustained tonal lines and even patterns more fretwork and *gamak*-s appear on the scene. In all the four phases of *dhrupad*, i.e. *sthayi, antara, sanchari* and *abhog vilambit* tempo can be used. Yet, it is generally true to say that from *sthayi* to *antara*, the tempo is gradually on the increase. In order to emphasize the basic *shadja* or a particular note in a *raga*, a *mukhada* is constructed and it is used in all *alap*-s. After the completion of each 'note-sentence', *mukhada* is employed to suggest the completion. Yet, the *tala* is not activated. The specific circularity of the *tala*-cycle is absent. It is due to repetition of *mukhada* that the *alap* displays sections.

According to some, the *vilambit* is itself divided into three types as: (a) *vilambit+vilambit*, (b) *vilambit+madhya*, (c) *vilambit+druta*.

(a) The progression is to begin from the note of commencement (*graha swara*) to reach the central note (*ansha swara è*) and to end on the final note (*nyasa swara è*). This is what happens in the *Auchar*.

(b) Commencing from the fundamental ('*shadja*') and reach main (*ansha*) or the controlling note (*vadi swara*) and end on the *nyasa*. *Bandhan* and *Qaid* have this kind of elaboration.

(c) From *ansha* to *samvadi*. This occurs in the phase known as *vistara*.

Vilambit+madhya = the *drut* tempo is introduced. *Bidhar* (see *bidar*) kind of elaboration takes place. The *chikari*-work in instrumental music forms a part of this phase.

Vilambit+drut = Tempo increases though the *mukhada* remains *vilambit*.

Madhya = Determined in relation to *vilambit* but notably less than *drut*.

It must be remembered that many times the *vilambit-madhya-drut tempi* are determined by the kind of music possible on a particular instrument.

Even this phase is according to some scholars divisible in three phases: *madhya+vilambit, madhya+madhya, madhya+drut*.

It could be said that what is characterised as *chhanda* is first felt in the *madhya* tempo. *Chhanda* can be defined as generation of a definite, repetitive line of recognisable duration that bestows a definite length on the concerned tonal phrase.

Madhya+Vilambit = Known as *Dagur ki badhat* it consists of embellishments and *chikari*-work.

Madhya+Madhya = Also known as *'madhya jod'* or *'barabar ki jod'* it abundantly consists of musical embellishment known as *'Gamak'*. In *'tata'* instruments, fretwork is on the increase in this phase.

Madhya+drut = The phase is also known as *'ladi-jod'*. It has a faster tempo than the *madhya+madhya*.

Drut = Three types: *drut+vilambit, drut+madhya, drut+drut*. *Chikari*-work is on the increase. In fact, the increasing tempo is the chief characteristic.

Jod: *Jod* (coupled)-phase of *alap*-s is in double the tempo of *vilambit* and succeeds the latter. It is in this phase that complicated fretwork and fingerwork on the high-pitched string (*chikari*), otherwise used chiefly for the drone-cum-rhythm function, become prominent.

Jhala: In this phase *chikari*-work comes to the fore. Sometimes a small *tukda* (>) is also allowed an appearance.

Increasing tempo registers a movement towards musical climax. In this phase the entire musical expression comes nearest to a metrical quality. *Jhala* is the phase in which *alap* gets a definite *chhanda*. Strokes identified as *'da ra ra ra'* are employed in quick tempo to realise the phase. One or a few notes on the main string followed by one or more quick strokes on the *chikari* string — this is the general plan. *Chikari*-work is obviously on the increase. *Ta na na na* and such other meaningless syllables are used in vocal music to carry out the work done by *chikari* strings in instrumental music. Accompanying rhythm instruments are also able to have a little more say in this phase — chiefly by sounding the *matra* after the *mukhada*.

Thok: This post-*jhala* phase of elaboration is replete with accents. The plectrum, etc., is actually struck on adjacent wooden or metal portions of the instrument to introduce the *'thok'* (strike) effect. After the *jhala alap* reaches the *drut+drut* phase because of the *'thok'*, stresses become important. In vocal music, more stressed, meaningless syllables such as *'dretum'*, etc., actualise the phase.

Ladi: This phase is more or less confined to instrumental music. A nucleus of notes (of sound-syllables in case of *pakhawaj* music, etc.) is formed and patterns are woven around the nucleus, which is thus repeated in varied contexts. *Ladi* means series. For example, in *mridang*-music, to include syllables such as *'tak dhum kit'* and then to elaborate them as *'tak tak dhum dkit, kit tak tak tak dhum kit'* is to prepare a *ladi*. *Ladi*-s can be presented in a similar fashion on other instruments.

Lad-gutthi: (a plait with a knot). In this phase a *ladi* with a 'knot'-effect is created by introduction of harder sound-syllables and their groups. *Lad-gutthi* is to tie a knot in the *ladi*. In other words, in the comparatively straight syllables of the *ladi*, to introduce joint sound-syllables such as, *kredhetete*, would create a *lad-gutthi*.

Lad-lapet: It consists of *ladi*-effect alternating with places that employ *meend* and other enveloping sound-progressions. The essence of *lad-lapet* is to introduce *meend* and *aans*, etc., along with *ladi*, *lad-gutthi*, etc.

Paran: In this phase patterns in string-music, analogous to the accompanying *pakhawaj*-passages, are presented. In this phase, a player on string instrument begins a *tala*-pattern on the *chikari* string. Then simultaneously, he plays on the main strings patterns responsive to the patterns played by the *pakhawaj*-player, subsequently to return to the original pattern on the *chikari*. The rhythm accompanist plays correspondingly. This is known as *paran* or *tar-paran*.

Sath: In it string-player and rhythm-accompanist proceed in strict correspondence with each other. It is similar to the *paran* but in it the main musician as well as the accompanist play in identical mode and come to the first beat of the *tala*, i.e.'*sama*'. In a true sense they are 'with one another'.

Dhuya: For this phase *chikari*-string is used to phrase *ladi*-s alternating with other patterns played on the main strings. In *dhuya* the main elaboration is on the main string and *ladi* or *lad-gutthi* are introduced on the *chikari*.

Matha: In it alternating movements on *chikari* and main strings are played. *Ladi* on the main string and *lad-gutthi* on the *chikari* or to continue playing so alternatively is a good example of *matha*.

Paramatha = to bring a *paran* to an end by playing a part of the *paran* on the main string and the rest on the *chikari* is known as *paramatha*. However, some hold that this phase has gone out of vogue.

On this background provided by the contemporary practice, it is interesting to note exposition of the theme *'giti'* in *Ratnakara*. It maintains that in vocal music *alap* are actualised with the help of linguistic, non-meaningful vowel-sounds. In ancient days *alap* must have been presented with the help of Sanskrit *sloka*. It is interesting to note that two types of melodic elaboration are clearly mentioned. One identified as *ragalapti* does not need a *tala* or a genre and to that extent it is absolutely melodic. The other variety, called *roopakalapti* is melodic but with the help of a composition set in *tala* and with a song-text. To that extent it is less absolute than the *ragalapti*.

In general *alap* is that elaboration of *raga* in which aspects of *graha, ansha, mandra, tara, nyasa, apanyasa, alpatva, bahutva, shadava, audava* are clearly brought out. In the *roopaka-alap*, presence of different sections, i.e. *geet-khanda* is felt. In *prabandha*-singing, the *vilambit* (slow) *alap*, which is in a notable tempo but without *tala* is known as *vartani*. In case the *vartani* is in fast tempo, it is called *karan*.

While describing the *alap* in greater detail the ancient tradition has noted the following sections of the elaboration of a *raga*:

Akshiptika = the section in which *raga* is outlined. It has four sub-sections called *swasthana*:

Prathama swasthana = to express sentiment of *raga* by pausing on the *sthayi* note of the *raga* as also by going 'below' and 'above' it.

Dwitiya-swasthana = to pause on the *dvyardha swara* (*dvyardha samvadi* is the middle. To the lower limit of this note extends the scope of the *prathama swasthana*.)

Tritiya swasthana = to end on the *ansha* after moving among the *ardhasthita swara*-s. (The *ansha swara* of the second *saptaka* is called *dwiguna swara*. *Swara*-s between the *dwiguna* and the *dvyardha* are called *ardhasthita swara*-s.)

Chaturtha swasthana = to pause on the *dwiguna swara*, execute movements and come back to the *ansha swara*.

It could be maintained that, in some measure, *swasthana*-s are also detected in the modern tradition. For example, the following details are noted after considering the *sthana* or *mukam* as section of the *alap*:

(a) First *sthana* = to take the prominent *swara* and come back to the *shadja*.

(b) Second *sthana* = from the *shadja* to the prominent note. This is called *roopaka*.

(c) Third *sthana* = from the lower to the *tara shadja*. This is known as *chik swara*.

(d) To pause on the fundamental *shadja* then move to the *shadja* in the second and third octaves while depicting the nature of the *raga* by regular ascending and descending. This is known as *vishramaka*.

Ragavardhani = *Prathama*: elaboration in the *madhya* and the *tara*. This is *vilamba kala sanchara*. *Dvitiya*: Elaboration in the *mandra* and *madhyama*. This is *madhya kala sanchara*. *Tritiya*: Elaboration in the three *sthana*-s. This is *drut kala sanchara*.

Sthayi: The elaboration begins from the *ansha swara*. According to the *rupa*, this has 10 and according to the *karya* this has 33 varieties. In the *Aprasiddha sthayi*, there are 36 *sankirna* and 26 *asankirna* varieties. The total comes to 96. Every *sthayi* expresses a different picture of the *raga* concerned (*sthya* and *thaya* are synonymous).

Makarini: This section of the *alap* literally caps (*mukuta*) the *alap*. It moves in all the octaves and is completed on the *nyasa swara*.

Nyasa = *Alap* is completed.

Geet = From the earlier ages *salagsood* was the kind of *prabandha* which the *Ratnakara* period inherited. In this type, *prabandha*-s were known after the *tala*-s they used. *Geet* is useful to realise the *raga* through easy, with-*tala* and brief movements.

Prabandha: It is realised through the 4 *dhatu*-s and 6 *anga*-s.

2.9 *Amukta* (S not free, *a* = not + *mukta* = free)

The term refers to a feature in fingering technique employed in playing wind instruments such as *bansuri* (>). In it sound-holes are completely blocked. *Mukta* (open) and *ardhamukta* (half-open) are the two other related varieties.

2.10 *Anga* (S. = noun meaning division or department, a portion or part of the whole which marks a division, or demarcates a portion or part of a whole, and which is not further divisible)

- In the *Sangeet Ratnakara*, a *prabandha* is stated to have six *anga*-s. In fact the *prabandha*-s were classified according to the number of *anga*-s it consisted of. Even today, the genre-name *chaturang* displays this feature.
- *Historical aspect*: The term is ancient and it has two important sub-types, namely *talanga* and *varnanga*.

While describing the *tandava* dance, Bharata deals with two kinds of *geetaka*, the first of which consisted of *vastu*, while the second was made of *anga*. For him, *anga* was a component of *tala* with less scope while the *vastu* offered more. Obviously, *varnanga* was related to musical notes. Rules pertaining to ascending-descending, dynamics of notes within a phrase, places in the *geetaka* where it was possible to rest/remain steady, etc., were determined by the *varnanga*. However, this statement of the position does not explain relationship between *talanga* and *varnanga*.

- Dattila has emphasized *anga* as *varnanga*. On this background, four subtypes of *anga* according to Dattila and three according to Bharata are to be understood. They are: *ekaka, avagadha, pravritta* and *vividha*.

- *Ekaka* is that which has no sections or divisions. In other words, the related phrase, etc., is not divided by resting on notes, etc.

- *Avagadha* and *pravritta* are to be considered as a pair because the only difference between them is on account of emphasis either on ascent or descent. Dattila holds that *avagadha* stresses ascent and *pravritta* the descent. Bharata, however, holds the contrary view. In his opinion *avagadha* is completed on the *ansha* note and *pravritta* on the *nyasa* note. Dattila goes on to lay down some more features of the related phrases.

- If a phrase could be assumed to have at least two major sections, i.e., the *vidari*, then their interrelationship is what determines the nature of *vividha*.

Vividha, the third type, therefore consists of specific kinds of internal distribution of musical notes, and hence it has three sub-types in *samudga*, *ardhasamudga* and *vivrudha*.

- These relationships can be of three varieties: *sama*, *madhya* and *vishama*. For example, according to Dattila, if both *vidari*-s are similar in all three respects, i.e. *pada, varna* and *swara*, the relationship is known as *sama*, if the similarity is partial (i.e. *varna* or *pada* or *swara* are similar, or a part of one *vidari* is similar to a part of the other *vidari*) it is known as *ardhasamudga*. If the two *vidari* are completely different, the relationship is known as *vivritta* or *vivrudha*. Vemabhupala, a later theoretician, suggests that while deciding on the *vividha* relationship, it is advisable to take into consideration the component of *pata*, i.e. sound-syllables produced by instruments.

- During the period of *Ratnakara*, the term could be said to have become more definite in meaning as well as wider in application. In it, while discussing the *prabandha*, *anga* is identified as the indivisible and *dhatu* as the divisible component. It helps to note that, *geetanga* and *talanga* are stated to be the indivisible components of *geeta* and *tala* respectively.

- The question arises: what is the position today? Today the term *anga* does not have rigidly structural meanings as it had in the past. The first half of the octave-range (i.e. from the *shadja* to *pancham*) is known as *poorvanga* and the second half (consisting of notes including and between *pancham* to *tara shadja*) is known as *uttaranga*. The term is also used while describing characteristics of *tala*. Both these modern applications certainly suggest relationship with the ancient *varnanga* and *talanga*. However, one senses that their meaning as well as semantic fields have undergone considerable changes.

- The octave space is divided into two main sections consisting respectively of *sa re ga ma* and *pa dha ni sa* (upper). The former is called *poorvanga* and the latter *uttaranga*. Both have equal number of notes and both string together four notes each in sequence. The two *anga* are similar in construction and in number of their respective constituents. In Indian *raga*-music, in order to determine the *vadi* note this equality of the two *anga*-s plays an important role. Hence, we have pairs of *vadi-samvadi*, e.g. pairs of *sa-pa, re-dha, ga-ni* and *ma-sa* (upper). The *shadja-pancham* relationship (*bhava*) is employed to determine components of these pairs. It may appear that the pair *sa-ma* is an exception but it is argued that this pair is merely the reverse of the *sa* (upper)-*pa* pair and hence does not constitute an exception to the general rule. It would be obvious that to finalise member-notes of the pair one note is taken from each of the two *anga*-s. Thus perfect consonances (that is arrangements realised through a note and its fifth) of *sa-pa, re-dha, ga-ni* and *pa-sa* form the pairs and the role of *anga* is quite evident.

The *anga* concept also generates a sub-characteristic of *raga*. The *anga* in which *vadi* of a *raga* is located is regarded important. *Anga-pradhanya* (importance of the *anga*) therefore becomes a guiding principle in performance. It also serves as a distinguished mark in musicological descriptions.

2.11 *Aas* (H S *as* = to abide, to remain, continue to be in any state)

The term refers to persistence of sound after the cessation of the original stimulus, which creates it. The term is often used to denote a continuous or uninterrupted action. Alternatively the term *aas* is also derived from *ansha* = part.

2.12 *Antarmarga* (S *antar* = internal + *marga* = path)

A very useful term, which unfortunately is not in general circulation today! It refers to characteristic movement of notes *within* a particular *raga* indicating thereby their abundant or limited use. For example, a note may be used but not repeatedly, or it may be slurred or stepped over. These two distinctive ways of using notes are respectively known as *anabhyasa* and *langhana*. However, *vadi* (>), a note being repeatedly used by definition, is kept out of the purview of these terms.

Thus *antarmarga* are expressed through *alpatva* (scarce, infrequent use) and *bahutva* (abundant, frequent use). The former is realised through *anabhyasa* (a single time, non-repetitive use) and *langhana* (stepping over, cross over). For the latter (that is, *bahutva*), *abhyasa* (repetition) is the royal road.

2.13 *At/i* (H *at* = obstacle, objection; S *atani* = that end of the bow which has a niche to tie the bow string)

Additionally, '*at*' also means an obstacle, objection etc. It is not a coincidence that in the evolution of chordophones, reference to a bow can be made naturally in the context of this term. A tightened string of a bow works as a single stringed chordophone.

The strip located before the first fret of *sitar*, etc., is to provide a supporting niche to the string passing over to the peg. This is known as *at*. A string proceeds to the peg after resting on the *ati*.

2.14 *Avanaddha* (adj. S *avanaddha* = covered; a common term for membrane-covered instruments of rhythm broadly described as drums)

Sometimes *'Bhand'*, *'Bhand vadya'* are used as variants.

Instruments are classified into four classes, namely *Tata, Ghana, Sushira* and *Avanaddha*. The last is described as an instrument, the mouth of which is covered with a membrane of hide/skin. This class of instrument is specifically mentioned for its capacity to add *'ranjakata'* (i.e. colour) — meaning recreational value to sung expression.

In the ancient tradition *avanaddha* has 23 varieties as mentioned below:

(1) *pataha*, (2) *mardal*, (3) *hudukka*, (4) *karata*, (5) *ghat*, (6) *ghadas*, (7) *dhavas*, (8) *dhakka*, (9) *kudukka*, (10) *kuduva*, (11) *runja*, (12) *damaru*, (13) *dakka*, (14) *mandi-dakka*, (15) *dakkuli*, (16) *selluka*, (17) *jhallari*, (18) *bhana*, (19) *trivali*, (20) *dundubhi*, (21) *bheri*, (22) *nissan*, (23) *tumbaki*.

As if to emphasize importance of these instruments, the palm and fingers of hands which play them is allocated certain deities. For example, thumb = Brahmadeva, forefinger = Shankar, middle finger = Vishnu, ring-finger = all deities, little finger = sages and seers, palm = sun, outer surface of the palm = moon, right hand = Indra, left hand = Varun.

According to Bharata, from among *avanadhha* instruments, *mridang* and *dardura*, are the chief, and *jhallari* and *pataha* are secondary. That all *avanaddha* instruments are not equally important is also suggested in other ways. For example, it is stated that from *avanaddha* instruments *pushkar* is the most mature. It is stated that Lord Maheshwar used the following *avanaddha* instruments for his famous *Tandava* dance: *mridang, bheri, pataha, bhand, dindima, gomukha, panav* and *dardura*. Bharata has specially mentioned the *tripushkara* drum while discussing the *marjana* procedure. The three *ang*-s of the *tripushkara* are mentioned as *vamaka, savyaka* and *urdhvaka*.

It was laid down that *avanaddha* instruments are to be employed in dance in accordance with the playing-styles adopted. These styles are mentioned as: *sama, rakta, vibhakta, sphuta* and *shuddha*.

Some details in the ancient tradition about playing *avanaddha* are worth-noting: *Natyashastra* states that *pushkara* can produce what is producible through voice, that it can precisely follow *laghu-guru, yatibheda* in the words of *Geeta*. The exposition of *avanaddha* class holds up *mridanga* as a model. The discussion of playing of *avanaddha* includes as many as 15 themes/topics. Even if everything stated is not clear today, it becomes certain that *avanaddha* instruments were seriously regarded.

According to the usage in Pali literature, *avanaddha* instruments were described, rather confusingly, as *vitata*. Another minority tradition subscribed to the view that rubbed *avanaddha* instruments with strings (to which the term *vitata* has a direct reference) are better described as *tatanaddha*.

Anaddha is obviously an alternative term.

A large number of *avanaddha* instruments operate today in various musical categories and different performing contexts. A number of individual instruments necessitate separate descriptions for fuller appreciation of their distinctive identities and special contributions. However, some important structural features commonly found in *avanaddha* instruments are noted below:

Mukh: (S *mukha* = mouth) face of a drum covered by membrane

Khod/ar: (H *kotar* = hollowed trunk of a tree from which body of an *avanaddha* instrument is made)

Bhanda: (H S *bhand* = body of an *avanaddha* instrument made of metal)

Patal: (S, *Pudi*: (H) membrane)

Gajra: (H *ganj* = group) a plait of leather or thin rope holding the membrane evenly stretched over the face

Rassi/*dori*: (H) small rope of leather or cloth used to stretch the membrane. Leather strips that perform a similar function are called *baddi*.

Ghera/*kada*: (H) a metal ring around which a leather plait is woven

Gatta: (H) wooden blocks inserted under the *rassi* to tighten the latter and thereby increase tension on the membrane — in the process increasing its pitch

Ghar: (H S *griha* = house) section of a *gajra* formed by a *rassi* passing through it. Stroking the sections upwards reduces tension on *pudi* and decreases pitch. A downward stroke has an opposite effect.

Masala/*siyahi*: (H P *syaha* = blackness) a thin circular coating of iron filings, carbon, boiled rice, etc., applied on membranes to improve their timbre

Chhalla: (H S *challi* = creeper) small brass rings passed through *rassi* to tighten or loosen *rassi* and hence membrane, in order to heighten or lower pitch

Gittak: (H) small piece of metal, wood, etc.

Kinar: (P *kinarah*) edge of a strip, membrane, etc.

Ghundi: (H S *guntha*) button-shaped knot of cloth, rope, etc.

Shanku: (S) a cone-shaped solid body

Indavi: a ring of cloth to keep/rest an instrument

Lav: minuscule hair, wool in animal skins, etc., used to tan/prepare membranes

Dhancha: skeleton

Dandi/danda: bar

Penda/pendi: base

Chano: key screw

Ghat/ghada: clay-pot

Lakadi: wooden stick

Poolika: circular coating of paste

Jhanj: metal disk

Jhilli: a thin coating, covering

Udarpattika: strap going over player's stomach to hold an instrument

Skandh pattika: strap going over player's shoulder to hold an instrument

Chaddar: metal sheet

Khapacchi: a thin strip of bamboo, wood, etc.

2.15   *Avartana* (S. turning round, revolution)

It means a complete cycle of a prosodic or rhythmic pattern. The concept is of special importance because the phenomenon of *tala* depends on circularity of temporal progression. The term is also applied rather loosely to indicate repetitions (*avritti*). *Avarta* is synonym.

2.16   *Badhat* (H *badhana* = to increase S *vardhana* = increase)

It generally means 'to move from slow to fast tempo'.

More specifically it means elaboration of *raga* according to established norms by stressing qualities of gradualness and attention to detail. A concern to project a larger musical pattern is also evident. The concept simultaneously suggests expansion as well as exploration of subtle ideas *raga* may consist of.

2.17   *Barabar* (adj. H P *var* = equal)

It is a term mainly used in connection with tempo and rhythm. In its tempo-related connotation the term suggests a relationship of correspondence between units of song, etc., and units of accompanying rhythmic framework.

2.18   *Bahutva* (S abundance, plenty)

In particular *raga,* or even in non-*raga* manifestation some specific notes are used oftener than some others. The term *bahutva* indicates significance of notes in abundant use. The antonym is *alpatva.* (see *Antarmarga*)

2.19   *Baj* (H *baja* S *vadya* = mode of playing)

1. *Style.* The term is used in connection with certain forms e.g. *dhrupad*, *khayal* or with instruments (e.g. *mridang*).
2. It also denotes one particular 'string' in musical instruments, namely the string chiefly employed to 'make' music. For example, the first string in *sitar,* etc., is mainly used for producing prominent notes or effects in musical elaboration and this string is therefore described as *baj ki taar.*

2.20   *Bant* (v. H *bantna* = to distribute)

Distribution: It is an important procedure adopted in musical elaboration. According to it components of a musical composition are redistributed through variation of their rhythmic, tonal and timbre-contexts to introduce element of novelty.

2.21 *Bemancha*

It is a term in *pakhawaj / tabla*-music. In case a performer foresees overshooting of *sam* (while completing a *paran*-composition, etc.) he is allowed to improvise and add a *tihai*, etc., to the composition to reach the next *sam*. The procedure is called *bemancha*. Etymology of the term is unknown.

2.22 *Chalan* (H S *chal* = to move)

It is a characteristic manner or movement of organising tonal/rhythmic material in musical manifestations of all kinds. A very inclusive term, *chalan* may also allude to grammatical peculiarities of rhythmic/tonal groupings as also to changes introduced in them due to stylistic considerations.

2.23 *Chal* (H S *char* = gait movement)

It means style in a narrower sense. Today it also means a 'tune'. Till recently, in context of older poetic compositions, the term indicated a change in metre, and along with it change of tune.

Tarz is clearly, and *chalan* is broadly, synonymous.

2.24 *Chapak* (v. H *chipakana* = to glue, to move closer)

It is a special way of producing sounds by striking left-hand fingers on the edges of the bass (left-hand) drum in *pakhawaj* and *tabla*-music. While the technique is known as *chapak*, compositions in need of employing it are known as *chapak ke bol*.

2.25   *Chhanda* (H S= to please)

Even though the term primarily connotes a characteristic feature of poetry, it has contributed to evolution of the concept of *tala* in a major way. Through this concept others such as *matra* and *laya* have secured a place in music.

A unique feature of the Indian *chhanda* is their invariable association with definite tunes. The tunes, being tonal moulds, raise the performance of *chhanda* much above a simple *pathan* (recitation). Instead of remaining a prosodic mould *chhanda* also thus becomes a tonal mould, a basic framework of musical notes. Prevalence of Sanskrit and Prakrit *chhanda* has certainly contributed to the high musical literacy Indians generally enjoy.

2.26   *Chayalaga (S = ?)*

The term indicates an important class of *raga*. *Raga*, which is manifest only along with a shadow of another *raga*, is described as *chayalaga*.

2.27   *Chhoot* (S *syoot* = sewn, stitched)

This is an important melodic embellishment, which involves intonation of a note, or a cluster of them, in successive octaves without touching the intervening notes. (For example, *sa* followed by *Sa* in the higher octave). Sometimes the term is loosely applied even when any two or more notes are intoned with some intervening notes omitted (for example, *sa ga*).

2.28 *Darja* (H A *darj* = prestige, designation)

This is a term employed to indicate subtler distinctions between notes in the melodic aspect of music as well as in aspects of production of syllables in rhythm-music. For example, terms *chadha ma* (heightened *ma* note) or *druta madhyalaya* (fast-medium tempo) respectively point to subtle distinctions in melodic and rhythmic aspects. The concept of *darja* is used to bring this out. It is clear that like many other facets of performance, *darja* is demonstrable, perhaps describable rather than explainable! The use of the term as well as concept is therefore more or less confined to the performing tradition.

2.29 *Deshi* (adj. S regional)

The term can roughly be translated as 'regional'. Musicologically, *deshi* as contrasted with *margi* way of making music has been described "as less governed (or at least more flexibly governed) by rules pertaining to *raga* and *tala*, comparatively recent in origin, preferred by common people and changing according to the region of its origin."

The Deshi in music:

Matanga, who probably hailed from southern parts of India wrote *Brihaddeshi* (The Great Treatise on the Regional) — a work important for many important reasons. To begin with, it is the first to describe music in the post-Bharata period, the state of music before the advent of Islam and Islam-influenced music in the country. Secondly, it is the first major and available text to describe *raga*, which has been the key-concept in Indian art music for centuries.

Thirdly, it introduced *sargam*, i.e. notation in note-names, *sol-fa*.

One of Matanga's major contributions is his scholarly assertion about the independence/musical autonomy of the Regional element in music — as the title of the book suggests. *Deshi* is a term to be understood in contrast to the *Margi* music, which was regarded sacred and was pan-Indian in scope. Over the centuries music in India had became more diverse and moved away from early *Sama-Vedic* tradition, which was, perhaps more uniform. Matanga took a positive stand about the variety in music as it became apparent in the country between 600-800 AD.

It is significant to note that the term *dhvani*, i.e. sound, is used while posing the basic question," What is *Deshi* (regional)?" To which Matanga does not answer in geographical terms but in terms of basic features of the said music. He says "*Deshi* music is that which is sung voluntarily and with delight/pleasure by women, children, cowherds and kings, etc., in their respective regions." Obviously the focus is on secular music as also on music, which is produced by persons directly and normally involved in the mundane affairs of the world in various regions of India. While explaining the *jatiraga*-s Matanga refers to the ground rule that no *Margi raga* can have less than four notes. But with his declared intention to recognise the *Deshi* element in music it is not surprising that he draws attention to the fact that music of the Shabar, Pulinda and other clans consists of less than four notes. With a remarkable consistency of approach Matanga employs the word *Deshikar* in the title of the chapter on *Prabandha*-s — compositional types.

He classifies *nada*, i.e. sound, into five categories namely subtle (residing in secret places), very subtle (in the heart), expressed (in the throat), indistinctly expressed (in the cerebrum) and artificial (i.e. created in the mouth) — certainly a new way of looking at the basic material of music. In his discussion of scales and microtonal intervals he takes a position, which largely clarifies what Bharata had said in the *Natyashastra*.

One may use the term today to describe folk music in India.

2.30   *Dhakit* and *dhumkit baj*

The two terms, taken together, aptly and fundamentally describe the overall style of *pakhawaj*-music. Firstly, they indicate preponderance of specific sound-syllables, namely, *dhakit* and *dhumkit*. Secondly, they serve as pointers to patterning of produced sounds based on three or four units respectively as well as sonorous timbre created by these specific clusters. The former is also described as *kattak baj* following a similar logic of relying on criteria of duration, pattern and sonority to describe the style (*baj*) of playing.

2.31   *Dhruvaka* (S *dhru* = invariable, stable)

The term indicates line/s or stanzas of compositions that recur at the conclusion.

Palavapada is a synonym.

2.32   *Druta* (adv. S fast)

Indian music and musicology do not subscribe to the principle of absolute time. Hence *druta* is defined as a state of time-management or organisation, that is in a tempo which is double the medium, which, in turn, is identified as double the slow (*vilambita*) tempo.

2.33   *Gamaka* (H S *gam* = to go, one who is going/moving)

This is a term with a wide-ranging connotation. In effect it points to an important group of melodic embellishments in vocal and/or instrumental music. The core meaning of *gamaka* is intonation in which a contextual use of musical notes is brought out. In such applications a note of primary application is accompanied by a touch of preceding and/or succeeding note/s — thus enlarging its tonal context. Traditionally and appropriately, *gamaka* is described as 'a vibrating effect employed in producing tone to the delight of listeners'.

The medieval *Ratnakara* tradition refers to fifteen varieties of *gamaka*, the later *Sangit Parijat* to twenty, and some later performing traditions claim twenty-two types of *gamaka*! Unfortunately the typology is not clearly explained.

Gamaka can be further classified according to its required duration, covered range of notes it covers and finally according to the special effect it may produce. One may also distinguish between vocal and instrumental *gamaka*.

Some interesting and identifiable *gamaka*-s are:

- *Tirip*: four notes in a short beat, producing in the process an effect of *damaru* (a folk membranophone).
- *Tribhinna*: use of notes in a vibratory manner in three successive octaves.
- *Ahata*: use of an accent on the next, i.e. the higher note.
- *Humphit*: use of the *'hum'*-sound.
- *Mudrita*: use of a closed mouth while singing.

It is interesting to note that the word *gamaka* in Hindi also means fragrance! As an embellishment *gamaka* surely adds to the beauty of music.

2.34 *Gana* (S singing)

This is a very basic and generic term. *Gana* refers to that linguistic/syllabic composition which provides base for elaborating *swara* or *raga*.

The two main divisions of *gana* are respectively known as *nibaddha* (bound, tied, fettered, stopped, closed, formed of) and its opposite *anibaddha*. *Nibaddha gana* consists of five compositional sections (*dhatu*); and it is set in *tala*. The five *dhatu*-s are:

1. *Udgraha* = initial section
2. *Melapaka* = section intervening between the first and the third
3. *Dhruva* = section regarded mandatory
4. *Abhoga* = section which completes the piece
5. *Antara* = section optionally placed between third and fourth sections

2.35 *Ghana* (S compact, hard)

Perhaps the most thickly populated of the instrumental categories, *ghana* is described traditionally as 'that made of bronze'. Thereby solidity is suggested as the chief characteristic. Modern organology identifies this instrumental category with the term idiophonic.

This variety of instruments had a very significant role to play during the medieval period. Some major instruments current during that period were:

Tala, Kansyatala, Ghanta, Kshudraghanta, Jayghanta, Kamra, Shuktipatta, Tal, Manjira, and *Chimta.*

However, today circulation of these and such instruments has been mainly restricted to folk music. Some important structural features of these instruments are:

- *Dand/danda*: a bar to hold and lift the heavier of the *ghana* instruments
- *Dolak/lolak*: a clapper inside bells etc.
- *Ankada*: a hook to hold the clapper
- *Hathoudi*: hammer
- *Nabhi*: navel, centre
- *Chhalla*: a small metal ring
- *Chaukhat*: frame
- *Tukada*: piece of wood
- *Patti*: strip of wood
- *Ghundi*: a button-shaped knot of cloth, rope, etc.
- *Gol* (ref. *ghungroo*): sphere-shaped metal body
- *Goli* (ref. *ghungroo*): pebble-like small objects
- *Dori*: rope.

2.36   *Gharana* (H *Ghar* S *griha* = family, dynasty)

Performing arts have been carried on as family traditions in a majority of cases. This has been so at least till the very recent past. The term *gharana* may therefore be more appropriate in performing arts than in other arts. As has been often pointed out, disciplines dependent on book-learning do not seem to have used the concept. Further, today the term has come to connote comprehensive musico-aesthetic ideology changing from *gharana* to *gharana*.

At one point of time *gharana* were understood to be indications of the place of origin of hereditary performing musicians. Hence the use of place names was regarded inevitable while describing *gharana*. For example following are names of some major *gharana*-s in *khayal*:

Agra, Gwaliyar, Patiala, Kirana, Indore, Mewat, Sahaswan, Bhendibazar, Jaipur, and *Bishnupur,* etc.

Of course hereditary musicianship is hardly confined to vocalists, and hence *gharana* names also occur in instrumental contexts. For example in *tabla*-music we have Delhi, Ajrada, Farrukhabad, Punjab, Benaras, etc. It is interesting to note that *gharana* in *pakhawaj,* an instrument established earlier than *tabla,* are person-oriented, viz. Kudausingh, Panse, etc.

Dhrupad-singing is done in many *gharana*-s but their names have been chiefly described as *bani* and descriptions have been mainly in terms of musical and stylistic characteristics (see *dhrupad*).

Another important point has been the prominence of this concept during the nineteenth century. It has been plausibly argued that it was during this period that hereditary musicians were compelled to move to urban centres as after the advent of British rule they were deprived of the munificent royal patronage. In cities they stuck to place-names of *gharana* in an attempt to preserve their respective musical and regional identities.

However, since then, during the modern period *gharana*-s are being interpreted on the basis of their explicit or implicit musical ideologies. In the process, regional or familial explanations are naturally replaced. During the modern age persons with no musical background in the usual sense began taking to music, seriously and studiously. As a consequence, today music-related affiliations are formed on ideological and not familial or regional basis. This is also true in respect of *gharana* in other musical forms that have, comparatively speaking recent history. For example, one may think of genres such as *thumri* (>). The more mature a genre or an instrument etc. is, the more the possibility of emergence of *gharana*. This is the reason why there is a strong, logical and justifiable possibility today to have *gharana* in *sitar* or *ghazal*, etc.

Even today *gharana*-s, are discussed, proclaimed and justified with much passion, heat and pride! However, it is clear that new musical alignments are taking place. In face of the media-explosion leading to easy and general accessibility to all kinds of music, the validity and utility of *gharana* as an institution is being repeatedly and widely questioned. It is up to musicians to reinforce aesthetic basis of the *gharana* if the concept is expected to continue contributing meaningfully to musical life and thought.

2.37 *Ghasit* (H *ghasitna* S *ghrisht* = rubbed, dragged)

It is a melodic embellishment prominently used in music produced by string instruments. The term connotes a playing technique in which note is produced through rubbing a string. *Ratnakara* calls the procedure as *khasit* and adds that it consists of a vibrating sound production in a descending movement of notes.

2.38 *Graha* (H S *graha* = to receive)

The core meaning is 'to take or grapple or join with'.

In the early tradition the term *graha swara* indicated note with which it was mandatory to introduce/commence *raga*. Later, when music became more *anibaddha*, i.e. free or improvised, rules regarding *graha swara* were observed with less rigidity.

Today the term indicates ways in which song/singing, etc., and rhythm come together. Thus:

- *Sama* (equal) *graha*: Both commencing on the same beat.
- *Anagata* (not arrived) *graha*: Rhythm commencing before the singing, etc.
- *Atita* (beyond) *graha*: Rhythm commencing after the singing, etc.

2.39 *Guna* (H S quality, merit)

An acoustic term indicating quality of sound as contrasted with the other two dimensions of sound, namely pitch and intensity.

Traditionally *guna* also means merit of artistes, instruments, etc. For example *Naradiya Shiksha* (c. 500 AD), the earliest musicological text, refers to *dashaguna* (ten merits) of a singer.

2.40 *Guru (S.* = Guide, preceptor or teacher, when used as a noun)

In oral tradition of music in India *guru* has a special place. In fact *guru-shishya-parampara* is still held up as the distinctive feature of Indian music as a whole. Hence it may not be out of place to deal with it in some detail.

Guru-Shishya Parampara:

Guru, as a socio-cultural institution, has a long history. Some of its features may appear novel even to the contemporary performing community.

For example, in the *tantra* tradition, women could become *guru*-s and receive worship, etc., from disciples. However, it is to be noted that Kalhana, in his *Rajtarangini*, satirically refers to the practice of women *guru*-s receiving worship.

Gurukula is a word, which is in vogue from the period of the *Vedic sutra-grantha*-s. The *Gurukula* system was established from this period. The *guru*-concept does not seem to have developed during the *mantra*-period, which preceded the *sutra*-period. The *mantra*-s were composed on inspiration or in imitation of the inspired *mantra*. In other words, till then no special class had evolved to systematically teach them. When the *mantra*-s were systematised into *samhita*, a need arose for specialists devoted to the task of learning, teaching, transmitting and preserving *mantra*-s. The main reason was that the sacrifice-based religion (*yadnya-pradhan-dharma*) was becoming increasingly complex. It also underscored the need of a class of experts in various departments (e.g. *hota, adhvaryu, samagayan*) related to the sacrificial religious practices. It is from the *samhita*-period that we have names of *Acharya* — such as Angiras, Garga, Atri, Brihaspati and Vasishtha.

It is instructive to note that all along there were also people who did not believe in ritualistic religion and *aranyaka-literature* emerged to concentrate on *adhyatma-vidya* with importance accorded to analysis of fundamental questions about reality, nature of god, contemplation etc. However, even these thought-systems needed to be taught, learnt, transmitted and preserved and *guru-shishya* tradition worked towards it. During the period prior to the Buddha, 82 such traditions have been listed! As the issues were fundamental, numerous approaches were evolved and thus each *darshana,* i.e. philosophic school, had its own *guru-shishya* tradition. *Guru-*s became necessary and inevitable.

During the medieval period, and after the advent of the Islam, India notably recorded a marked proliferation of esoteric religious cults, including the *tantra.* Most of them were meant for the initiated few and were therefore described as *guhyadarshana.* Expectably, the institution of *Guru* attained its highest prestige as well as inevitability. For example, in the *natha-*cult, it is the *guru-vansha* and not *pitru-vansha* with which one is identified!

Panini refers to four kinds of *guru-*s: *Acharya, Pravakta, Shrotriya* and *Adhyapak. Acharya* was the one who taught *Veda* to disciples who had had their sacred thread ceremony. *Pravakta* taught *brahmana-*s, *shrauta-sutra-*s and *vedanga-*s. *Shrotriya* gave *santha* (training along with rituals etc) of the *Veda. Adhyapak* taught secular and scientific literature.

Namachintamani lists 12 types of *guru* — and the nomenclature is colourful or ecological as one may choose to describe it! :

1. *Dhatuvadi-guru* = Makes the disciple undertake pilgrimage and follow other helpful procedures before giving the final *upadesha.*
2. *Chandan-guru* = As the sandal wood spreads fragrance, even among the ordinary people, similarly this *guru* helps common people by just being near.
3. *Vichar-guru* = Teaches the disciple to think and attain realisation by *Pipilika marga.*
4. *Anugraha-guru* = Imparts knowledge to the disciple by *anugraha,* i.e. Grace.

5. *Paris-guru* = The stone which when touched, turns the touched into gold. Similarly, by mere touch, this *guru* imparts divine knowledge to the disciple.

6. *Kashyapa-guru* = The tortoise-mother nurtures her offspring by merely looking at them. Similarly this *guru* imparts knowledge.

7. *Chandra-guru* = There is a stone which oozes when moonlight falls on it. This *guru*, named after this stone, helps by the stream of compassion in his heart for the disciple.

8. *Darpan-guru* = As the mirror shows yourself to you, this *guru* shows your real self to you.

9. *Chhayanidhi guru* = A big bird called *Chhayanidhi* soars high in the sky. The person, on whom the bird's shadow falls, becomes a king. A *guru* whose shadow makes the disciple king of his own self / or a king of the kingdom of the inner joy is named after the bird.

10. *Nadanidhi guru* = *Nadanidhi* is a bead which immediately turns any metal it touches into gold. A *guru* turning a person into a self-realised soul the moment he prays for it.

11. *Kraunch guru* = The fabled bird only thinks of her offspring while flying in the far away regions to nurture them. Similarly, the *guru* takes disciples to the blessed state merely by remembering them.

12. *Suryakant guru* = The bead fires up on being touched by sunlight. Similarly, the said *guru* fires up disciples with the blessed state.

Another *tantra*-text, *Kulagama* refers to six types:

1. *Preraka* = one who creates an initiative about initiation in disciples' mind.

2. *Suchaka* = one who describes both initiation and practice.
3. *Vachaka* = one who describes various devices to attain the goal.
4. *Darshaka* = one who explains how to discriminate between proper and improper *sadhana* and *deeksha*.
5. *Bodhaka* = explains philosophical differences between *sadhana* and *deeksha*.
6. *Shikshaka* = initiates and teaches sadhana.

Guru is regarded the metaphysical father of a disciple and is ranked higher than biological parents. Even the Buddhist monks were recommended to stay with the *guru* for ten years, though Buddha admitted of no other *guru* for himself! Some have opined that scarcity of the writing material and skill etc. — along with the preponderance of oral tradition — probably contributed to *guru*-s growing importance. It is important to note that most of the *guru*-s were from *grihasthasharma*, very few were from *vanaprastha* and still fewer were *sanyasin*-s.

It appears that institutions making monthly payment to *guru*-s did not come in existence till about 8th–9th century. From the 11th century onwards, we have records to show that a *guru* teaching grammar, Mimamsa, etc., was paid a fixed quantity of rice per year and that the one teaching *vedanta* got more rice than him. Kulkarni, a village administrative officer received less than *guru*-s. There were cases when *guru*-s entered into a prior contract with disciple for imparting training on a pre-determined *gurudakshina*. Such *guru*-s were not regarded highly, and were aptly described as *bhritakadhyapaka* (servant-*guru*-s!)

Kalidasa succinctly expresses the consensus in this matter when he says in his play *Malavikagnimitra*:

"One who sells his learning for earning his livelihood is called a trader who sells his knowledge."

The general feeling was that *guru* should teach a poor but deserving student free and the student should try to get free from *guru*'s debt through offering *gurudakshina*.

Guru-s were expected to teach everything they knew to a disciple and hold back nothing out of fear that they will be outclassed by the taught. As the well known aphorism puts it, "One should wish for defeat from one's disciple!" If a *shishya* died while doing chores for the *guru*, the latter had to undergo severe *prayaschitta*. Opinions differ on the propriety of *guru*'s resorting to corporeal punishment to the disciple.

Gurukula:

Gurukula literally means *guru*'s dynasty or family. However, the term came to mean an institution of teaching. A student would be admitted to it after the sacred thread ceremony. The student would stay with the *guru* for a period of 12 years to learn the *Veda*-s. He would be permitted to enter the *grihasthashrama* on completing training. The institution was accessible only to the three upper classes (as is known Eklavya, a *nishad*, and Karna, a charioteer's son were denied benefits of the *gurukula*!). However, there was apparently no discrimination between poor and rich.

Similar to the *gurukula*-s, there were also *vidyashrama*-s of different sages. The *gurukula*-s were well supported by kings who considered it their duty to make *gurukula*-s financially viable. Many kings established *agrahara*-s to ensure continued financial support to the *gurukula*-s. The *guru*-s and *shishya*-s lived together in the *agrahara*-s. I must state in anticipation that the *gurukula* was the direct precedent

of the reputed concept of *Gharana* in Hindustani music —
with of course the religious foundation nearly replaced for
scholastic, performing as well as cultural reasons.

Gurudakshina:

It is understood to be an offering made by disciple to
guru after completing training — this nearly being the final act before entering the *grihasthashrama*. It is to be noted
that *guru*-s, who head different religious cults, also receive
gurudakshina-s from time to time, for example, on various
sacred occasions including birth, initiation, marriage, or
death in the family of followers. It appears that *guru* could
ask for anything he desired as *gurudakshina* and the *shishya*
was expected to achieve the feat! (Koutsa was to give 14
crore gold coins to his *guru* Vartantu or, Uttanaka was
asked to procure queen's (king Poshya's wife) ear-rings
for the *guru-patni,* and Sandipani asked Krishna to bring
back Sandipani's son — who was drowned in the sea!)

Gurupournima:

It is celebrated on the full moon day of the month of
Ashadh and sage Vyasa is worshipped. As per the belief,
Sankaracharya was a reincarnation of Vyasa and hence
the monk-community also worships Sankaracharya. Finally, all disciples worship their respective *guru*-s, i.e. those
who have initiated them as also parents on this day. In
the overall tradition of *guru*-s, Vyasa is regarded supreme
and he is venerated as the source of all knowledge.

Gurumantra:

It is originally the *mantra* associated with Brihaspati.
It is to be properly 'made' (i.e. *siddhi*) before it can be used

to fulfill wishes (*ishatasiddhi*). By analogy the term is used to refer to any effective advice given by the elder or teacher, etc., to the disciple.

Shishya:

He is *guru*-s partner in the educational adventure, and was of two types. One, who paid fees to the *guru* was known as *acharya-bhaga*; the other, who learnt by doing domestic chores in *guru's* house, etc. was described as *dharma-shishya*.

Manu records instructions on how a disciple should behave in *guru's* presence, as also in the latter's house. For example, he mentions that a disciple should eat and wear dress in a manner inferior to his *guru's*. He should go to bed after the *guru* has done so, and should wake up earlier than the *guru*. He should be obedient and should not sit on a level higher than the *guru's* seat. He should not imitate guru's walk or talk, etc. He should not listen to criticism of his *guru*. If it falls on his ears, he should shut his ears and go away from the place.

Post-training contacts with the *guru* were encouraged and sometimes the disciple married the *guru's* daughter — even though the custom had obvious incestuous overtones.

Chhatra:

Chhatra is generally understood as one who lives with the *guru*, i.e. under his 'umbrella', i.e. protection and this is not far off the mark. However, a traditional definition throws up a surprise as it says:

"A *chhatra* is one who covers, conceals defects of a guru." *Chatra*-s have been (of course!) classified.

Dandmanav:

According to *Patanjali* he is the one whose training in *Veda*-s has not yet commenced. According to *Tatvabodhini,* he is the one whose sacred thread ceremony has not yet taken place. *Matang-jatak* has an interesting variation to offer: the term refers to those children who play in the *ashram* with a stick treating it as a horse! Obviously they are very young.

Sabrahmachari = One who stays with one's *guru.*

Antevasi = One who after the sacred thread ceremony devotes himself to the *guru* with mind, deed and speech.

Piturantevasi = Learning from his father.

Chhatra-s were often identified on other basis such as *kaksha* (grade), *guru, grantha* (the studied texts), *vedakrama* (according to the mode of studying *Veda*-s) and *ritu* (season in which he attends). For example:

Grantha = *agnishtomik, vajapeyik*

Ritu = *varshik* (i.e. monsoon), *sharadik, haimantik, masik, sanvatsarik* and *ardhamasik*

Vedakrama = *pathak, kramak*

Acharya is defined variously. For example, see the following definitions:

* One who explains *mantra*-s.
* From whom the *shishya* learns the dharma.
* One who teaches behaviour, collects *shulka-dhan* or enriches the intellect of the *shishya*-s. — Nirukta.

According to *Manusmriti:*

* One who performs a sacred thread ceremony of a Brahmin *shishya* and teaches him *Veda* and *Upanishad* is known as *acharya.*

- The second, more technical meaning of the term *guru* refers to unit of long duration in prosody and music (when used as an adjective).

2.41   *Jabadi* (H. *jabda* = *jaw*)

The term is used to describe one specific variety of *tana*. A straightforward explanation connects the term to a notable use of jaw in executing *tana*. However, the term is also connected rather fancifully with the Sanskrit word *jabal* meaning "yoke on a bull's neck".

2.42   Jamjama (U to employ notes)

Reportedly, this melodic musical embellishment uses pairs of notes in perceptibly fast tempo, repeatedly and successively (for example *sa re sa re, ga ma ga ma*).

2.43   *Jarab* (A stroke)

In melodic instrumental music the basic 'up'/'down' strokes of the plectrum, etc., are called *jarab*. These are then named after associated onomatopoeic sound-syllables (for example *da* and *ra* in sitar, etc.). In case of *avanaddha* instruments the up and down strokes are respectively known as '*pata*' and '*tali*' with '*bhari*' hovering around as a synonym to *jarab*.

2.44   *Jawab* (A answer)

The term has a larger, as also a narrower application. The former refers to any composition, part of it, or a melodic/rhythmic phrase alluding to, or suggestive of another part, within the same performance of music through positioning, structural similarity or characteristic use of units concerned.

In a narrower sense *jawab* suggests relationship between notes distanced by four/five intervals (for example, *sa – pa, sa – ma*).

2.45 *Jawari* (H. *sawari* = to ride over or go over?) (H S *jawa* = speed)

The term indicates a special effect of sound creating an unforgettable timbre. A lingering, rounded sound, a characteristic resonance added to the sound of the original plucked/strummed sound of strings through a special arrangement of strings passing and resting over the bridge and the intervening thread is called *Jawari*.

In string-instruments strings pass over a bridge made of wood, brass, ivory, ebony etc. For creating the effect described as *jawari*, a thread is inserted between string and the bridge as a part of permanent construction or as a part of the procedure readying the instrument for strumming the string or playing the instrument. It is interesting to note that actions undertaken for improving *jawari* are usually described with words such as 'opening, cleaning or taking out'.

It is reported that in *tabla too*, a thread is inserted between tensed membrane and leather strip pasted over it at the edge to create a similar effect. Some harmonium manufactures also refer to the term *jawari*. Voices are often described as voices with or without *jawari* (*zar* appears to be a synonymous term as far as voice is concerned).

It appears that from the specific usage in relation to string instruments the term and its connotation have spread over other modes of music making to describe similar and desirable sound effects.

Jiwa is a synonymous term.

2.46   *Jhatka* (H *jhatakna* S *jhatta* = sudden shake or pull)

It is a melodic embellishment consisting of a fast movement from one note to another and in which the embellishment ends by stressing the latter note.

2.47   *Jila* (A shine or *jil* = region)

A term indicating departure from a *raga* mentioned e.g. *jila* Kafi. It may also indicate that the concerned *raga* is a *raga* enjoying a rather loose structure and hence it is identified only by naming it along with a *raga* that is adjacent to it.

2.48   Jod (< S *jud* < H *jodna* = to pair, coupled)

Jod is a phase of *alap* in medium tempo (often in music of the string instruments and in *dhrupad* singing). It is so called perhaps because it is located between two main varieties of *alap,* namely, *nibaddha* and *anibaddha.* It almost provides a conceptual link between them.

Another connotation of the term clearly refers to the paired aspect. In instruments such as *tanpura* and *sitar* two brass strings are tuned in the main note 'sa' (*shadja*). These two as a pair are called *jod*-strings.

2.49   *Jod-nawaz* (< S *jud* < H *jod* = to join + *nawaz* P favour)

A term used to indicate a person proficient in *alap* and especially the *jod* phase of it in elaboration of *raga.*

2.50 *Kaku* = > A (S tonal changes introduced to signify musical content)

Broadly it is true to say that the term represents phenomenon known as "changes introduced in intonation to express the inner meaning". The term is often translated as modulation — but this is to be avoided as the latter indicates a technique or a device of changing the keynote one begins with for musical elaboration or composition.

The Indian performing tradition with firm roots in composite sensibility and expression has rightly treated the phenomenon in at least three contexts: behaviour in the mundane world, drama and finally music, i.e., singing. Bharata's exposition, Abhinavagupata's enlightening elucidations and musicological texts by Sharangadeva etc., together provide evidence of a thorough discussion of this phenomenon which is a bridge between music and speech-behaviour.

The etymology is: The change sound undergoes because of fear or pathos is *kaku*. Abhinava explains the term with reference to *pathya* and clarifies that it means *Swaravaichitrya*, i.e. variety/variation in intonation. He adds that because of this change, the meaning gets completed. In fact Abhinavagupta rightly points out that these kind of expressive tonal changes take place even in the world of animals. Sharangadeva, the authoritative musicologist, refers to the phenomenon in his listing of characteristics of singers as well as composers. Expectably the discussion leads to *Gamak* — a major type of musical embellishment that depends on variations in vocalisation. However, another near-contemporary of Sharangadeva, namely, Parshvadeva has musicologically elaborated the concept in his *Sangeetsamayasara* (c.1250 AD). Taking off from the core-thrust of the concept, namely introduction of subtle/marginal deviations to enhance the quality of the ultimate result he has classified *Kaku* in six types as shown below:

Name	What does it mean ?
Swarakaku	Addition/elimination of sruti of a note
Ragakaku	Addition /diminishing of the inherent impression of a *raga*
Anyaragakaku	Introduction of an impression of another *raga*
Deshkaku	Introduction of variations in a *raga* according to regional vogue/practice
Kshetrakaku	Characteristic changes/additions due to the individual singer's voice, etc.
Yantrakaku	Characteristic changes/additions due to the individual quality of an instru-ment

2.51   *Kampana* (H S *kamp* = to vibrate, tremble)

It is an important class of melodic embellishment in which a note is produced in such a manner that the entire range between the preceding and the succeeding notes is suggested.

2.52 *Kana* (S *kan* = v. to go small or as a noun = grain, particle)

It refers to a melodic embellishment in which a higher or lower note is attached to the main note with a very light touch. The attached note is called *kana swara*.

2.53 *Kanthadhvani* (H S *kantha* = throat + *dhvani* = sound)

It means 'the sound of voice'. Medieval musicological observations on merits and demerits of voice were rich and thorough. In fact the tradition took a step further than merely describing voice as used in music. It traced particular voice qualities to specific states of human organism in terms of three basic humours namely *kapha* (phlegm), *pitta* (bile) and *vata* (wind) as propounded in *Ayurveda*, the Indian science of longevity.

However, basic distinctions made in contemporary musicology in respect of *Kanthadhvani* are few. They are also loosely employed and vaguely understood. Three terms used with general agreement and in alignment with three acoustic parameters of pitch, volume and timbre need to be noted. They are: *uccha* (high pitched), *gambhira* (voluminous) and *madhura* (sweet). Usually accepted antonyms are *dhali* (bass), *patli* (thin) and *karkasha* (harsh). Three other terms employed to describe subtler voice-qualities are: *halki* (quick in movement), *bhari* (heavy in movement) and *jhardar / jawaridar* (resonant).

2.54 *Kharaj* (H S *shadja* = derived from six organs)

It indicates the bass octave. A special method of cultivating voice by practising singing in lower octave is known as *kharaj sadhana*.

2.55 *Khatka* (H *khatakna* = to create a sharp clashing sound)

A melodic embellishment in which a cluster of notes is quickly and forcefully produced prior to the note projected as the important note in the particular cluster of notes.

According to some, two synonymous terms are *gittakadi* and *murki*. A minority holds that *khatka* is *gamak* (>), which has only two component notes.

2.56 *Khula-band* (H *kholna* = to open + *bandh* = tie, close)

This paired term includes in it two terms generally applied to two general ways of singing/playing. These are respectively described as open (*khula*) and closed (*band*).

2.57 *Krama* (S sequence)

The term indicates the initial sequence of musical notes in an ascending order.

2.58 *Krintana* (S)

It is an important playing technique in string-music. In it forefinger of the left hand touches the fret lightly while middle finger stretches the string out.

2.59 *Laghu* (H S short)

It indicates an important unit of measuring musical time. When duration of time required for pronouncing a letter is equivalent to batting of an eyelid it is described as one *laghu*. It is also known as *ekamatrika*, that is, of one measure. However, the minimal time-unit prescribed for use in ancient (*margi*) music is five *laghu*. Significantly, *deshi* (regional) music is stated to deviate from this requirement.

2.60 *Lakshana* (H S a mark, token, characteristic)

It is a general term indicating identifiable qualities of diverse musical phenomena such as *raga, tala and gana*. Traditional statement of *lakshana* is unfailingly perceptive and very detailed.

In contemporary practice *lakshana* is used as a near-synonym of aptitude in context of music teaching-learning process. Veteran *guru*-s or performers use the term to assess and indicate disciples' or young/new performers' potential.

While *lakshana* refers to qualities realisable in future, *guna* indicates quality already possessed and expertise achieved. Some important terms related to *lakshana* are:

Lakshanakara = an authority on musicology.
Lakshana geet = (>)
Lakshana grantha = A work on musicology.
Lakshana-Lakshyagrantha = A work consisting of theory as well as compositions that are in actual practice or circulation.

2.61 *Lakshya* (H S *Laksha* = to perceive, to define)

Lakshya refers to a classical work, composition, etc., that belongs to performing tradition as opposed to the scholastic. It is, in other words, an effort of a representative character presenting authentic rendering of *raga, tala*, etc. It holds up as it were a model or standard for new efforts.

2.62 *Langhana* (H S *langh* = to jump over, to cross over)

It means an act of going 'over' a note without touching it, or only slightly touching it. The technique helps in defining the way in which specific note/s are emphasized as well as chief components involved in the process.

2.63   *Laya* (S *lay* = to move, to go)

Regulated motion is *laya*. Duration of rest between two strokes which determine the extent of the rest, i.e., *matra* (measure) is *laya*.

Laya is of three main types: *vilambita* (slow), *madhya* (medium) and *druta* (fast). *Madhyalaya* provides the required reference to determine the other two; and *matra* determines the *madhyalaya*.

Drutalaya is double the *madhya*, and *vilambitalaya* is half of the *madhya*.

The two major applications of *laya* are in metrics and music. Both applications expectably interact with each other. While time-measurement in poetry employed the triad of *laghu*, *guru* and *pluta*, that in music has ultimately settled on the trinity of *vilambita*, *madhya* and *druta*.

A related concept is *laya khanda*. The term refers to segmentation of an otherwise continuous movement into sections through a deliberate grouping of strong-weak accents.

2.64   *Layakari* (S. H *laya* = rhythm, temporal segmentation. + *kari* = to work on rhythms)

It is an introduction of rhythmic variations with reference to an assumed *laya*. It is also aptly described as *alankarik* (decorative) *laya*. Five important varieties of *layakari* are stated as:

Chatusra = four in one *mantra*
Tisra = three in one *mantra*

Khanda = five in one *mantra*
Mishra = seven in one *mantra*
Sankirna = nine in one *mantra*

2.65 *Lopya/lupta* (H S *lup* = to cause to disappear)

It means a note omitted or selected from omission in a particular *raga*.

2.66 *Madhya* (H S = medium, middle)

It is an important term indicating a reference-state to help comprehend relative highness and lowness in matters of pitch, and slowness and fastness in matters of tempo. Concepts of *mandra* (bass) and *tara* (treble), *vilambita* (slow) and *druta* (fast) are established in relation to the state identified as *madhya*.

2.67 *Manjha* (H < S. *madhya* = middle)

In melodic compositions for vocal as well as instrumental music a section located between *sthayi* (>) and *antara* (>) is called *manjha*. Such middle-units traceable in some *khayal* (>) compositions are also found in some other genres which were in vogue prior to the heyday of *dhrupad*.

2.68 *Marga sangeet* (S)

Ancient music that has 'offering devotion to God', as its main aim. It was expectably to be performed with a strict adherence to rules elaborately laid down. Music-making contrastive in character to *marga sangeet* was described as *deshi* (>). Alternatively known as *margi sangeet*; today *marga sangeet* does not claim an identifiable separate vogue or corpus of forms or compositions.

2.69   *Mata* (H S doctrine, tenet)

Opinion: During the course of its long history Indian musicology had to repeatedly attempt to classify the ever-growing number of *raga*-s. A very early formula was codification of *raga*-s into *raga-ragini-putra-vadhu* families. Approaches to the problem were crystallised in various codifications that came to be known as *mata*.

Prominent *mata*-s were *Hanuman mata, Shiva mata,* and *Naga mata.* Today the concept of *mata* enjoys merely an academic significance.

2.70   *Matra* (H S measure)

It is the basic unit of measuring musical time in general and particularly in *tala.* Different opinions are expressed in respect of the precise time-value of a single *matra.* For example, it is suggested that one *matra* is:

a. Time required for pronouncing five *laghu* letters.
b. Time required for batting an eye-lid.
c. Time required for pronouncing one letter.

The concept of *matra* is also employed to define two time-values with longer durations namely, *guru* and *pluta.* *Guru* is time required to pronounce ten *laghu*, and *pluta,* fifteen *laghu.*

2.71   *Matu* (S.)

It is a general term referring to the language-component in musical compositions. The tonal component is described as *dhatu.*

2.72 *Misal (misil* A *misla)*

This term in *pakhawaj*-music refers to the conventional sequence in which various composition-types /compositions are to be played in solo performances.

2.73 *Meend* (H. < S *meedam* = in a low tone, softly)

It is an important melodic embellishment in which continuity of intonation is maintained while moving from a higher to lower note.

Musicological texts have dealt with the concept very precisely in describing *meend* as a *karshankriya* (an act of stretching, with clear indication of use of a string in instruments). The embellishment has four subtypes as shown below:

- *Anagat meend* = that which terminates before the desired note is reached
- *Atikrant meend* = that which terminates after the desired note is reached
- *Vicchhinna meend = that which* breaks in between
- *Vishamahata meend* = that which displays unevenness of strokes; hence resulting in temporal unevenness in the effect of continuity.

Even though the terms clearly betray a chordophonic bias, the phenomenon is also observed in vocal music.

2.74 *Mela* (S. H = meeting, union, assembly)

The generative scale formulated through sequential ascending and descending arrangement of eight notes from the fundamental to its octave was known as *mela*.

Vidyaranyaswami of the Vijayanagaram Empire (est. 1336 AD) was the first to use the term. Later terms *sansthan*, *sansthiti*, *thata*, as well as the Persian *makam/mukam* are nearly synonyms.

2.75   *Melakarta* (H S *mela* + *karta*)

It is a generative scale of seven notes sequentially arranged in their ascending and descending orders. Vyankatmakhi who laid foundation of modern *raga*-codification in Carnatic music and influenced Pt. Bhatkhande's similar work related to Hindustani music advocated seventy-two *melakarta* scales by basing his formulations on a total number of twelve notes placed in one octave.

2.76   *Mishra* (H S mixed, blended, combined)

This is a term widely used to classify sound, *raga*, and many other constituents of Hindustani music. For example:

Mishra-nada = Combined sound produced by human breath and instrument.
Mishra-raga = *Raga* resulting from a combination of two or more *raga*-s.
Mishra-tala = A *tala* combining two or more basic *tala*.
Mishra-swara = Sharp/flat states of the fundamental seven notes in the scale.

2.77   *Mudra* (H S = face, stamp)

Certain informational material is included in many musical compositions through a feature called *mudra*. *Mudra* is usually placed in the last line. Though *mudra* does not find a place in all forms of music, it is however present in music of art, religious categories of music as also in some genres from the folk category. Twenty-one types of *mudra* are noted though all of them are not included in each case. Examples of *mudra* are:

i. Name of a composer
ii. Pen-name of a composer
iii. Name of a *raga/tala*
iv. Name of a patron
v. Name of a *guru*
vi. Name of a hero

2.78 *Mukh/a* (S. = mouth)

A recurring portion of a melodic composition, which is placed prior to the *sama*, is called *mukha*. It virtually acts as a clue to identify the composition. In addition, it fulfills the aesthetic function of providing a constant reference for variations, which performers may introduce from time to time. *Mukhada* is a diminutive of *mukha*.

The term is also employed to describe constructional parts of instruments especially of aerophonic (*sushira*) and membranophonic (*avanaddha*) categories.

2.79 *Mukhari* (H S *mukha* = mouth)

A person knowledgeable enough to compose, recite and teach rhythmic compositions used in dance is known as *mukhari*. A *mukhari* controls singer, rhythm-accompanist as well as the main dancer in dance performance.

2.80 *Murchana* (S)

It is a sequential arrangement of seven notes, in ascent and descent, but beginning every time on a different note.

The Western concept of key-modulation may come nearest to *murchana*.

Application of *murchana* principle obviously enables generation of new basic frameworks for further patterning of melodic material.

2.81   *Nada* (S)

It is a generic term for the concept of Sound as a basic element of music both as art and science. The fact that *nada* is regarded basic also to *yoga* suggests an intrinsic relationship in Indian culture between music and *yoga*. From the term the syllable *'Na'* is stated to symbolise *Prana*, i.e. breath and syllable *'da'* stands for fire. Two basic types of *nada* are *ahata* that is produced through 'striking', and *anahata*, that is produced without recourse to the process of striking. The former is used in music.

Subdivisions of musical *nada* are *anudatta* or *mandra* (base), *swarita* or *madhya* (medium) and *udatta* or *tara* (high). The basic principle applied to determine relative highness/ lowness holds that later the variety, double the pitch, and vice versa. It is therefore clear that Indian musicology does not accept the principle of Absolute pitch.

Expectably many other classifications of *nada* are possible. For example Matanga in *Brihaddeshi* (800 AD) suggests the flowing:

Sukshma = subtle
Ati sukshma = very subtle
Apushta = not filled/not full
Pushta = full
Kritrim = artificial

It is usual, though strictly not correct to consider the following as synonyms: *dhvani, rava, swana, kolahala*.

2.82   *Nara* (S man, male)

The term refers to bass tonal quality in instruments such as *pakhawaj*, harmonium, etc. *Madi* (P *Madah*) suggests the opposite quality.

2.83   *Nibaddha* (S bound, fettered)

The term indicates the fundamental musical characteristic of being rigorously regulated by rules, especially those pertaining to *tala, chhanda, yati*, etc. The term *anibaddha* suggests a contrastive tendency of being free of such constraints. Also see *gana*.

2.84   *Nikas* (H < S *nishkasa* = to produce)

The term indicates production of sound syllables in instrumental music relevant to particular instruments. It clearly refers to playing techniques in *pakhawaj, vina, sitar*, etc.

In most cases, actual sounds, which instruments produce, are roughly indicated by the 'alphabet' of the 'language' of the instrument. Hence, a change in the *nikas* of a particular sound-cluster may actually bring about a considerable change in the final impact achieved. Therefore, *nikas* is of primary importance in performing traditions. To a great extent, *gharana*-s are distinguishable on the basis of how they develop, follow and advocate particular techniques of *nikas*.

2.85   *Nikharaja* (H S *ni* + *kharaj shadja*)

It is a description that indicates a highly diminished presence of the note *shadja* (*sa*, the fundamental) in *raga*. In view of the overall importance of the principle of tonality, this feature makes the concerned *raga* sound very different. A prominent example is that of *raga Marwa*.

2.86   *Nimisha* (H S = winking, shutting the eye)

It is the minimal unit of measuring musical time and it is suggested that it is approximately equivalent to 9/32 of a second. It must, however, be remembered that in spite of similar exact descriptions and a terminology to match the effort, Indian performing tradition does not recognise principle of Absolute time.

2.87   *Nirgeet* (S)

The term, though not in general use, indicates an important musical practice of ancient lineage as also an ever-present musical tendency. The core meaning of the term is 'song without words'. Performance of instrumental music without a song was aptly described as *shushkageet on* account of this connotation of song. A further sophistication of usage brought into circulation another term — *bahirgeet*, meaning a song irrelevant to the matter of drama/play. Such a song could therefore be independently performed outside the performance of a play. A mythical explanation described *bahirgeet* as a composition couched in *laya, tala*, etc., with *shushkakshara*. As demons created these songs (i.e. *bahirgeet)* in competition with gods, the latter named the variety *bahirgeet*!

2.88   *Nishkala* (S)

The term describes a string instrument that does not consist of a drone or sympathetic strings (e.g. violin). The opposite term is *sakala*.

2.89   *Nishabda* (S)

The term refers to soundless measurement of musical time in *tala*. *Sashabda* is its opposite.

2.90   *Nyasa* (H S *nitaram* = in an effective manner + *asa* = to sit, to stabilise)

The term describes a musical note with a special status. In a musical scale *nyasa*-note is a class/type of note, which helps in clearly bringing out nature of a specific *raga*. In most cases, *nyasa-swara* points to   long duration, i.e., time-value which the concerned note enjoys. Along with other terms such as *graha, apanyasa* and *vinyasa, nyasa*-note was important in Indian music in the historical phase of musical evolution when *raga* was *not* the predominant concept and secondly when music was mostly pre-composed. *Nyasa* etc. made way for *vadi, samvadi* and related terms when *raga* became the reigning concept, and improvisation, a ruling strategy of music elaboration.

2.91   *Pada* (S)

In a rough translation *pada* means 'a phrase'.

1. In *raga*-music *pada* may be described as the minimal unit of notes indicative of a *raga*. In majority of cases, two notes suffice to make a *pada*.
2. It also means portion of a musical composition consisting of meaningful language units. Of its two types, the *nibaddha* music is regulated by rules pertaining to metres etc., while *anibaddha* is free from such constraints. Significantly, the latter is also de-

scribed, as *churnapada* while the former is known as *padya*.

2.92   Padhant (H *padhna* = to read, to recite)

In *pakhawaj*-music (and by extension in *tabla*-music), *padhant* indicates the convention of 'reciting compositions aloud prior to playing them'. Prior *padhant* is especially useful in case of compositions consisting of syllables, which match meaningful words. Performance of a composition subsequent to its *padhant* is called *bajant*. 'Translation' (transliteration) of meaningful words by matching them with sound-syllables could be illustrated thus:

- *Ganapati = gadikat*
- *Jagat = digat*
- *Shankar = dingan*

2.93   Pakad (H *pakadna* = to grapple, to hold)

A group of minimal number of musical notes characteristic of any *raga* is described as *pakad*. To performers and auditors alike, *pakad* literally offers a good grip on the *raga!*

2.94   Pata (S)

The term is related to the process of making *tala* concrete through procedures that employ sound (e.g. claps). The opposite mode of operation employing silence towards the same end is known as *shamya*. In a wider context the term *pata* connotes sound-syllables (*akshara*) used to describe sounds producible from various musical instruments of almost all categories.

2.95 *Pat* (H)

It is the process of accelerating *tempi* in a predetermined manner. The short and long durations of *'pat'* add a dimension to any pattern selected in instrumental music.

2.96 *Poorab* (H S *poorva* = eastern)

It is a term employed to describe characteristic styles of singing, playing or dancing, especially in singing of *thumri* and *tabla* playing. Regionwise the term indicates eastern areas of Uttar Pradesh in which the styles referred to have their origin or with which they had a very strong association.

2.97 *Pukar* (H *pukarna* = to call)

The term refers to one particular and effective way of intonation in vocal music. It consists of a repeated use of a high note indicating intensity of emotion and one leading to heightening of musical effect.

2.98 *Punjab ang*

It is a descriptive term employed to denote characteristic way of singing and *tabla* playing. Flashy presentation, intricacy of design and occasional inclusion of folk idiom are some of the easily perceivable features of this idiom related to the area known as Punjab in the undivided India.

2.99 *Raga* (S)

The traditional definition is wide enough to accommodate even harmonic music within its ambit! It runs, *"Raga* is a group of stationary, ascending or descending notes, moving in violation of sequence or enjoying other liberties. The notes are delightful to the hearts of men."

In Hindustani music, *raga* as understood today is a result of processing the basic scale to create melodic frameworks that are foundational and generative. Contemporary *raga* formation directly explores a span of twelve notes with seven notes regarded *shuddha* (authorised) and five *vikrut* (changed) notes as the components.

Important characteristics of *raga* stated by Pandit Bhatkhande are briefly described below:

1. No *raga* can be made of less than five notes.
2. A *raga* cannot omit both *madhyama* and *panchama*, that is, fourth and fifth note.
3. A *raga* should not consecutively employ two 'states' (i.e., sharp and flat) of the same note.
4. Notes occurring in the scale of *raga Bilawal* are to be treated as *shuddha* for reference.
5. All *raga*-s are principally classifiable into three groups according to their inclusion of *shuddha re*, *dha* or *komal re*, *dha* or *komal ga*, *ni*.
6. All *raga*-s are bound by rules, pertaining to *vadi* that is the principal note.
7. A *raga* has either its *poorvanga* or *uttaranga* as the chief area of its elaboration depending on location of *vadi*.
8. Relationship of *raga* with *diurnal*, as well as seasonal, time-cycle is one of its defining characteristics.
9. To determine the *raga*-time relationship, importance of *tivra madhyama* in a *raga* serves as a prime indicator.

10. In accordance with their association with either of the two twilight periods, *raga*-s are classified in two broad divisions. *Raga*-s belonging to the two twilight periods display structural features describable as 'question-answer'.

11. In a *raga*, *vivadi* is not to be understood as an entirely omitted note. It is a note, which is sparingly and judiciously used to add colour to *raga*.

12. *Raga*-s in the twilight periods follow sequence vis-à-vis the time of their performance. The group of *raga*-s including notes *komal re* and *komal dha* are followed by those consisting of notes *shuddha re* and *dha,* and this group is followed by those that include notes *ga* and *ni*. Finally come *raga*-s using *ga, ni komal*. *Raga*-s with *sa, ma, pa* as important notes precede twilight *raga*-s.

13. *Raga*-s strong in *poorvanga* are strong in ascending movement; while those strong in *uttaranga* are strong in descent.

14. To mix/combine *raga*-s and *ragini* is a legitimate procedure of enriching *raga* music.

It is possible to classify *raga*-s in many ways. These numerous classifications based on different criteria throw important light on formative elements of Hindustani *raga* corpus taken as a whole. Some classifications, along with criteria that they employ, are mentioned below:

a. *Sampurna* = seven notes
   Shadava = six notes
   Odava = five notes
   The criterion employed is number of notes *raga* includes.

b. *Shuddha* = pure, original
    Chhayalaga = with a shadow of other *raga*-s
    Sankirna = mixture of many *raga*-s
    The criterion is the type or kind of grammatical ex-
    clusiveness a *raga* enjoys.

c. *Pratargeya* = sung/rendered at mornings
    Sayamgeya = sung/rendered in evenings
    The criterion is time of the day at which a *raga* is to
    be conventionally performed.

d. *re-dha* (*shuddha*) included
    re-dha (*komal*) included
    ga-ni (*komal*) included
    The criterion applied is the presence/absence of a
    particular structural weightage resulting from use
    or otherwise of the indicated notes.

e. *Prachalita* = in easy circulation
    Aprachalita = rare circulation
    The criterion is the general vogue enjoyed by a *raga*.

f. *Sarala* = simple in movement
    Vakra = convoluted in movement.
    The criterion is tonal contour prominently displayed
    by a *raga* through sequential or out of sequence
    movement of notes regarded mandatory in a *raga*.

g. *Alapapradhan* = conducive to elaborations in slow
    tempo.
    Tanapradhan = conducive to elaborations in fast
    tempi.
    The criterion applied is prominence given to differ-
    ent elaborational phases and associated *tempi* —
    preferably fast-paced.

h. *Poorvangapradhan* = predominantly to be elaborated
    in the first half of the scale, i.e. lower half.

Uttarangapradhan = predominantly to be elaborated in the second half of the scale, i.e. the higher half. The criterion is prominence enjoyed by one or the other half of the scale.

i. *Aam raga* = an expansive *raga* allowing elaboration which is free, varied and abundant.
Dhun raga = *raga* with limited but unrestricted inbuilt melodic structuring.
The criterion employed is elaborational potentialities of different *raga*-s and the kind of freedom enjoyed in doing so.

j. Spring = *Hindol raga*
Summer = *Deepak raga*
Monsoon = *Megha raga*
Winter = *Bhairava raga*
Hemant = *Shri raga*
Shishir = *Malkauns raga*
The criterion employed is seasonal associations a *raga* enjoys according to the tradition.

k. Many *raga*-s are classified according to their reported place of origin.

l. *Raga*-s are also classified according to an implied sexual symbolism.

m. Some *raga*-s proclaim their ethnic origin.

2.100 *Raganga paddhati*

Pandit Narayan Moreshwar Khare, a disciple of Pandit Vishnu Digambar Paluskar, attempted a new system of *raga* classification called *Raganga*.

He maintained that as a first step towards a scientific classification, *raga*-s that fulfill all fundamental conditions of *raga*-formation are to be identified. He felt that exploita-

tion of selected aspects (*anga*) of fundamental *raga*-s leads
to creation of other *raga*. He advocated twenty-six groups
formulated according to his theory.

2.101 *Raga-ragini*

The paired term operates at various levels.

At the metaphysical level it mirrors Shiva-*Shakti* or
Purush-Prakriti pair from Indian philosophy and metaphys-
ics to represent manifestation of male-female principle in
music.

In a narrower musical context, musicological tradition
in India refers to six major *raga*-s and thirty-six *ragini*-s. It
is possible that the aesthetic theories of *Natyashastra* advo-
cating the evocative *nayak-nayika-bheda, i.e. hero-heroine*
differentiation, influenced musicological thinking and thus
emerged the *raga-ragini* phenomenon. Whatever that may
be, diverse   criteria have been advocated to distinguish
raga from *ragini*. A few are noted here:

a. The original seasonal *raga*-s, six in number, are
   raga-s, other being *ragini*-s.
b. *Raga*-s are rendered in slow movement and their
   mood is also more serious/grave.
   On the other hand *ragini*-s are light-hearted in mood
   and faster in pace.
c. Names of *raga-ragini* indicate their genders.
d. *Raga*-s consist of larger tonal intervals as opposed
   to *ragini*-s which consist of smaller ones.

It appears that *raga-ragini* classification was one of the
attempts made to systematise the growing number of *raga*-
corpus and the immense variety. After *mela* or *thata* principle gained ascendancy, *raga-ragini* classification became
redundant.

2.102 *Rasa* theory

Natyashastra of Bharata is the oldest known text on the theory of theatre and literature. The text is dated to 200/ 300 AD.

The theory of *rasa*, as enunciated by Bharata and especially as interpreted by his major commentator Abhinavagupta (10th century), has stimulated followers of both scholastic and performing traditions in India for the last 2000 years. It must be noted that the original statement of the theory and a large portion of later commentaries , discuss the theory mostly in literary and dramatic contexts. And yet, the *rasa* theory has provided invaluable aesthetic framework to literary arts (chiefly poetry, fiction, drama), performing arts (which mainly include dance, theatre and music), fine arts (basically painting and sculpture), and combined arts (for example, architecture).

Natyashastra deals with the *rasa* theory in chapters VI and VII. The 31st *sutra* of Chapter VI provides the premise for an immense body of material produced through centuries by philosophers, aestheticians, artists and students of culture in India and abroad.

In translation the *sutra* reads "*Rasa* comes/arises from a (proper) combination of the *vibhava*-s (the stimulants), the *anubhava*-s (the physical consequents) and the *vyabhicharibhava*-s (the transient emotional states)."

What is an analogy? We say "Just as flavour/taste is produced by a proper combination of different spices (*vyanjana*), leafy vegetables (*aushadhi*) and other substances (*dravya*), so *rasa* (in drama) is produced by a combination (*upagama*) of many *bhava*-s. Just as food-substances such as *shadava* (a combination of six flavours), taste is created from substances such as molasses, spices and vegetables, similarly, the permanent emotions attain the status of *rasa* when they are accompanied by different *bhava*-s. One may ask: What is this you call *rasa*? The answer is: (It is called *Rasa*) because it can be savoured. How can it be savoured? As people in contented state of mind (gourmet?) are able to savour the flavour of food prepared with many spices, and attain pleasure, so the sensitive spectators savour the primary emotions suggested by the acting out of the various *bhava*-s and presented by appropriate modulation of voice, movements of the body and display of involuntary reactions and attain pleasure. Therefore they are called *natyarasa*."

The first known commentary on the work is of Udbhata — which came after 500 years or so after *Natyashastra* was in circulation.

1. To say that *rasa* is produced or created is only true in a limited sense as otherwise it would appear to be an external entity. Similarly to describe art-experience, as imitation is also partially true because the emotion felt by the listener is not due to imitation on his part. *Rasa*-phenomenon has an external element to the extent that there is an objective work of art, which sets the *rasa*-process into motion. *Rasa*-experience cannot be dismissed as non-existent, or false. It must be accepted as a matter of perception.

2. The aesthetic experience cannot be fully described as production, imitation or even revelation leading to relish or enjoyment. It is in essence, revelation through intuition. For example, in Kalidasa's play *Shakuntala*, the hero-king Dushyanta, because of a curse, has forgotten that he had married Shakuntala. He is sitting in a happy and normal

state of mind, hears a song sung by his maid Hansapadika, and he feels disturbed/affected by it. What happens in such a case?

(a) Sensory perception (Something is heard.)

(b) Scientific/technical perception follows (The sound is recognised by Dushyanta as musical.)

(c) Identification, and placement of the experience through familiarity and previous information (What is heard is a song by Hansapadika, a maid.)

(d) Further interpretation, through specialised knowledge (The singer is rendering a classical/scientific melody, the words are charged with emotion.)

(e) Personal response to the experience of being affected (Dushyanta understands the ironic content of Hansapadika's song as a generality of human life.)

(f) Emotive reaction (Dushyanta is personally and unaccountably restless/disturbed.)

(g) Aesthetic judgment (Beautiful sight and sweet melody have a disturbing effect.)

3. What is important is to note that the experiencer passes from a particular personal experience to a generalisation. This is due to a mental vision, a vivid intuitive realisation.

4. It is implied that the emotion and its relish are potentially present in a work of art. What is emotional experience for the creator is for the receiver/perceiver an aesthetic relish.

5. What is the role of components of the work leading to the final relish? They are symbols or instruments

for conveying an emotion to the reader/spectator/
listener. They are the means for producing an
awareness or perception of the emotional experience projected by the work of art (i.e. singing, etc.)

6. Obviously there are certain prerequisites for the *rasa*-
relish.

    The experiencer must have a mirror like mind to
    permit the reflection of the experience presented to
    him. He must have the aesthetic sensibility, which
    can be cultivated by guidance, and studies. He must
    be free from prejudice. He must have the ability to
    forget himself.

7. There are certain handicaps an experiencer may be
    plagued with: for example, he may not believe in
    the validity of the experience of art as such. He may
    be in the habit of treating every experience 'person-
    ally'-identifying with the characters/music-makers,
    etc.

8. Artists' inadequacies may also hamper the experi-
    ence. For example, he might have insufficient skills,
    he may lack in projection or he may lack the ability
    to balance the components of the art concerned.

Finally, the *rasa*-experience is pure joy or delight irrespective of the nature of the individual emotion involved.
The art experience brings in fact a temporary repose to the
mind. It is extraordinary as it is unique and distinguishable, not only from the familiar perceptions on the empiri-
cal level but also from perceptions from the meditative/
spiritual kind. However, on account of the repose element
in art, there is an affinity between religious/spiritual experience and the art-experience.

In various kinds of musical expressions in India following broad equations appear to have been used indicating the existing *rasa-raga* relationship.

Rasa	Raga
Karuna	Jogiya, Bhairavi, Asavari
Shringara	Bahar, Khamaj, Kafi
Shanta	Darbari Kanada, Puriya, Kalyan
Veera	Adana

2.103 *Ritusangeet* (H S *ritu* = season + *sangeet* = music)

Indian musicology has firmly associated six *raga*-s with six seasons of a single calendar year. According to *Hanuman-Mata*, the correspondence is:

Season	Raga	Months
Grishma	Deepak	Jyeshtha-Ashadh
Varsha	Megh	Shravan-Bhadrapad
Sharad	Bhairav	Ashwin-Kartik
Hemant	Malkauns	Margshirsha-Pausha
Shishir	Shree	Magh-Phalgun
Vasant	Hindol	Chaitra-Vaishakh

2.104 *Sachala* (S = shiftable)

1. *Sachala-swara*: notes with variations/states such as *komal*, *tivra*, etc. In Indian musicological tradition only *Shadja* (*sa*) and *Panchama* (*pa*) are regarded unchangeable notes.

2. *Sachala thata*: An arrangement of shiftable frets in musical instruments such as *sitar* effected to facilitate easy use of variations in notes. See *achala thata*.

2.105   *Sakala vadya*

Refers to an instrument, which provides drone as well as melody.

2.106   *Sampurna* (S = complete)

As a technical term it refers to a scalar arrangement of notes, which includes all seven notes of the gamut. The other two arrangements are *odava* and *shadava* respectively including five and six notes from the available seven.

2.107   *Samvada-tatva* (H S *samvada* = harmony + *tatva* = element)

The term refers to an important musicological principle of organising tonal/melodic material by establishing mandatory relationships between two or more notes or elements. The principle may in fact also become applicable to rhythmic material, though some conceptual reinterpretation and employment of new terminology might become necessary.

Primarily and traditionally the first application of the *samvada-tatva* is exemplified through the relationship of two notes distanced by nine or thirteen microtonal intervals (*sruti/shruti*). Pairs of notes resulting from such applications display a special degree of consonance. Further, applications of the first-fifth relationship (called *shadja-panchama bhava*) or the first-fourth (called *shadja-madhyama bhava*) make available pairs displaying second degree of consonance.

Secondly, *samvada-tatva* may refer to similarities in larger melodic structures. For example, two major *triads*, *sa, re, ga,* and *pa, dha, ni,* reveal a constructional correspondence.

Thirdly, *samvada-tatva* is also applied to *raga*-s because they are often formulated/positioned in the total corpus in such a way that they appear to function as 'questions and answers'. For example, *Deshkar*, a morning *raga* and *Bhoop*, a *raga* for early night, exemplify the *samvada-tatva* because, even though they differ in dynamics on account of shift of emphasis, they have similar ascent and descent.

2.108   *Sangeet* (H S *sam* = good + *geet* = sung)

It is a generic term for a combined manifestation of the sung, the played and the danced.

It is significant to note that the term 'music' used in the Western tradition also indicates a combined operation of performing arts which came to be treated as separate entities in later period.

2.109   *Sangeetlekhana* (H S *sam* = good + *geet* = sung) + *lekhana* = writing

This should be the proper term to indicate notation of music in India. The generally used term *Swaralekhana* seems to be a literal translation of the Western term 'notation' — a sure indication of the fact that the concept is foreign to Indian musicology. The term 'notation' would, strictly speaking, rule out inclusion of items such as linguistic texts, sound-syllables employed by the melodic and rhythmic instruments, suggestions about use of specific sound-production techniques.

2.110 *Sangitshastra* (H S *sangeet* = music + *shastra* = science)

Musicology, earlier known as *gandharva-tatva* is today indicated by this term. It includes studies broadly classifiable in three categories as shown below:

1. Directly related to study and performance of music:
    a. Characteristics of *raga, tala* forms of music and musical instruments
    b. Rules related to elaboration of musical ideas, rhythmic as well as melodic
    c. Playing techniques for four types of instruments
    d. Musical embellishments and *gamaka*
    e. Musical scales and their manipulations
    f. Accepted merits and demerits of performers

2. Indirectly connected with performance:
    a. Metrics
    b. Notation
    c. Musical mnemonics,
    d. Musical aesthetics

3   Having no connection with performance:
    a. Music and mathematics
    b. Musical history

2.111 *Sansthan* (S)

The term is synonymous with *thata* (>), *makam* and *mela* (>). Lochana probably was the first to use the term in his work *Ragatarangini* (1675 AD).

2.112   *Saptaka* (S.< *sapta* = seven, a group of seven)

The group of basic seven notes from *Shadja* to *Nishad* is known as *Saptaka*. As the count proceeds in an ascending order, the eighth note is counted and becomes the first note of the next *saptaka*, hence it is not included in counting the first *saptaka*. More plausible reason is that the count is related to intervals between two notes and not to the notes themselves as they act as dividers.

Three generally accepted *saptaka* are respectively known as *mandra* (bass), *madhya* (medium) and *tara* (treble). The name of notes within a *saptaka* are:

Note name	Meaning	Short form	Position
Shadja	Born of six or from which six are born	Sa	First
Rishabha		Re	Second
Gandhar		Ga	Third
Madhyama	In the middle	Ma	Fourth
Panchama		Pa	Fifth
Dhaivat		Dha	Sixth
Nishad		Ni	Seventh

The order of notes as indicated above was accepted sometimes during the medieval period. The ancient gamut, employed in *Samagayana* was arranged in a descending order had less number of notes in initial stages.

2.113 *Shabdalapa* (H S *shabda* = articulated sound + *alap*)

The term refers to the early practice in which *alap*, i.e. tonal or melodic elaboration was superimposed on words of a song. The modern term *bol-alap* is synonymous with *shabdalapa*.

2.114 *Shabdadosha* (*shabda* = articulated sound + *dosha* = demerit)

Indian musicology pays adequate attention to merits and demerits of singers. Unfortunately, all descriptions are not clear today and overlaps between terms and concepts are confusing. The eight *dosha*-s are:

    i.   *Ruksha* = dry

   ii.   *Sphurita* = with breaks

  iii.   *Nissara* = lacking in inner strength

  iv.   *Kakolika* = like a crow

   v.   *Keti* = ranging over three octaves but without quality

  vi.   *Keni* = experiencing difficulties in *tara* and *mandra* elaboration

 vii.   *Krisha* = weak

viii.   *Bhagna* = lacking in effect

Shabda guna is the antonym.

2.115 *Shabda guna* (*shabda* = articulated sound + *guna* = merit)

See *Shabdadosha* (>)

The fifteen *shabda guna*-s are:

1. *mrishta* = filling ears without causing pain
2. *madhura* = full in all the three octaves
3. *chehala* = possessing six characteristics
   The six are:
   > *Shasta* = easily perceivable
   > *Proudha* = mature
   > *Natisthool* = not thick
   > *Natikrisha* = not thin
   > *Snigdha* = loving
   > *Ghana* = solid
4. *tristhana* = clear and pleasant in three octaves
5. *sukhavaha* = delightful to the mind
6. *prachura* = thick
7. *gadha* = strong, powerful
8. *sharowak* = possessing carrying power
9. *karuna* = capable of producing pathos
10. *ghana* = possessing inner strength
11. *snigdha* = loving
12. *shlakshna* = continuous
13. *raktibhav* = entertaining
14. *chhaviman* = clearly articulated
15. *komala* = soft

2.116 *Shadja-chalana* (S *shadja* = produced from six organs + *chalana* = to shift)

Refers to shifting the beginning note without altering the sequence of notes.

2.117 *Sparsha* (S touch)

It is an important playing technique in string-music. The forefinger of the left hand is kept on one fret while the next fret is touched by the middle finger.

2.118   *Sthana* (S place)

According to tradition, chest (*hridaya*), throat (*kantha*), and head (*shira*) are respectively responsible for producing bass (*mandra*), medium (*madhya*) and treble (*tara*) octaves in vocal music. *Hridaya,* etc., are called *sthana*. With a slight shift, the term is also applied generally to mean an octave and hence the usage is extended to describe tonal ranges of different instruments.

2.119   *Stobha*

To employ for musical elaboration syllables or letters not in the original hymn was a legitimate procedure of *sama*-singers. These special syllables were known as *Stobha*. There were three types of *stobha*-s: *varna-stobha* = use of extra letter, *pada-stobha* = i.e. use of extra words and *vakya-stobha* = use of extra sentence. For example, the following are detected quite often: *hau, hai, atha, haha, ee, oo, aa, hin, hun,* etc.

2.120   *Sruti* (S one which is heard)

The term refers to microtonal intervals. The use of such intervals is a feature Hindustani art music is well known for.

Sruti is the minimal notional unit employed to measure the progressively increasing pitches of successive notes within a musical scale. It is so called chiefly because mainly a fine auditory sensibility determines it. Sounds possible within the range of a scale are obviously infinite. The reason why the number of identifiable *sruti*-s is limited to twenty-two is yet to be conclusively stated.

According to the scholastic tradition, these twenty-two *sruti*-s are further grouped into five classes.

Almost every aspect of the *sruti* phenomenon has raised controversies that are raging even today. Important points on which controversial positions have been taken are:

a. All *sruti*-s are not equal.
b. Every note is established on its first *sruti*.
c. It is possible to state/present the *sruti* system in terms of Western acoustic concepts of frequency, cents, etc.
d. The conventional natural scale in the Western system and the Hindustani *Bilawal thata* would appear to correspond if the modern acoustical explanation of the Western scale on the one hand and the *sruti* tradition on the other are shown to be similar.

Diametrically opposite views have been expressed on each of these and similar other points argued.

2.121 *Sur* (H S *Swara* = note)

The term has many meanings:

1. It may refer to *Shadja,* the first note of the Indian *saptaka* (>). This may correspond to the Western concept of a keynote.
2. Drone.

2.122 *Sushira* (adj. S perforated, full of holes)

Refers to aerophones, i.e. wind instruments, an ancient category of musical instruments. Some important technical/structural terms related to these instruments are listed below:

Phoonk = blown wind
Nadachhidra = sound hole

Chabhi = key
Mukh Patti = reed
Mukha = mouth
Tumba = gourd
Penda = base
Pet = belly
Kalash = top-portion (ref. conch)
Nali = pipe
Nabhi = navel, centre (ref. conch)

2.123 *Swara* (H S sound, noise)

Refers to any musical note. It is necessary to remember that all sounds are not musical and all musical sounds are not notes. Musical sounds are called *sruti* and *sruti*-s, which are members of scales, are known as *swara*. The first and the fifth notes, respectively called *shadja* (*'sa'*) and *panchama* (*'pa'*) are regarded immutable in Indian musicology. Remaining five notes have two states each, thus resulting in the contemporary framework of twelve notes. In this manner at the first level, the *swara*-s are stable and unalterable or unchanged.

The changes in *swara* are brought about in two ways:

1. By application of the *murchana* (>) process. For example, to shift the beginning of the *saptaka* to *re* instead of from the note *sa* would give us *komal* states of notes *ga* and *ni*. This is the *murchana*-way.
2. By changing the established microtonal values.

An example of the second method is to heighten pitch-values of earlier notes by 'borrowing' microtonal degrees from the quota of the higher note. It is obvious that changes introduced in this manner are 'notional'. Such changes in intervals and demarcation points help in permutation and combination of *swara*.

Many classifications of *swara* prevail from earlier periods, though all of them do not continue to have the same contemporary relevance. For example:

1. *Udatta, swarita* and *anudatta* (mainly in *Vedic* music), *graha, nyasa, ansha* (during the phase of *nibaddha* music), *komal, tivra* (understood respectively as lowered and heightened), *chetana, achetana, mishra* (respectively referring to human voice, sound-producing lifeless objects and a combination of both as producers of *swara*).

2. *swara dhun*: a group of notes composed, executed, or elaborated without having to conform to restraints of *raga*-grammar. It may or may not have a *tala*.

Hindustani art music is rightly equated with *raga*-music. The development of the melodic aspect of music to the stage of *raga* was dependent on evolution of the *swara-saptaka*. This in itself seems to be a culmination of a logical development from very early times. A rough time-chart can be noted.

Hindustani swara-saptaka:

In a manner of speaking there is a steady development from the *Vedic* times to the contemporary framework of twelve notes used for making *raga*-music. Broadly, the developmental phases can be listed as shown below:

1. *Archik gayan* = of one note. (4500 BC) with 'hrasva' (shortened), 'deergha' (lengthened),

'*pluta*' (more lengthened) as their respective durations.

2. *Udatta* and *Anudatta* = *Gathik*, i.e. of two notes (3500 BC, i.e. pre-*Rgveda* times).

3. *Udatta, anudatta, swarita* = In *Yajurveda*.

4. Three *grama*-s (*shadja, madhyama, panchama*), *Samaveda* times (3500–2500 BC).

5. Three *grama*-s consisting of seven notes in each = Brahmana and Upanishad times, (2500 BC to 1500 BC).

6. Seven notes in each of the three *saptaka*-s. In *Panini* and *Yadnyavalkya* (*anudatta mandra, swarita madhya* and *udatta tara* mentioned) = Aranyaka times (1500–500 BC).

7. Singing of *grama*-s. *Grama* from every note = Puranic times to 500 BC.

8. Bharata. Singing of *Jati*-s = 500 BC to 400 AD.

9. Seven *shuddha* and 12 *vikruta* notes = Ratnakara-period   (400-1300 AD).

10. Seven *shuddha* and seven *vikruta* = Ramamatya (1550 AD).

11. Only *shadja grama*, 7 *shuddha* and 5 *vikruta* notes = Vyankatmakhi (1620 AD), Tulajirao Bhonsale (1635 AD).

2.124   *Swaralipi* (H S *swara* = note + *lipi* = script)

During the nineteenth century, notation systems were usually described as *swaralipi*.

A skeletal system of notation was in operation in ancient India but *swaralipi* came into prominence and use in the latter part of the nineteenth century. Many systems were devised and advocated but two, which Pandit Vishnu Digambar Paluskar (1900 AD) and Pandit Vishnu Narayan Bhatkhande (1910 AD) formulated, gained considerable following. The major notational signs employed by them are given in the following table. (pp. 258-59)

2.125 *Swaradnyana* **(H S *swara* = note + *dnyana* = knowledge)**

It means sensitivity or aptitude for tunefulness, i.e. a feeling for the right/exact location of notes in the accepted gamut. Though the modern concept of just noticeable difference may apply, *swaradnyana* has actually nothing much to do with the sense of absolute pitch. A finer sense of the subtleties of tonal intervals is described by adding the adjective *sukshma* (subtle) to *swaradnyana*.

2.126 *Swarasanchalana* **(H S *swara* = note + *sanchalana* = to move)**

It means changing the keynote to build a new melody. The practice seems to have a direct connection with the ancient vogue of *murchana*. However, after the acceptance of the principle of tonality, which enabled music makers placing all twelve intervals within the space of one octave, the *murchana* strategy was sidelined. Since then, there is a vogue of treating the fourth note, i.e. *madhyama* as the base note to present semi-classical forms such as *thumri*. This is may be treated as an example of *swarasanchalana*.

2.127 *Swayambhu* **(H S *swayam* = oneself + *bhu* = to become)**

This is a term usefully coined to refer to harmonics created by, and heard from, the first and the fourth strings of

Major Notational Signs Employed by Paluskar and Bhatkhande

	Paluskar-System	Bhatkhande-System
1. To indicate Lower Octave (Shuddha Swaras)	ṅi ḋha ṗa ṁa	ṅi ḋha ṗa ṁa
2. To indicate Medium Octave (Shuddha Swaras)	sa re ga ma (No symbol is used)	ṡa ṙe ġa ṁa (No symbol is used)
3. To indicate Upper Octave (Shuddha Swaras)	re ga ma pa	ṛe ġa ṁa ṗa
4. To indicate 'Komal' i.e. Flat Swaras	re ga dha ni	re ga dha ni
5. To indicate 'Tivra' i.e. Sharp Swaras	ma	ma
Division of Time		
(a) To indicate 'Sam' i.e. the first 'Matra' (beat)	'9' symbol is used below the note-name	'X' symbol is used below the note-name
(b) To indicate kal or khali	'+' symbol is used below the note-name	'O' symbol is used below the note-name
(c) To indicate Tali (Clap): 2nd, 3rd, 4th & so on...	Respective number is put under the note-name	Respective number is put under the note-name
7. To indicate four Matras.	'x' symbol is used below the note-name. (The symbol is named as 'Chatasra')	
8. To indicate two Matras.	'~' symbol is used below the note-name. (The symbol is named as 'Guru')	

(Continued)

	Paluskar-System	Bhatkhande-System
9. To indicate one Matra	'—' symbol is used below the note-name (The symbol is named as 'Laghu'.)	
10. *Division of Matras:* To indicate ½ Matra.	'0' symbol is used below the note-name (The symbol is named as 'Drut'.)	
To indicate ¼th Matra.	'‿' symbol is used below the note-name (The symbol is named as 'Anu-Drut'.)	
To indicate ⅛th Matra.	'⌣' symbol is used below the note-name	
To indicate ⅓rd and ⅙th Matra.	⅓ and ⅙ numbers are put below note-name respectively	
11. To indicate a sustained use of word—	ja •• vo ••	ja s s vo s s
12. To indicate meend, i.e. sustained use of a Swara	ma s pa s s dha	ma— pa— —dha
13. To indicate Kan-Swaras i.e. Grace Notes—	ga ma / sa re ga	ga ma / sa re ga
14. To indicate continuous tonal production—	ma pa dha ni	ma pa dha ni
15.		Notes brought together with a curve below are to be sung or played in one Matra e.g. dha ni sa sa ni dha pa
16. Bracketed note, is to be used along with the succeeding and preceding notes respectively, in one Matra	(pa) = dha pa ma pa or (re) = ga re sa re	(pa) = dha pa ma pa or (re) = ga re sa re

a *tanpura* (>). It is also applied to similar other sounds in case of other instruments.

2.128   *Syunt* (S)

It is one of the three basic techniques of tone-production, the two other being *gamaka* and *meend*. It involves passing smoothly to a higher note from a lower. Continuity of an upward movement characterises *syunt*, while downward movement indicates *meend* (>).

2.129   *Takrari bol* (*takrar* = repetition + *bol* = meaningful words)

Very often a part of song needs repetition for effect. To facilitate the repetition, as also to help in meeting demands of the *tala*-cycle, a singer adds on the spur of the moment short words not originally included in the song, e.g. *'ab'* = now, *'are'* = oh you, *'re'* = yes, my love. These are known as *Takrari bol*.

2.130   *Tala* (H S *tal* = the palm of the hand)

Amarkosha succinctly defines *tala* as 'measure employed in the act of keeping time'.

Ancient *Vedic* recitation required use of different pitch-levels leading to formation of the scale range. The recitation inevitably required control and manipulation of recited words also on the temporal plane to ensure faultless prosodic arrangements. Scale-manipulation and exploitation of time-frame together led to metre as well as to *tala*. On this background of close and intrinsic association with prosody, it is understandable that a number of *tala*-terms bear mark of genetic relationship with linguistic and literary terminology.

Tala is that measure of time, which through the process of lengthening and shortening of durations, controls manifestations such as singing, instrumental music and dance. *Tala* becomes recognisable through purposeful and well-designed employment of sound, silence, rest, variation of intensity and *tempi*.

Theoretically infinite number of *tala*-s are possible though musicological texts have settled on 108, probably to correspond with the mythical one hundred and eight dances of Lord Shiva, the patron deity of all performing arts.

Major characteristics of *tala* are well codified in the tradition and they are collectively known as *dashaprana*. Significantly, basic characteristics of *raga* also number ten and they are known as *dashalakshana*. *Dashaprana* are briefly explained below:

1. *Kala* (time): Temporality as opposed to spatiality is the essence.
2 *Anga*: Reportedly refers to six sections of *tala* described according to their respective durational values. The significance of the term is not clear.
3. *Kriya* (action): Connotes procedures adopted to keep time by using sounds, silences, hand movements, etc.
4. *Marga* (path): Refers to the relative density of notes in the duration-span of one *matra*. Six ways of manipulating duration are indicated. However, the *marga*-concept as such is no more in circulation in performing traditions.
5. *Jati* (kind): A *tala*-unit may consist of three, four, five divisions or combinations of these. These types,

depending on the number of divisions included, are respectively known as *tisra* (3), *chatusra* (4), *khanda* (5) and *mishra* (combination).

6. *Kala*: Refers to subdivisions or segments, which constitute the essence of any significant patterning activity.

7. *Graha* (to grapple, to grip): Taking to or joining with. The *graha* of *tala* in use is described either as *sama, atita, anagata* or *vishama* depending on the relationship of the onset of melody with the beginning of *tala*. *Sama-graha* is exact correspondence of the two, *Atita-graha* is over-reaching/crossing of the *tala*-onset by the melody onset, and *anagata-graha* is the under-reaching. *Vishama-graha* is an indifferent relationship between the two.

8. *Laya* (tempo): Basically it is the equidistance between two beats (minimal basic dividers) in a *tala*.

9. *Yati* (a pause, break in a metre): the term speaks of the ways in which *tempi* are distributed in a *tala*. Thus, *sama-yati* is to have the same *laya* in the beginning, middle and end of a *tala*. *Srota* or *srotogata yati* is successive doubling of *tempi* in the beginning, middle and end-sections of a *tala*. *Pipilika-yati* features random slow, medium and fast movements. Finally, *Gopuccha* (cow's tail) *yati* displays fast, slow and fast movements in successive sections.

10. *Prastar* (elaboration): It is at this stage of evolution of *tala*, that genres or forms of rhythm-music take over.

It must be admitted however, that the minute systematisation evident in the early period has not been assiduously followed in the contemporary performing tradition. Instead, a new set of terms, rather tenuously connected with the *dashaprana* systematisation, has come into circulation. Some important concepts in the present-day *tala*-system are explained below:

Sam: The first, and usually the stressed, beat of *tala*-cycle.

Kala: The unstressed or the weakly stressed division-point. When *tala* is marked by hand-movements, an outward and downward movement of an open palm indicates the *kala*. It is also known as *khali* (empty).

Matra: Measure of the duration between two normal divisions of a *tala*.

Khanda: Sections in which *tala* is divided.

Bhari: *Tala*, taken as a whole, exhibits sections relatively more or less sonorous due to the character of sound-syllables included. More sonorous sections are described as *bhari*.

Khali: Sections of a *tala* described as less sonorous. Sometimes the term is also used, though rather confusingly, in the sense of *kala* (see above).

Tali: Refers to clap-point in the *tala*-pattern when the latter is marked by hand-movements. To indicate the point with a clap is to suggest that the beat so marked represents sonorous element. These points are to be matched by appropriately sonorous sound-syllables when the *tala* is played on an instrument.

Theka: In order to create varied sound-patterns, a *tala*-design needs to be expressed through different sound-syllables. Thus one *tala* may have many *theka*, depending of course on potentialities of the instrument employed.

Bol: Syllables formed by instrumental sound. Richness of any instrumental language depends on availability of identifiable, reproducible, isolable and minimal sound-patterns, which, if so employed, become sound-syllables.

Tala:

   Tala is the second concept that Indian musical genius has explored, especially in the art music traditions, for instance the well-known Hindustani and the Carnatic. In importance and evolution, *tala* is on par with *raga* in Indian music. As already pointed out, *raga* and *tala* taken together, go a long way in distinguishing Indian music from many other music systems of the world. Of the two major dimensions of music, namely, melodic and the rhythmic, the former is mainly expressed through musical notes while the latter chiefly explores dimension of time through operation of time divisions, popularly (though loosely!) called beats. The melodic dimension evolved into *raga* after many processes took place and *tala* resulted from an equally fascinating and lengthy evolution in the rhythmic dimension.

   The term *tala* is derived from the Sanskrit root-word *'tal'*, meaning 'to strike with palms'. Early music-makers could easily be imagined to have employed hand-claps, or palm-strokes and so on, to mark time in dance and music, the two performing arts in which *tala* plays a vital role.

   Tala, as an idea is embedded in the concept of Time, which, of course, has many varieties. For example, 'clock time' enables us to count seconds, minutes and hours; as also to refer to past, present and future. Secondly, we have 'psychological time' which seems to shorten hours of happiness and lengthen minutes of sorrows as it were! These two varieties of Time are clearly beyond our control. Further, they, in themselves, do not have value or quality attached to them. It is in music that Time acquires an intrinsic value just as space becomes valuable and qualitative in spatial arts such as painting and sculpture. Different musical cultures bring about the miracle of transforming 'Time' into 'musical time' through adoption of various procedures. A brief examination of the manner in which Hindustani music achieves the feat is our present concern.

As in the case of *raga*, it is the artist, the creator, who takes the basic decision of bestowing quality on Time by differentiating musical time from the two other varieties, mentioned earlier (or from similar other kinds of time — one may add). Clock-time cannot be manipulated, a feature which distinguishes it from musical time because, the music-maker creates, manipulates his time and gains control over it. (This can hardly be imagined in case of clock time, hence the maxim, 'time and tide wait for no man'.) As far as the psychological time is concerned, it varies from person to person as also from moment to moment. On the other hand, musical time severs its connections with the day-to-day world and evinces a vitality of its own. How does an artist accomplish this astonishing task?

A musician creates his time by thinking out, imagining a beginning to, and a divided flow of, Time as his first step. A musician can therefore, decide to have a beginning of a *tala* whenever he wants. The other two varieties can hardly allow taking such liberties! This act creates the first time-division or 'beat'. The time-flow is now released as well as channeled or directed.

However, a mere release of time flow would hardly suffice, as an unimpeded time flow would simply go on and on, and thus, fail to create a pattern or make musical sense. Hence, the artist puts in the second stroke, a beat to mark the first division or segment. By virtue of his first division the flow becomes comprehensible. As it has been often pointed out, the vast expanse of the sky becomes comprehensible if and when you place a star into it! The artist proceeds to put in successive and equidistant strokes and thus makes available to us the *matra*-s, a measure to compute musical time. The duration between two *matra*-s is known as tempo. Faster the tempo, lesser is the intervening duration and vice versa. The release of the time flow and determination of the measure to compute it are the primary requirements towards making of *tala*. This is so, chiefly because to satisfy the two conditions is to throw up an unmistakable rhythmic pattern.

An unvarying repetition of these patterns would cease to be meaningful and the next logical step is, therefore, to form a bigger pattern to accommodate many smaller ones (and something more). Patterns of longer and shorter durations are grouped together and these are known as *gana*-s. One is easily reminded of the strategy employed in creating metrical units in poetry. As we know, differing patterns of arresting beauty are created in the prosodic activity by combining and permuting longer and shorter durations. To that extent, a metrical line comes close to the idea of *tala*. However, a metrical pattern can claim to be a *tala* only when, (in addition to being a pattern of longer and shorter durations) it displays circularity. How is this achieved and to what end?

The question to be asked is: what happens when a metrical line is completed? The answer: the second line may or may not follow. A metrical line can exist singly and even one single line is adequate to create a metre. However, a single rhythmic line without language soon ceases to be exciting because it also ceases to be creative. If the line is repeated in its entirety without a break it creates a series of circular patterns conducive to generation of musical patterns, either melodic or rhythmic. Cyclical and repetitive time-patterns composed of groups of longer and shorter durations are thus *tala*-s, as we know them today. To speak of a *tala* of four or six or sixteen *matra*-s is therefore, to refer to cycles the circumference of which are dotted with four or six or sixteen equal divisions to provide dynamic patterns of time points.

However, the insatiable patterning urge of humans soon finds itself thwarted if it is to go round and round with the unchanging duration-patterns. Hence, some of the dividers are accentuated and some others less so. The result is the creation of a new and complex pattern — once again to throw up a series of new patterns!

In a manner of speaking, the entire process described so far was mental. Unless it is married to sound and silence, how can it become music? Can one describe colour without bringing into picture light and darkness? Hence, gradations of sound and silence are brought into action by recourse to claps, finger-taps and waving of palms. For example, a sonorous *matra* (comparable to an accented divider) is turned into a clap, a lesser degree of sonority is marked by light finger-taps while waving of palms suggests domination of silence over sound. In other words, a rhythm pattern is woven out of sound and silence. For instance, in *teentala* of 16 beats (*matra*-s), there are claps on the first, fifth and the thirteenth *matra*-s; palm waving is placed on the ninth *matra* and finger-taps mark rest of the *matra*-s. Every *tala* in Hindustani art music has an analogous distribution of claps (*tali*), finger-taps and palm-waving (*khali* or *kal*). Ancient treatises enumerate 108 *tala*-s, presumably intended to correspond to the number of sacred dances credited to Lord Shiva, the patron-deity of all performing arts. However, contemporary performing tradition is normally restricted to about 15 *tala*-s.

What began as an idea became a relief map or a soundscape when expressed in terms of claps, finger-taps, etc. However, *tala* gains life and body when instruments play their role. In the present context, instruments of rhythm are those objects capable of producing intense, discrete and comparatively non-sustained sounds. Instruments of rhythm and their sounds give life to the idea of the *tala*. Instrumental sounds, when expressed onomatopoetically, formulate sound-syllables. These sound-syllables, when fitted suitably to the *tala*-divisions create *theka*-s — these being the actually played and heard *tala*-expressions in Hindustani music. Theoretically speaking, innumerable *theka*-s are possible for any *tala*, provided instrumental sounds of the required variety and richness are available. *Theka*-s provide content to *tala*-s and raise them above the level of mathematical formulae. Whether in accompaniment or in solo renderings, the *theka*-s convince listeners by a kind of compositional beauty.

Thus realised, Hindustani *tala*-s become musical components that function as accompanying entities in dance and music. They also serve as the basis for solo renderings in rhythm-music. Instruments such as the *tabla* and the *pakhawaj* enjoy a rich repertoire of rhythm-music. Mastering rhythm-music requires years of training and rigorous practice if performing competence is to be achieved. It is no surprise that Hindustani rhythm-music has acquired an expansive audience of its own, at home and abroad.

2.131 *Talim* (A teaching, towards expertise)

Learning and teaching of music according to the norms
of the *guru-shishya* tradition. Initial imitating *guru* seems to
be one of its important features. However, as the ancient
Naradiya *shiksha* wisely pointed out this was not the final
goal. In translation the relevant direction of the *shiksha*
reads, "One should imitate the teacher so that the intellect
is prepared to receive knowledge."

2.132 *Tana* (S *tan* = to stretch, spread, expand or to compose)

Etymology suggests that melody or *raga* is expanded
through the use of *tana*. The term possibly owes its origin
to a technique in instrumental music whereby notes could
be added to a melody by stretching a string.

Two main varieties of *tana* are mentioned, *shuddha* ('as
they were originally'), in which notes are employed in sequence and *kuta* ('puzzling') wherein notes are employed
out of sequence. These two basic structural strategies, when
applied to scale-range, yield seven types of *tana* identified
in the ancient tradition as follows:

Archika = consisting of one note
Gathika = consisting of two notes
Samika = consisting of three notes
Swarantara = consisting of four notes
Odava = consisting of five notes
Shadava = consisting of six notes
Sampurna = consisting of seven notes

Thus understood it appears that *murchana* (>) is also to
be considered a *tana*. However, it has been argued that

while *tana* enjoys only the ascending order, *murchana* enjoys both ascending and descending orders and both are different. Applying the formula rigorously to scales evolved from each of the seven notes, musicology has enumerated the number of possible *tana*-s to a total of 5040! It is however obvious that combined with words, *gamaka*, tempi-changing, etc., an infinite number of *tana*-s are possible.

It must be admitted that the contemporary tradition displays a rather confused classification but the rich variety of *tana* employed in performance is well reflected in the terminology used. Some of the terms are noted below:

1. *Utarti* (descending) = *sa ni sa, dha pa dha, ma ga ma,...*
2. *Kaki* = in a crow-like voice
3. *Khuli* = using open vowel-sounds, especially 'a'
4. *Jabadi* = produced with the help of jaw movements
5. *Tangan* (hanging) = produced with the use of the vowel-sound '*ee*'
6. *Palti* (inversion) = *sa re ga ma, ma ga re sa*

2.133   *Taranga-vadya* (S *taranga* = ripple + *vadya* = instrument)

The term appears to be a new addition facilitating more inclusive instrumental typology.

Ghana (>) instruments such as *jalataranga* are able to produce a kind of musical sounds otherwise not producible in the usual instrumental categories. The term represents a special plea made to create a category to include them.

2.134   *Tarata* (H S *tara* = high)

An acoustic term referring to parameter of sound identified as pitch, the two other parameters being intensity and timbre.

2.135   *Tata* (H S *tata* = stringed)

Refers to category of musical instruments described as chordophones. Some important structural and technical terms are:

Dhancha = skeleton
Gaj = bow
Kaman / dhanush = curved bow
Ghodi/ghudach = bridge
Mijrab = wire plectrum
Nakhi = wire plectrum
Tantri / tar = string
Tumb/tumbi/kaddu/tumba = gourd-round or flattened
Dand / danda = stem
Khunti = peg
Tabli = disc to cover resonator
Sarika/parda = fret
Kon / trikon / jawa = wooden or metal striker of strings
Tarab / taraf = sympathetic strings
Mooth = grip
Adhar / apar shikha = respectively lower & upper end
Chikari = high pitched accessory strings
Pet = belly
Kamar = waist
Baj ke tar = main string (also called *nayaki tar*)
Ghat = clay pot

Patra/patrika = plate

Meru = edge

Kakubha = crooked end-piece of a string-instrument

Shalaka = small and thin stick

Keel = a wooden or metal nail

Jawari = cotton string inserted between string and the bridge

Kamrika = a curved bow (small)

Shanku = cone, conical instrumental part

Nabhi = navel, centre

Chibuk = chin/chin-rest

Khal = leather covering

Langot = a triangular thin plate

Atak =   end-part beyond which a string does not extend

Gulu = gum used to stick wooden strips, etc.

Sajawat = decoration

Gardan = neck

Jod ki tar = accompanying string customarily tuned in the key selected by the instrumentalist

2.136 *Tatavanaddha* (*tata* = stringed + *avanaddha* = covered)

Stringed instruments with a membrane, it is argued, need to be described as *tatavanaddha*. This appears to be a better term than the ancient term *vitata*.

2.137 *Teep* (H *teepna* = to utter forcefully)

Today *teep* means higher octave or notes from the same. The term is probably connected with medieval description of the important instrument *bansuri* (>). According to the medieval tradition, sound-hole located near the blow hole and used to produce high notes was known as *teepa*.

2.138 *Tenaka*

According to medieval tradition, meaningless sound-syllables such as *tena, na, ri* were employed as components of musical genres. They were regarded auspicious. Even today musical genres such as *tarana, chaturang, ras* employ meaningless sound-syllables though they seem to have lost their earlier auspicious aura.

2.139 *Thap* (H *thapna* S *sthapana* = installation)

A characteristic playing technique in *avanaddha* (>) instruments such as *tabla, pakhawaj,* etc., is described as *thap*. This technique involves lifting up palm immediately after it has struck the drum-face. This action is designed to produce an open sound. The stroke requires a skilful coordination of finger-closure, placement of fingers on *syahi* (>) and maintaining an angle at which the membrane is struck. Hence *thap* is regarded to be a 'test' of the technical virtuosity attained by a performer.

Pakhawaj-music relies more on *thap* and hence the resulting style of playing the instrument is aptly described as *thapiya baj*.

2.140 *Thata* (H *thath* = group)

A sequentially arranged and complete scale of seven primary notes in ascending as well as descending order is known as *thata*. In the older, Sanskrit tradition, the term *krama* probably suggested a similar phenomenon. If one combines and permutates all notes including *vikrut* notes (changed, i.e. varieties such as *komal, tivra* etc.) within a septet, numerous *thata*-s are possible. Vyankatmakhi derived seventy two *thata*-s and explained the systematic derivation in his *Chaturdandi-prakashika* (1660 AD). Lochana in his *Ragatarangini* (1675 AD) also used the term and in fact names of *thata* he lists are very similar to the much later list given by Pt. Bhatkhande! It is not generally known that Sadiq Ali — a very early *sitar* player had given descriptions of ten *thata*-s in his *Sarmaye Isharat*. Drawing on such many earlier formulations Pandit Bhatkhande propounded a system of ten main *thata*-s and one hundred and ninety five *raga*-s derived from them. It is clear that *thata* resulted from a systematisation of *raga*-s, which existed prior to the *thata*-formulation. However, Pandit Bhatkhande proceeded to name each *thata* after one prominent *raga* in the same *thata*. In this way the prominent *raga* came to be installed as *janak* (creator) *raga* and other *raga*-s in the same *thata* became *janya* (created) *raga*-s. The *janak* *raga* is also described as *ashraya* (support) or *melakarta* (creator of *mela*) *raga*.

Historically speaking *thata* was, in all probability, a necessity for accompanists on string instruments who had to establish all notes (including the *vikruta*) in one octave-range to facilitate changes in the fundamental note. This is · why they resorted to the immovable (*achala*) *thata*.

Sansthana, mela and *thath* are synonyms.

2.141   *Tivrata* (H S *Tivra* = intense + *ta*)

It is a term in acoustics referring to the dimension of sound known as intensity. The other two parametres are, respectively pitch and timbre.

2.142 *Tuk* (H *tuk* – piece)

A number of terms such as *amsha, kali, dhatu, charan,* and *tuk* are employed to indicate parts or sections of larger musical entities. In case of compositional genres such as *dhrupad, khayal,* etc., presence of a definite number of *tuk*-s is a distinguishing trait, a clue to their identity. The term is also used in instrumental music.

2.143 *Upaj* (v. H *upajna* = to be created)

The term refers to improvisation on a short phrase from a musical composition — the product being described as *upaj* in order to stress the aspect of creativity in the venture. It is a procedure of embellishing small phrase (e.g. *mukhada*) in a *gat* or song with the help of *swara* or *raga*. Independent elaboration of a musical idea is the main feature. There is of course no reason why the term should be restricted to the melodic aspect of music.

2.144 *Ucchara* (S utterance, pronunciation, declaration, or v. H *uccharna* = to utter)

Though somewhat metaphorically, the term is used to describe many initial acts/steps in music-making. For example, it often refers to commencement or beginning of *tala* in vocal or instrumental music.

2.145 *Uthan* (H *uthana*< S *utthana* = the act of rising or standing up, getting up)

It is a short preparatory piece played prior to playing *tala* or the associated *theka* in *tabla* or *pakhawaj* music.

2.146   *Vadana* (H S *vad* = to sound, to converse)

All instrumental music is described as *vadana*. Five kinds of basic *vadana* are defined:

Tatva = strictly follows the song in matters of tempo, *tala*, pauses, rests, style, syllables, general contour, scale, etc.

Anugata = follows song but also consists of independent playing.

Ogha = independently repeats entire musical content of earlier elaboration at the end of a composition.

Chitravritti = overshadows song.

Dakshinavritti = song overshadow, instrumental expression.

A *vadana* without a song is described as *nirgeet* or *shushkavadya*.

2.147   *Vadi* (H S *vad* = to converse, to sound)

It is obvious that if musical activity is to yield significant patterns, the inter-relationship of notes within *saptaka* (the basic scalar arrangement of notes) needs to be regulated.

Notes of *saptaka* are therefore classified into four classes, respectively known as *vadi, samvadi, anuvadi* and *vivadi*.

In its stabilised and unelaborated state *saptaka* does not have these four classes in operation because in *saptaka* all notes are of equal importance at all times. The foursome comes into existence when *saptaka* becomes dynamic and when it is developed for patterning. It is to be remembered that the quartet came into reckoning only after the *murchana* (>) system of creating new bases for musical development was replaced by a system, which established all intervals/ notes in one octave-range. According to the contemporary understanding, the four classes can briefly be explained as follows:

> *Vadi* = the most important note.
> *Samvadi* = a note next in importance to *vadi*. It is located in that half of the octave, which does not include the *vadi*.
> *Anuvadi* = all notes included in a *raga* but other than *vadi* and *samvadi*.
> *Vivadi* = notes entirely omitted or very sparingly used (in a *raga*).

2.148 *Vaditra* (S)

An older and a general term for musical instruments taken collectively — *atodya* — was yet another ancient and synonymous term.

2.149 *Vadya* (S)

Refers to an instrument designed to express musical sound and movement. The definition appears to be wide enough to include human voice. One view in Indian musicology however, holds that human voice is not man-made and hence it constitutes a class by itself. Thus it is safer to say that according to Indian musicology the term *vadya* connotes four man-made and one divinely created *vadya*. Tradition divides man-made *vadya* into four classes, namely, *tata*, *avanaddha*, *sushira* and *ghana*. *Vitata* was once regarded as a separate category. Modern thinkers advocate *tatavanaddha* and *tarangvadya* as additional categories. One must also add a class of electronic instruments to the traditional listing.

2.150   *Vaggeyakara* (S *vak* = voice + *geya* singable)

Composer. The word/text aspect of a composition is known as *vak* or *matu* and the melodic/musical aspect as *geya* or *dhatu*. A person proficient in both is known as *vaggeyakara*.

2.151   *Varjya/varjita* (S)

Refers to note/s omitted from a particular *raga* in conformity with the relevant rules.

2.152   *Varna* (S)

1. A letter expressed through combinations of vowel and consonant sounds.
2. *Jati,* i.e. the basic way of bringing together or combining musical notes. Four basic strategies of organising tonal material in a melodic treatment are laid down:

    a. *Sthayi* = repetition or prolongation of a single note, e.g. *sa, sa, sa.*
    b. *Aroha* = arrangement of notes according to their respective pitch in an ascending order.
        It is also known as *anuloma,* e.g. *sa, re, ga.*
    c. *Avaroha* = arrangement of notes in descending order according to their respective pitch, e.g., *sa, ni, dha,* etc. It is also known as *viloma.*
    d. *Sanchari* = employment of notes by incorporating all the three possibilities described so far. *Sanchari* may allow notes in *krama* (that is, in

the grammatically sanctioned sequence) or as *santara* (that is omitting or stepping over certain notes).

Using embellishments, etc., further develops these *varna*-s.

As fundamental strategies, *varna*-s are relevant to all music and hence to recitation as well as singing. Hence, *pathya* (recitation) too has four types of *varna*-s. They are:

Udatta = high pitched
Anudatta = low pitched
Swarita = having sustained high or low pitches
Kampita = vibratory

All *varna*-s are employable in any octave.

2.153   *Vidara* (S inundation, overflowing)

Notes within a *raga* have a certain flow. To open new possibilities of elaboration by changing their sequence, etc., and yet to keep the flow uninterrupted is known as *vidara*.

2.154   *Viloma* (S reverse, contrary)

Refers to the inversed melodic sequence of notes, that is, *avaroha* > *varna*.

2.155   *Vistara* (S)

Elaboration or development of melodic or rhythmic ideas in music. *Prastara*, a term that appears to be synonymous with *vistara* needs to be confined to highly regulated elaborations, especially in rhythm-music.

2.156   *Vritti* (mode of action)

It is a term used to classify three basic interrelationships between song and instrumental music in combined rendering:

i.   *Chitravritti*: instrument leads, song follows.
ii. *Vartikvritti*: song and instruments are equal in importance.
iii. *Dakshinavritti*: song leads and instruments follow.

3

MUSICAL
INSTRUMENTS

This section has a limited purpose of describing instruments active on the Hindustani concert platform. Not more than a score are in operation and expectably all of them do not enjoy equal musical potentiality as well as prosperity.

Hindustani musical instruments appear to carry out three major tasks. Firstly, they present music solo, secondly, they provide tonal or rhythmic accompaniment or finally they produce drone. Some instruments are capable of accomplishing more than one task while some others have an exclusive application. But generally, occasions on which an instrument performs two or more roles at the same time are rare. In other words, Hindustani instrumental usage displays considerable division of labour or functional specialisation.

While in solo or accompanying mode, instruments are chiefly required to explore one of the two dimensions: melodic or rhythmic. However, it must be noted that when instruments make music, voice does not take up the mantle of accompaniment and thus for all practical purposes Indian music-culture stresses primacy of vocal music. This in fact is one of the distinguishing marks of Indian art music.

The overall abundance of musical instruments has inevitably led to formulation of a meticulously defined classificatory system, which, in turn, has led to a number of ways of classifying the instruments. It is to the credit of Indian tradition that contemporary musicological, and especially organological, thinking approves of the four-fold classification of instruments formulated in ancient India.

According to this thinking, instruments are classified through identification of the major sound-producing agent in a specific instrument. Therefore, *tata* (with string), *ghana* (solid), *sushira* (with holes), and *avanaddha* (membrane-covered) form the four major classes. Sometimes one more class namely, *vitata* is also mentioned. Instruments in this class consist of strings and membrane-covered (bodies). With the arrival of advanced electronics it is also rightly suggested that now electronic instruments need to be treated as a separate class. Many other classifications and sub-classifications are put forward through application of different criteria based on playing methods/techniques, etc., and they are relevant at more academic levels.

Before moving to description of contemporary instrumental scene, one medieval classification should be of interest for its patent performance-orientation. According to this classification, the criterion is the lead instruments follow in the process of music making. For example, instruments that followed dance were described as *nrittyanuga*, those guided by vocal music were called *geetanuga*, and those played independently, were set apart as *prithagvadya*. Even today it would be difficult to brush aside the highly relevant functional bias displayed in this classification!

In theory it is possible to hold that any instrument can find a place in any set-up. Yet, in reality, instrumental mobility is considerably restricted, and for valid reasons.

Firstly, acoustic properties of every instrument tend to limit its circulation. Secondly, the patently melodic (as opposed to polyphonic and harmonic) thrust of Hindustani music places a premium on instruments capable of sustained tonal production. Thirdly, non-musical cultural associations also play notable part in determining scope allowed to an instrument. For example, taboos and sanctions play a role in music, which, after all, is merely a segment of the total life-pattern in a specific culture.

To know about an instrument is useful. Even information (as distinguished from knowledge) helps to have right expectations from instruments and its user. It is not an exaggeration to say that correct information about instruments is conducive to right reception of music they make.

It is perhaps necessary to note one more minor point. Instruments are music making mechanisms but they are also objects. They also store social information and prove fascinating carriers of culture. As has been often pointed out, instruments migrate more easily than their users or inventers! However, such information may often be tenuously linked to actual performance. It is, therefore, proposed to concentrate only on the following eight items/features to describe/discuss instruments in vogue in Hindustani art music:

1. Name/s
2. Etymology
3. Classification
4. Legend

5. Constructional features
6. History
7. Hold, posture and playing technique
8. Tuning method

3.1   *Bansuri*

- *Bansuri*, flute
- (H *bans* S *vamsha* = bamboo)
- *Sushira*

Rather loosely, references are often made to the instrument with other names such as *murali, venu, algooz, vamshi,* flute, etc. However, these different names should actually be specifically *applied* to definite kinds. As far as concert music is concerned, *bansuri* is an influential instrument. Names of its two main varieties, namely, horizontal and vertical, clearly indicate origin from bamboo. In fact other names such as *venu, vamshi* also reflect the fact. Horizontal *bansuri* is aptly called *aad-bansuri, ad* meaning 'that which is held in front of the eyes, from left to right or vice-versa'.

Kalidasa (634 AD) in his *Kumarasambhava* has recorded a legend about the instrument. A black bee bore through a slender bamboo. Winds blowing through it created so haunting a musical sound, that the music-loving demi-gods, *kinnara* cut away the portion in order to make an instrument!

Horizontal *bansuri* is a simple cylindrical bamboo tube of a uniform bore. Closed at one end, it ranges in length from 30 cms. to 75 cms. Longer *bansuri*-s are lower in pitch and deeper in tone. A few centimeters from the closed end is located the blow-hole or embouchure through which a player blows. There are six to eight holes placed in length to produce notes of different pitches. *Bansuri* has a com-

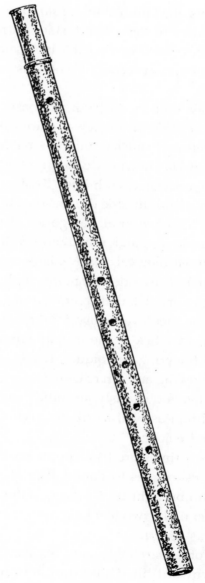

Bansuri

pass of about two and a half octaves. Unlike similar Western instruments, the Hindustani *bansuri* does not consist of mechanical valves or keys. Hindustani art musicians prefer *bansuri* made of bamboo available in Assam though flutes can be made of various types of wood, as well as of ivory and metals.

The prototype of the instrument boasts of a long history. During the *Vedic* period it was employed in *samagana*, the earliest genre of musico-religious recitation in India. The instrument was however called *tunava* or *nadi*. Later, it was closely associated with Lord Krishna. This association endowed it with mythic dimensions. It is perhaps the only instrument active in all categories of music, namely primitive, folk, art, popular, religious as well as confluence. The ancient musicological text *Naradiya Shiksha* (600 AD) pressed it into service to identify notes employed by reciters of the *sama*. A very detailed treatment is given to the instrument in the medieval *Sangeet Ratnakara* (1247 AD) in which fifteen varieties of the instrument are dealt with. Five types of fingering techniques, twelve merits and five demerits of blowing and ten chief merits of the player also find place. This is obviously an indication of a long performing tradition as well as durable scholastic attention the instrument enjoyed.

In modern times credit of popularising the present horizontal *bansuri* goes to Pandit Pannalal Ghosh (1911-1960 AD) who brought to it concert status and matching musical content. The two feet long *bansuri* of Pandit Ghosh was known as *tipperi*.

A player of *bansuri* holds it in a horizontal position with a slight downward tilt. Thumbs of both hands are often employed to hold it. Three fingers of the left hand (exclud-

ing the little finger) and four fingers of the right hand ma-
nipulate finger holes. The basic playing techniques include
completely covering the sound holes, keeping them half-
open and finally cross-fingering. To vary blowing pressure
(especially employing over-blowing), is an important aspect of the player's virtuosity.

The other main variety, the vertical *bansuri,* has its blow-
ing-end shaped into a narrow opening known as *beak.* Near
the *beak,* and along the tube is located the edge of the fipple
to produce sound. Manipulation of finger holes yields various notes. The vertical *bansuri* has nearly disappeared from
the concert platform though it has not gone into total
oblivion. Its high pitch has its uses especially in presentation of orchestrated music.

3.2 *Batta been*

- *Vichitra been*
- (H *Batta* S *vatuk* = rounded piece of stone used for
  grinding spices, etc., in Indian households; *vichitra*
  = adj. S various, painted)
- *Tata* (see *been*)

In general appearance it is similar to the widely respected *been.* The fretless *batta been* has a wooden stem and
two gourds below it at both ends. Each gourd (each 45
cms. in diameter) is fitted with screws to the stem. The
stem (135 x 20 x 3 cms. in length) has an ivory bridge covering the complete width at one end. Six playing strings of
brass and steel run the whole length of the stem and they
are tied to pegs at the end — opposite to the bridge. Twelve
sympathetic strings of varying lengths run parallel to, and
under the playing strings. *Batta been* has two high-pitched

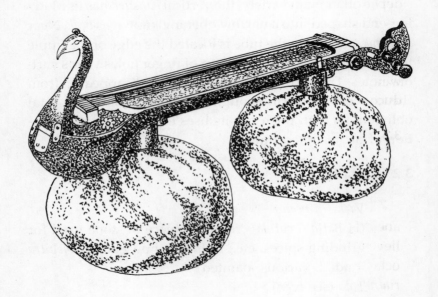

Batta Been

side-strings mainly for the climactic *jhala* (>) phase of musical elaboration.

A prototype of *batta been* appears to have existed in the medieval *ekatantri vina* (one-string lute). However, Ustad Abdul Aziz Khan of the Patiala court has been credited for inventing the contemporary version during the pre-independence period.

Placing the instrument on the ground, the player plucks strings with steel-wire plectrum worn on the right-hand fingers. A piece of rounded glass, looking like a paper-weight, is held in left hand to slide across strings to produce required notes.

3.3 Been

- *Rudra vina, Saraswati vina*
- (n. H S *vina* = lute)

The variant name *rudra vina* may be taken to suggest ancient lineage of the instrument in some form. It is believed that the name is traceable to twelve intervals in the octave as they numerically symbolise twelve *rudra*-s, (eleven *rudra*-s and one *maha-rudra*) enumerated in Hindu mythology. Sometimes the name *Saraswati vina* is applied to the *been* though a majority favours restricting the former name to the South Indian *vina*.

Been has a wide fingerboard of wood. An earlier practice was to use bamboo for it. It has two gourds of 35 cms diameter each, under the two ends of the stem. Other important features of the instrument are: a flat bridge at one end and twenty-four metal frets fixed with wax over the fingerboard. Four playing strings are supplemented in the *been* by two drone-strings, one on each side.

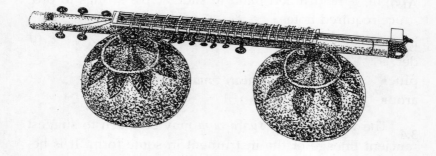

Been

The ancestry of instrument goes back to *kinnari vina* described in great detail by many and early musicological texts. It is also widely depicted in medieval sculpture. The earliest assignable period of *kinnari vina* is placed around 500 AD. A smaller version of the instrument, described as *laghavi vina* seems to be the direct predecessor of the instrument under discussion. Historically, Mughal period, and especially the reign of Akbar (1542-1605 AD) proved to be the heyday of *been*. Even today prominent *been* players trace their musical genealogy from Tansen (1506-1589 AD), the legendary court-musician of Akbar.

The *been* is held in front and across the body in a slanting position with the upper gourd resting on the left shoulder, and lower gourd on the right knee. Playing strings are plucked by the right hand, and the left hand, passing around the stem, presses strings on the frets as required.

3.4 *Dilruba* (adj. P *dil* = heart + *ruba* = attractive)

- *Tata, Vitata*
- *Dilruba*, a fretted and bowed instrument with its declared romantic Iranian name presents an interesting combination of *sitar* and *sarangi* — two major chordophones (i.e. *tata*) instruments popular in India.

On its wooden stem are fitted nineteen, gut-tied, movable and elliptical frets. The bridge at the neither end is placed on a skin-covered, waisted, wooden belly. Four playing strings run over the frets and eleven sympathetic strings pass underneath. Pegs for playing strings are located at the top while those for the sympathetic strings are at the

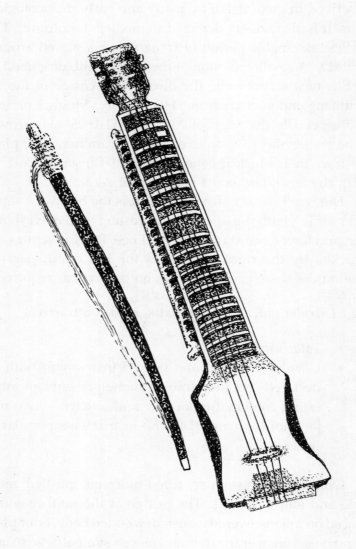

Dilruba

side. The bow, two feet and a quarter in length, uses black horsehair. It is held in a grip to ensure forceful bowing.

Held vertically, with lower portion placed on performer's lap, the top of the instrument rests against his left shoulder. Left hand slides over the strings to effect changes in pitch to create the required melody. The frets merely help to locate positions on the string as per the notes desired. The right hand does the bowing.

The instrument seems to be of recent origin. Probably it came into vogue after the *sitar* gained popularity during the early nineteenth century.

3.5   *Esraj/Israj*

• *Tata,Vitata*

The instrument shares similarities with *dilruba* (>) in appearance, playing technique and origin. While it has a *sitar*-like stem, its belly is like that of a *sarangi*. However, *israj* is rounder in shape and it is also shallow in the middle. Sixteen fixed frets and an equal number of sympathetic strings feature in it. The bow and its use are similar to their employment in playing of *dilruba*.

Esraj originated sometime in the early twentieth century and became popular in Bengal. It probably antedated *dilruba*.

It is argued that both *esraj* and *dilruba* were invented as less difficult instruments for the new, amateur music-lovers/performers of the nineteenth century. These amateurs, it was condescendingly argued, could not be expected to master traditional, dignified but difficult instruments such as *rudra-vina*, etc., and hence certain musical/organological concessions had to be made to their frailties!

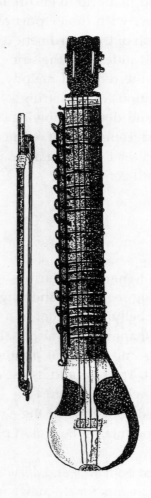

Esraj

3.6 Harmonium, *baja*, *samvadini* (*baja* H *vadya* = that which sounds, *samvadini* = A new term recently coined, edging away the English name from which it is loosely derived. It connotes an instrument that employs harmonious notes.)

- *Sushira* is the generally accepted classification of the instrument. However, it is rightly contended that in harmonium it is really the *reed*, which vibrates, and not the air-column. The instrument, therefore, needs to be classified differently.

Cabinet or the body is of primary importance in harmonium as it contains all other parts. It is made of wood and the size is determined by musical requirements such as tonal range, number of reed-lines, etc. Rectangular, box-like in shape, the harmonium has two bellows, outer and inner, made of cardboard and glued to the body. The outer bellow may have up to seven folds according to user's demand. The outer, vertical bellow sucks air into the cabinet and then the inner, horizontal bellow presses it into the sound–box. A reed-board, with a frame for each of the reeds, is fixed on the sound box. The base of the sound box is formed by a board (*kisti*), which controls air-supply to the sound box. In it, are located stoppers.

The harmonium-reeds (*sur*) are individually fixed in wooden frames. Made of brass, these *sur*-s are generally obtained in three kinds: *kharaj* (bass), *nara* (male), *madi* (female) — indicating three identifiable timbres as well as pitch-levels. The higher the pitch, the lesser remain the width, length and thickness of the reed. The three timbers are described as 'lines' and they are available in all three octaves namely, *mandra*, *madhya* and *tara*, customarily

Harmonium

employed by Indian music makers. To 'tune' *sur*, they are scraped or polished as required — a task, which needs to be carried out with great skill and care. The board on which *sur-s* are arrayed is known as reed board. Palitana in Saurashtra (Western India) is famous for the good quality of reeds manufactured there. The reed boards are joined to another board called *jali* in such a manner that the air pressed by bellow can (after passing through reeds) move through separate channels created by the *jali*.

The operation of the reeds is controlled by two types of keys, namely, 'straight', i.e. made of one single piece of wood, and 'stick or the English key' made of at least four wooden parts glued together. The keys — white for the major notes such as C, D, E, etc., and black for the sharp and flat varieties — number 12 per octave and are fixed on a board from left to right in ascending order.

The harmonium-player initiates the action of the bellow by pulling it by the left hand. Thus activated, the bellow sucks, compresses and finally pushes air via the sound box and through reeds. The player presses the keys with the fingers of his right hand to allow desired reeds to vibrate. Harmonium reeds vibrate freely, i.e. the vibrating edges do not touch frames in which the reeds are fixed.

The instrument which probably began its career in India as a pedal harmonium, soon evolved into the 'hand-harmonium' version obviously to suit the mode of music making in India in which performers usually sit down to perform. Since then, the instrument has developed many sub types such as plain, scale-change, folding and portable.

History of this instrument is not very clear. It is maintained that Portuguese soldiers brought it to India sometime during the 17th century. Maharashtra, one of the early

Jalatarang

centres of Western influence had accepted the pedal harmonium so well by 1880s that it was freely employed even in *keertana*, the a mode of musico-religious discourse extremely deep-entrenched in the region. Significantly it also became the mainstay of the music-drama tradition which came in its own from 1885 onwards. It is safe to deduce that the instrument was introduced at least a hundred years prior to its wide vogue around 1880s.

It is customary for the harmonium-player to sit cross-legged on the platform, etc., and keep the instrument in front. Sometimes the instrument partially rests on player's lap.

Harmonium, being a key-board instrument its tuning takes place while it is manufactured /constructed and one of its reported drawbacks is its comparative inflexibility in this respect.

3.7 Jalatarang (S. *jala* = water + *tarang* = ripple, *jalayantra* = *jala+yantra* = water instrument, a synonymous term sometimes used)

The instrument consists of a set of 15 to 24 porcelain (or bronze in early times) bowls of varying sizes and two slender bamboo sticks. Sometimes the tips of the sticks are covered with cotton or wool. Smaller bowls emit higher notes and larger ones expectably, can produce notes in the lower range. Further, more water in a bowl means lowering its pitch and less water enables producing higher notes.

The instrument does not receive a clear mention prior to *Sangeet Parijat* (1650 AD) of Ahobala.

The bowls are arranged semi-circular, in front and in easy reach of the player. From left to right the size of the bowls decreases. Having 'tuned' them according to his

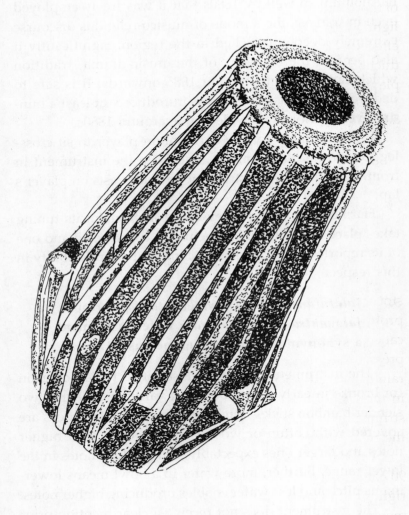

Pakhawaj

musical requirements, the artiste plays by striking on rims of these bowls. Water in the bowls is sometimes briefly and lightly touched (after having hit the bowl) to create special effects. The sticks, one held in each hand, encourage production of faster passages of music and they require alert playing.

3.8 *Pakhawaj*

- Loosely called *mridanga*
- Etymological explanations are varied (*pakshavadya*: *paksha* = side + *vadya* = that which sounds; *pushkarvadya*: *pushkara* = a thundering cloud + *vadya*; P *pakh* = *bass* + *awaj* = sound)
- *Avanaddha*.

Bharata in his *Natyashastra* has narrated an engaging story to explain origin of *mridang*, which is an obvious early prototype of *pakhawaj*. Sage Swati once went to the lake called Pushkara in a rainy season. He heard, and was impressed by the grave and sonorous rhythms produced by raindrops incessantly falling on lotus-leaves of various sizes in the lake. The sage was thereby prompted to create instruments of the *avanaddha* ('stretched membranes') i.e. of the membranophonic category.

A tapering wooden cylinder about 60 cm in length and 90 cm in diameter in the middle is so carved as to have its right and left faces respectively of 16 cm and 25 cm diameter. Both faces of this horizontal drum are covered with goat-skin, though the two 'faces' are covered with varying skin-layers. The skin on the right face is also thinner in comparison to one covering the left 'face'. On the right face, a mixture of iron-filings, glue, carbon, etc., is applied centrally and circular. It is rubbed to high polish and right density to ensure sonorous and clear tone. The left face gets a coat of a paste made of water, wheat flour, but this is applied every time afresh prior to performance. The left 'face' emits a bass, atonal sound. Membranes can be tightened or loosened by manipulating leather braces employed to stretch them. Cylindrical wooden blocks are inserted between alternate braces and the body, and these help altering the pitch as intended. Further, a braid which directly stretches membranes is struck with a pestle-like device for finer adjustments in tuning the instrument.

Prototypes of the instrument have a very long history. Especially as *mridanga*, the instrument dates back to the times of the two great epics, *Ramayana* and *Mahabharata* as well as to Buddisht texts which refer to it as *muing*. *Natyashastra* of Bharata calls it *pushkara*. Medieval texts describe many types of horizontal two-faced drums and deal in great detail in respect of forms of their music. It is described as an important drum by Abul Fazl, the perceptive chronicler of Emperor Akbar's times.

Player keeps the *pakhawaj* on the ground, in front, or takes it on his lap. Left hand plays the bass and the right the treble face. Compared to the *tabla*-playing, the playing-technique of *pakhawaj* relies more on open-palm strokes and the technique is described as *thapiya baj*.

3.9 *Santoor, santir, shatatantri* (*shatatantri* S *shata* = hundred + *tantri* = string)

- *Tata*

It is one of the rare dulcimer-type string instruments in the country. In its usually found sample, it consists of a trapezoid wooden box (60 cm x 30 cm x 3 cm) with fifteen

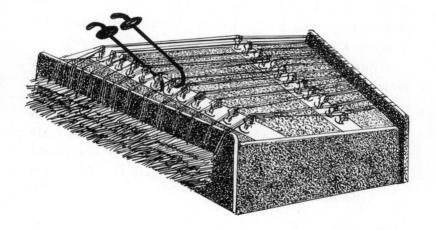

Santoor

bridges on each side, and four strings stretched over each bridge. Pegs located behind the bridges tighten/loosen the strings as required. More than one string is allotted to each note and a pair of sticks, curved at the striking end, helps produce the desired note/sound. Generally, the instrument has a range of more than two dozen notes.

Some authorities have tried to trace the *santoor* back to the ancient *shatatantri vina* or to one of the *vina* from the *Vedic* period. However, the conjectures are not well-supported. It is more likely that this instrument, circulating today in Kashmir, came originally from Central Asia.

The instrument is placed on the ground in front of the player who sits to perform with sticks held in both hands.

3.10 *Sarangi, saranga, sarang-vina* **(S** *saranga* **= deer or** *saranga* **= bow). Sometimes it is derived as** *sou* **= hundred +** *rangi* **= colours — a clear example of clever folk-etymology! Obviously this is eulogy, and not an etymology!**

- *Vitata*

It is carved out of one block of wood 60 cm in height, of adequate width and waisted at the bottom. The lower portion of the block is covered with parchment (thus forming the major resonator); while the middle portion is made of wood to form a finger-board. At the top is a box in which are fixed pegs at the right-back for the main gut-strings (four in number). To play on this fretless instrument the player operates, with his right hand, a bow with horsehair.

Bowed string-instruments are mentioned in Indian musicological texts from 700 AD. Medieval references are

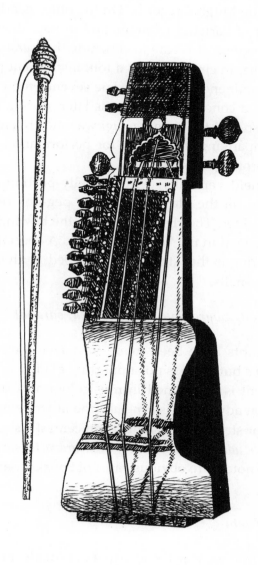

Sarangi

also numerous. Surprisingly the *sarangi* does not find a place in the Mughal records. On the other hand, there are a number of varieties in circulation in Rajasthan and contiguous regions. It is safe to conclude that *sarangi* was, for a long time, in circulation as a folk instrument prior to its urban prominence during the late seventeenth century. Its advent as a concert instrument is later, during the last 75 years or so. Till the time, *sarangi* was mostly employed as an accompanying instrument for performances of nautch girls or professional singers.

It is held vertically, with its belly-portion resting on ground or on the player's lap. The peg-box rests on the right shoulder. The right hand does the bowing while the left is engaged in the 'fingering'-work. A special feature of the fingering is that strings are 'stopped' with the back of the finger-nails.

3.11 *Sarod, swarodaya, swaravarta, sarabat*

Attempts have been made to derive the name from *sarada vina* but there is no supporting evidence, as no such instrument is mentioned in musicological texts. Another derivation advocated is *sur + ud*, the latter being the name of a major string instruments from central Asia. *Swarodaya* (S *swara + udaya* (rise of note) or *swaravarta, swara + avarta* (cycle of notes) are obvious cases of Sanskritisation in music!)

- *Vitata*

This fretless, waisted instrument is made out of a single block of wood, 1.5 m in length. It is similar to *rabab*, an instrument nearly out of vogue. The rounded end of the instrument (30 cms in diameter) is covered with parchment, at the centre of which is a bridge. From the bridge-end, the instrument tapers off towards the neck. Middle portion of the hollow body is covered with highly polished metal (silver or brass) sheet to form a fingerboard. On it are stretched six major playing strings that are melodically and acoustically supported by twelve sympathetic strings. All strings are of metal. Pegs for the main strings are at the top-end, while those for sympathetic strings are located at the side. A smaller and additional metal resonator is screwed at the top-back. A triangular plectrum made of coconut shell is held in the right hand to strum the strings.

Early Indo-Persian literature mentions *sarod*, though musicological texts do not refer to it. Reportedly, Khan Asadulla Khan introduced the instrument in Bengal in the early nineteenth century.

Held in front with a slight slant, the player's left hand slides over the strings and stops them as required. The right hand uses the stroking plectrum.

3.12 *Shehnai, sanai (shehnai. shah* = king + *nai* = pipe)

In Persia a player of *nai* (pipe) pleased the *Shah* (monarch) by his artistry and hence the name of the instrument. Alternatively, a player reportedly used a *nai* — longer than those in vogue, and with better results — thus, bestowing a special status on the instrument. As a consequence a suitable name was given to it!

This oboe-like double-reed instrument is basically a tube made of dark, close-grained, black-wood. The tube gradually widens to an end at which a metal bell, shaped as a *dhatura* flower is fixed. At the other end is inserted a reed traditionally made of *pala* grass cultivated in some regions

Shehnai

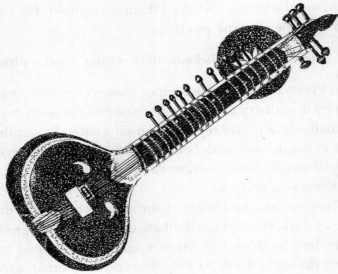

Sitar

of Uttar Pradesh. Spare reeds and an ivory needle to adjust them are attached to the mouthpiece to complete the structural set-up. There are eight/nine sound holes in the tube. A performer plays seven of them while others are stopped with wax or kept open at the discretion of the performer. An inevitable accessory to the playing of this instrument is the *sur* or *sruti*, which has a longer pipe with two or three sound-holes enabling the accompanist to keep a drone.

It is obvious that a prototype of the *shehnai* existed and enjoyed many versions in various parts of the country. Under the generic name *mukhavina*, instruments such as surnai, *mohir, madhukari, tuti, naferi* and *sundri* prevailed in Hindustan. *Shehnai* finds a mention in medieval times and an expert player is listed in *Ain-e-Akbari* (1596-97 AD). *Sangit Parijat* describes in great detail an instrument called *sunadi* that had an unmistakable resemblance to *shehnai*.

The *shehnai* succeeds as a music-maker on account of the skilful opening/closure of the sound-holes and on account of the adroit lip-tongue movements by the player.

3.13 *Sitar, satar* (H S *sapta* = seven + *tar* = string; P *seh* = three + *tar* = string)

* *Tata*

Legend, though uncorroborated, credits Amir Khusro (1310 AD) as its inventor.

Sitar has a hollow wooden stem made of two strips (34" x 35"), the upper concave and the lower hollowed. A wooden and slightly curved disc jointed to the stem at the bottom end covers a suitably cut gourd. The all-important bridge (2 ¾" x 1 ¼"), flat and made of ivory, ebony, etc., centres the disc. Sometimes, a second and smaller gourd is attached at the top-back mainly for additional resonance. Pegs for seven main strings and eleven sympathetic strings are distributed at the end of the disc. Metal frets, usually 19, are convex and moveable. Traditionally they are/were tied to the stem with gut.

In spite of claims to the contrary, *sitar* does not seem to have a long history. The Persian *seh-tar*, ancient *tri-tantri vina* and the Kashmiri folk instrument *setar/saitar* have been put forward as prototypes of the present day instrument. Neither Amir Khusro (who is credited to be its inventor) nor Abul Fazl referred to it. In the eighteenth century, it is interestingly described as *nibaddha tambura*, the latter (usually spelt '*tambur*') being an instrument similar to *sitar* was prevalent in West Asia.

The player holds the instrument in front, resting the main gourd on the ground or on his left in-step. Left hand fingers slide over frets to stop, stretch or vibrate main, i.e. playing strings. A wire plectrum worn on the right forefinger plucks the strings. A plectrum worn over the little finger is employed to play high-pitched side-strings mostly to create drone as well as strummed rhythm.

3.14 *Surbahar, Kachwa, kacchhapi vina, kashyapi vina* (*sur* = note + *bahar* = delight)

- *Tata*

It is virtually a larger edition of *sitar* (>) in every respect. Its flatter gourd resembles a tortoise and sometimes through craftsmanship it is deliberately made to resemble the mythical animal.

Surbahar

Tabla

The well known *been* player Umrao Khan is credited with the invention of the instrument, nearly century and a half ago.

The *surbahar* has thicker strings and flatter frets compared to *sitar* though the playing technique is similar. It is mainly employed for the slow-tempo musical elaborations known as *alap* (>). On occasions, *surbahar* was chosen for slow tempo elaboration to be succeeded by *sitar* for faster phases of music making — both presentations being two sections of one single rendering.

3.15 *Tabla, dayan* (adj. H *dahina* S *dakshin* = right), *bayan* (adj. H S *vam* = left), *tabla* (A *tabla* = a membranophonic instrument)

- *Avanaddha*

The usual simplification is to state that the ancient *mridang/pakhawaj* was divided into two in order to create an instrument easier to play, suitable to carry and conducive to brighter tonal colour.

In reality, *tabla* is a drum-pair. Normally a player plays each drum separately with his hands. Usually, bass drum is played by his left hand while the right hand plays the drum, which is tuned, in a higher pitch. However, today the term *tabla* refers to the drum-pair as well as the high-pitched drum.

The high-pitched member of the pair is carved out of wood block with dimensions: 30 cms x 17 cms x 20 cms. The bass drum made of clay or metal is 25 cms in diameter and tapers off towards the bottom. In both drums goatskin membranes — multi-layered in case of the treble drum — have an additional strip round the edges. This ring is fitted in a leather-braid through which pass braces tied together at the bottom. Tightening or loosening these braces leads to an increase or decrease in the tension on membranes and consequently to the desired pitch-variation. Cylindrical wooden blocks wedged between braces and outer walls of the treble drum enable players to bring about finer pitch-adjustments. Pitch-adjustments are also possible through hammer-strokes on the braid. An important feature is the circular, and centrally placed coating of iron-filings, carbon, etc., on the membrane of the treble drum. Many experts have pointed out that this feature distinguishes Indian drums from instruments in most other drum-traditions. This coating is placed eccentrically on the bass drum.

It is difficult to accept Amir Khusro as the originator of *tabla* (as also in case of *sitar*). On the other hand, ancient depiction of drums includes *mridanga* with three component drums, one to be kept on the lap and the other two kept vertically with their faces up in front of the player. In later centuries this distribution of component drums changed to one vertical and on the lap, and then two horizontal drums placed on the lap — one vertical drum thus getting eliminated in the process. The *Sangit Sar* of Sawai Pratap Sinha describes a variety of *mridanga*-s, namely, *hudukka*, which came into prominence only in the late eighteenth century.

In *tabla* playing, both drums are placed in front of the player who plays the left drum with wrist-pressure and curved palm combined with fingertips striking on the membrane. The right drum is played with fingers (palm down-facing the membrane).

3.16 *Tanpura, Tambora, tamboora* (P *tumbura*, S *tumb* = a long gourd)

- Tata

Tumbaru, the ancient *acharya* (preceptor) of music is credited with the creation of this instrument — which is so fundamental to Indian art music.

Chief features of *tanpura* are: gourd (70-90 cms in diameter), a hollow pinewood stem (105-120 cms in length), a slightly bulging wooden disc covering the vertically cut portion of the gourd and a bridge (of ivory or ebony etc.) centrally placed on the disc. Wooden pegs of the four main strings are at the top. A small sound-hole below the bridge probably ensures resonance. A piece of thread or silk is inserted between strings and the surface of the bridge in order to create characteristic resonance of *tanpura*. This characteristic resonance is described with the word *jawari*. Of the four strings that a traditional *tanpura* has, three are of steel, and the fourth bass string is made of brass. Strings are threaded through beads, inserted between bridge and end-attachment to allow subtler pitch adjustments.

The first unambiguous reference to *tanpura* is in *Sangeet Parijat* (1650 AD). It is neither mentioned by earlier texts nor does it find a place in sculptures. According to some authorities, a functional prototype of the *tanpura* is the medieval *tritantri vina*. Abul Fazl described an instrument called *swaravina* specifying it however as a *been* (>) without frets. *Sangit Samaya Sar* (1250 AD) refers to it. It is also important to note that *tamburi*, a four-stringed, one-piece drone used by non-elite musicians could easily claim to be a prototype of *tanpura*.

Tanpura

The traditional position to play this instrument is for a player in sitting posture to hold it upright by taking it on his lap or keeping the gourd on ground. Alternatively, the player may hold the instrument horizontally in front while sitting in a cross-legged position — though convenient, this hold and playing position is not approved by tradition.

To play *tanpura*, strings are strummed from left to right in sequence and succession. The third finger of the right hand plays the first string while the forefinger plays the remaining three.

3.17   *Tar-shehnai* (*tar* = **string** + *shehnai*)

* *Tata*

It is, virtually speaking, an *Esraj* with a gramophone sound box and a small megaphone attached to the resonator. Of very recent origin, its tone has a similarity with that of the *shehnai*. In addition, it has the notable capacity to produce a continuous sound as in a string instrument. The apparently confusing name has therefore a justification!

3.18   *Violin*

An obvious and a successful transplant from the West, the bowed string instrument is well established on the Hindustani concert stage at least from 1885.

Played in a sitting position and without the use of a chin-rest, the Indian playing style has often intrigued non-Indian observers of the scene in the past.

During the last hundred years, two kinds of playing techniques have crystallised. One is called *gatkari* and the other Carnatic, though the latter is also being employed to

Tar-shehnai

render Hindustani music. The former is conducive for a more rhythm-oriented and virile expression, while the latter encourages sustained, melodic production of sound.

Violin

BIBLIOGRAPHY

Naradiya Shiksha, Narada (4th century AD), critically edited with translations and explanatory notes by Ms Usha Bhise, Bhandarkar Oriental Research Institute, Pune, 1986.

Dattilam, Dattila (4th century BC), edited by Sambasiva Shastri, Trivandrum: Government Press, 1930.

Chatvarinshatrag Nirupanam, Narada (4th century BC), edited by B.C. Sukthankar, Bombay, 1914.

Bruhaddeshi, Matangmuni (6th or 9th century AD), edited by Chaitanya Desai, Khairagarh, 1961.

Sangeetsamayasara, Parshvadev (1165 AD), edited by Ganapati Shastri, Trivandrum: Government Press, 1925.

Varna Ratnakara, Jyotireshwara (1280-1340 AD), edited by S.K. Sen, Asiatic Society of Bengal, Calcutta, 1940.

Ghunyat-Ul-Munya, author not known (1374-75 AD), under the patronage of Malik Shamsuddin Ibrahim Hasan Abu Raja, the Naib of Gujrat (1374-1377 AD), Persian, edited by Sarmadee Shahab, Bombay: Asia Publishing House, 1978.

Sangeet Raj, Maharana Kumbh (1433-1468), King of Chittorgarh (Rajasthan), Sanskrit, edited by Premalata Sharma, Varanasi: Hindu Vishvavidyalaya, 1963.

Mansingh aur Mankutuhal (1486 AD approx.), Dwivedi Hariharniwas, Gwalior: Vidyamandir Prakashan, 1954.

Sangeet Damodar, Shubhankara (15th century), Bengal, Sanskrit, edited by Gaurinath, Calcutta: Sanskrit College, 1960.

Sahasrasa, Nayak Bakhshu (1501-1537 AD), Gwaliar, under the patronage of Raja Mansingh, edited by Premlata Sharma, Sangeet Natak Akademi, 1972.

Babarnama, Jahiruddin Babar (1530 AD), translated into Hindi by Yughit Naval Puri, New Delhi: Sahitya Akademi, 1974.

Swaramelkalanidhi, Ramamatya (1550 AD), Vijay Nagar: Shree Ganesh Press, 1910.

Ragmanjiri, Pundarik Vitthal (1556-1605 AD), edited by B.S. Sukthankar, Aryabhushan Press, 1918.

Sadragchandrodaya, Pundarik Vitthal (1556-1605 AD), edited by Ganesh Vajratank, Bombay: Nirnaysagar, 1912.

Rasakumudi, Shrikantha (1575 AD), a Brahmin from South India, worked for the king of Navanagar (Porbander), Sanskrit, edited by B.J. Sandesara, Oriental Institute, Baroda, 1963.

Kitab-I-Nauras, Ibrahim Adilshah II (1580-1627 AD), Bijapur, Persian, edited by Nazir Ahmed, Bharatiya Kala Kendra, 1956.

Ain-i-Akbari, Shaykh Abu 'I' Fazal (1590 AD), edited by S.L. Goomer, New Delhi: Naresh Jain (publisher), 1965.

Ragvibodh, Somnath (1610 AD), Andhra Pradesh, Bombay, edited by B.S. Sukthankar, 1911.

Sangeet Parijat, Ahobal Pandit (1620 AD), Dharwad State, translated by Kalind, Hathras: Sangeet Karyalaya, 1971.

Sangeet Darpan, Damodar (1625 AD), translated by Vishvambhar Bhatt, Hathras: Sangeet Karyalaya, 1971.

Ragtatvavibodh, Shreenivas Pandit (1650-1680 AD), edited by B.S. Sukthankar, Bombay: Aryabhushan Press, 1918.

Anup Sangeet Vilas, Bhavabhatta (1650-1709 AD), Dhavalpur (in Abhir State), Bombay, edited by B.S. Sukthankar, 1918.

Hridaykautukam & Hriday Prakash, Hridaynarayan (1667 AD), Gadha (Jabalpur), Bombay, edited by B.S. Sukthankar, 1918.

Ragtarangini, Lochana (1675 AD), edited by B.S. Sukthankar, Bombay: Aryabhushan Press, 1918.

Sangeetsaramrita, King Tulja (1729-1735 AD), Tanjore, Sanskrit, Bombay: Nirnaysagar, 1911.

On Musical Modes of the Hindus: *Music of India*, Jones William (1779 AD), Calcutta: Gupta.

A Treatise on the Music of India, Augustus Willard (1834 AD), Calcutta: Sunil Gupta, 1962.

Sangeet-Rag-Kalpadrum, Vyas Krishnanand, 1842.

Kanun Sitar, Sadik Ali (after 1853 AD).

Muladhar, Vol. I & II, Kelvade Meenappa Vyankappa, Bombay: Nirnayasagar, 1907.

Sangeet Darpan Masik Pustak, Ichalkaranjikar Balkrishnabuwa, Bombay, 1975.

Six Principal Ragas with Brief View of Hindu Music (1877 AD), Tagore Sourindro, Neeraj Publications, 1982.

Samay-i-Isharat (*Lit. Capital Stock of Bliss*, commonly known as *Laws of Music– Hindustani*), Delhi: Narayani Press, 1286AH, 1881 AD.

Sangeet Swaraprakash I, Abdul Karim Khan (1884-1937 AD), Belgaum, 1911.

Hindustani Music and the Gayan Samaj, Pune: Gayan Samaj Office, 1887.

The Music and Musical Instruments of Southern India and Deccan, Day C.R., London, 1891.

Navarathabhashya tatha Rasvilas, Shukla Krishnabihari, Bombay: Khemraj Shrikrishnadas, 1893.

Shree Sangeet-Kaladhar, Dahyalal Shivram (end of 19th century), Gujarati, Bhavnagar: Channalal Dahyalal Nayak, 1938.

Ragvilas, Malwe Anant Sakharam, Bombay, 1905.

Inayat-Geet-Ratnavali, Inayat Khan Rehmat Khan Pathan (1903 AD), Bombay.

Gayansamaj Pustakmala, Banahatti N.D., Pune: Gayan Samaj, 1906.

Ragvibodh Praveshika, B.S. Sukthankar, Bombay: Nirnaysagar Press, 1911.

Contribution to the Study of Ancient Hindu Music, Bhandarkar Praabhakar, Bombay: British India Press, 1912.

Introduction to the Study of Music, Clements E., Allahabad: Kitab Mahal, 1912.

The Music of Hindustan, Strangways A.H. Fox, Oxford: Clarendon Press, 1914.

Ganasopan, Gulabraomaharaj, 1914.

Theory of Indian Music as Expounded by Somnatha, Deval K.B., Poona: Aryabhushan, 1916.

Sangeetshastra, Shukla Nathuram Sundarji, Gujrati, 1918.

The Ragas of Hindustan, Deval K.B., Poona: The Philharmonic Society of Western India, 1918.

The Ragas of Hindustan, Vol. I & II, The Philharmonic Society of Western India, Poona: Aryabhushan Press, 1918.

Abhinavtalmanjiri, Kashinath Apatulsi, (–1920), edited by Vishnu Narayan Bhatkhande, Bombay: Nirnaysagar Press, 1914.

The Music of India, 1921, Popley H.A., New Delhi: Y.M.C.A. Publication, 1966 (Third Edition).

Git Sutra-Sar (translator's explanation and notes on grammar and theory of Hindustani music as spoken of in Bengali), Bannerji Himanshu S., 1925.

Rag Pravesh Lalit, Paluskar Vishnu Digambar, Nasik: Sangeet Printing Press, 1927.

Rag Parvesh Bhag 19, (Rag-Sorath-Desh), Paluskar Vishnu Digambar, Nasik: Sangeet Printing Press, 1929.

Gavaiyonka Jahaj, Mathura: Manohar Pustakalaya, 1939.

Gavaiyonka Mela, Mathura: Manohar Pustakalaya, 1939.

Padya Mimamsa, Sahasrabuddhe V.J., Kolhapur: G.V. Kulkarni, 1941.

Sangeet Sudha Sagar, Chattopadhyaya (Panubabu), Bengali, Banaras: Nripendrakrishna Chattopadhyay, 1941.

Marathi Chhandashastra (Nibandh), Patwardhan Govind Vishnu (Khasgivale), Miraj, 1947.

*Ragas and Ragini*s, Sanyal Amiya Nath, Calcutta: Orient Longmans, 1959.

Amir Khusrau's Contribution to the Indus-Muslim Music, S. Qudratullah Fatimi, Islamabad: Pakistan National Council of the Arts, 1975.

Ashtacchapiya Bhakti Sangeet: Udbhav aur Vikas I, II, III, Nayak C.C., Ahmedabad, 1983.

INDEX